The Road to Tingle Creek

S. Guetter

BALBOA.
PRESS

A DIVISION OF HAY HOUSE

Balboa Press books may be ordered through booksellers or by contacting:

Balboa Press
A Division of Hay House
1663 Liberty Drive
Bloomington, IN 47403
www.balboapress.com
1 (877) 407-4847

Because of the dynamic nature of the Internet, any web addresses or links contained in this book may have changed since publication and may no longer be valid. The views expressed in this work are solely those of the author and do not necessarily reflect the views of the publisher, and the publisher hereby disclaims any responsibility for them.

Print information available on the last page.

ISBN: 978-1-9822-2967-2 (sc)
ISBN: 978-1-9822-2968-9 (hc)
ISBN: 978-1-9822-3354-9 (e)

Library of Congress Control Number: 2019912408

Balboa Press rev. date: 09/16/2019

ACKNOWLEDGMENTS

To my wonderful, patient and encouraging husband, thank you!

To my friends and family who have put up with the writing crazies, thank you for your patience and support. I appreciate you reading the rough drafts and pointing out the speed bumps in the flow. John, Carol, Penni and Diana, I mean you!

To all the fantastic folks at Balboa Press: No one would be reading this without you and your support. Thank you for helping make a dream come true.

DEDICATION

To all those who have broken my heart and crossed the Rainbow Bridge ahead of me, human and animal.

CONTENTS

EPILOGUE

PROLOGUE

APRIL 10, 2014
MESQUITE BED and BREAKFAST
TINGLE CREEK, ARIZONA

CONNIE SULLIVAN HAD JUST CLEANED UP AFTER HER LATE AFTERNOON lunch when she heard a vehicle pull up to her B&B on the gravel drive. She looked out the window over the kitchen sink and saw that her friend Deputy Denise Porter had driven her Maley County Sheriff's Department vehicle into the yard. Deputy Jesse Lopez had followed Deputy Porter into the yard in his Sheriff's Department truck.

When Deputy Porter stopped, she put her SUV into park, set the emergency brake, and left the motor running. She picked up the mike for her radio and said, "Dispatch, show Mike-34 and Mike-29 out at the special assignment, out of radio contact."

Wondering why two deputies were in her yard while on shift, Connie went outside to meet them.

Deputy Porter's radio answered, "Mike-34, Radio copies. Fourteen thirty-two, (2:32 p.m.)"

Deputy Porter hung her radio mike on the clip on her dash, shut off the engine, exited her vehicle, and waited for Deputy Lopez. When he approached, he asked, "What if she heard that on the scanner?"

As they walked to the closed gate into the yard, Deputy Porter replied, "House rule, no scanner."

Deputy Porter led the way into the yard. When Deputy Lopez entered, she closed the yard gate behind him, then led the way to the porch. She asked Deputy Lopez, "By the way, you're not afraid of dogs, are you?"

"No, why?" As they approached the door, Deputy Porter pointed to the far end of the porch. Magic and Misty thundered around the corner of the house and raced to intercept them on the porch.

Magic yodeled her Akita greeting when she caught Deputy Porter's scent. She knew the deputy from past visits. Magic gave Deputy Lopez a sharp warning bark; his scent was unfamiliar. Misty danced around both deputies. She indiscriminately liked almost everybody and vocalized happy yips as she danced around their feet. Connie Sullivan stepped out onto the porch.

"Denise, Jesse, what are you guys doing here?"

"We need to talk to you for a minute," Deputy Porter said.

"Okay, but I need to leave soon. My shift starts at fifteen hundred, (3:00 p.m.)," Connie replied.

Deputy Porter led the way into the B&B. "Let's go inside for this, it's hot out here in a vest," she said as she tapped her knuckles against the bulletproof vest under her uniform shirt.

"Okay, but we need to make this fast," Connie replied as she and the deputies, accompanied by the dogs, went into the house.

Once they were all inside, she turned to Deputy Porter, "What's up?"

"Sit," Deputy Porter said and pointed at the couch.

Connie perched on the edge of the couch cushion, "You're scaring me."

"I don't mean to, but I need to tell you something, and I need you not to go all dispatcher on me by asking a dozen questions until I've finished," Deputy Porter said.

Connie nodded. She watched the deputies for any hint of what this was about. She saw they were both tense.

Deputy Lopez stood against the door. Deputy Porter sat next to Connie on the couch, adjusted her utility belt and vest then turned to Connie, and took one of her hands in hers.

"Connie, Tom was killed in New Mexico this morning," Deputy Porter said and watched as the color drained from Connie's face. Connie slowly shook her head, "no."

"No, I talked to him this morning, he was fine," Connie said, almost emotionlessly, her face pale. "They weren't going to be in the way of the fire, just clearing an existing fire break of vegetation that had grown up over the last couple years. Miles from the main fire."

"Connie," Deputy Porter said gently, "Tom was shot and killed in the fire break. And Ace is missing."

"No," Connie mumbled, fainted then slumped toward the floor.

The deputy protected Connie's head as she guided Connie's limp body in a controlled fall from the couch. Deputy Porter maneuvered Connie to a soft landing on the floor, lying on her left side.

The dogs milled around Connie, where she lay on the floor. Magic nudged her with her nose and licked her face. Misty lay down against Connie's back and rested her chin on Connie's shoulder. Deputy Porter knew Connie was safe with the dogs.

The deputy grabbed a blanket off the back of the couch to cover Connie and ordered her partner, "Find me a pillow for her head." Deputy Lopez grabbed a pillow from a nearby chair and threw it to Deputy Porter, who placed it under Connie's head. Deputy Lopez flung Deputy Porter another pillow that Deputy Porter then put against Connie's chest to keep her from rolling forward and blocking her airway.

Deputy Porter got on her cell phone and called Dr. Sharon Grant, "Hi, Sharon, it's Denise. I'm at the B&B with Connie. I just had to inform her that Tom was killed at a fire and she fainted on me. I don't want to leave her alone, and I know you two are tight. Any chance you could stop by?"

"Paul called me, I'm already on my way," Dr. Grant said and disconnected the call.

"Jesse, you might as well get back on patrol. I'll clear when I can," Deputy Porter told her co-worker. "Nothing more for you to do here anyway, I'll write the case report."

Deputy Lopez left quickly, not needing the suggestion to go to be repeated. He was uncomfortable around grief, especially intense grief. Connie's grief almost overwhelmed him.

PART ONE

MAY 12, 1994
CASPER, WYOMING

Ten-year-old Connie Daily was getting ready for bed with some supervision from her sitter, Barbara. She had brushed her teeth, but she was still barefoot and in her play clothes. She needed to put on her pajamas. Tonight was her parents' date night.

The rule for Connie on "date night" was, she had to be ready for bed when they got home. If she was in bed when they got home, she could get hugs, kisses and a short story before falling asleep for the night. If she wasn't ready, she only got hugs and kisses goodnight.

When the doorbell rang, Connie looked at Barbara in surprise. "Who is it?" Connie asked Barbara.

"I have no idea," she replied. "We'll go check and look through the peephole before we open the door."

As Connie followed Barbara to the front door, she thought to herself; the pizza delivery man already came hours ago. Mom and Dad never rang the doorbell. They just came in through the garage into the kitchen. Mom and Dad should be back from their "date night" any time now. Although why they needed to go on a date every month was beyond her. Dad had finally come home from Walter Reed Medical Center at Christmas. They had celebrated being married for fifteen years last week, and they had her. Connie watched as Barbara looked through the peephole in the front door.

When Barbara unlocked and opened the front door, Connie looked around her and saw two Natrona County Sheriff's deputies in their coats over full uniforms on the front porch.

"Can I help you?" Barbara asked through the still closed storm door.

"Is this the Daily residence?" asked the female deputy.

"Yes," Barbara replied hesitantly, "But they aren't home right now. I stay with Connie for them when they go out."

The male deputy said, "We know. May we come in, please? We have something to tell you both."

"Come sit in the living room," Barbara invited. She led the way with Connie at her side. The deputies entered, and Deputy Greg Johnson closed the storm door and front door behind them to keep the cold night air outside.

Once inside, the two deputies shook hands with Barbara as they introduced themselves to her, then crouched to do the same with Connie.

"Hi, I'm Michelle," said Deputy Smith as she squatted down in front of Connie to shake her hand. "What's your name?"

"Connie Daily," Connie replied and shook the deputy's outstretched hand. Connie gave her a thorough looking over. Short light blond hair with dark roots, tan eye make-up, a dark brown heavy coat with a metal six-pointed star badge on it, underneath the open coat was a tan-colored shirt, thick black belt with all kinds of stuff on it and a gun! She held a brick-sized portable radio in her left hand. It periodically squawked quietly. The rest of her clothes were heavy blue jeans and black boots with a thick tread on the bottom.

The male deputy was dressed the same, in a warm jacket over his uniform for the cold Casper evening. He had his portable radio hung on his belt. Deputy Johnson repeated Deputy Michelle Smith's actions. He squatted down and held out his hand to Connie, "Hi Connie, I'm Greg. I wish I could have met you under different circumstances."

The comment Deputy Johnson made to Connie increased Barbara's nervousness. "So why are you here?" Barbara asked.

"Let's go sit down, and we'll tell you," Deputy Johnson said. Everyone settled in the living room. The deputies each sat forward in matching recliners that faced the couch. Barbara perched on the edge of the sofa with Connie next to her.

Deputy Johnson took in both Barbara and Connie with his gaze, as he explained, "We are here to inform you that there has been a serious accident on C-Y Avenue at Poplar Street. Mr. and Mrs. Daily are both in critical condition and are currently undergoing treatment at Wyoming Medical Center."

Barbara sucked in a deep breath and let it out slowly before asking, "What? How? That's in Casper."

"The Casper Police Department asked us to come out and let you know since you're in the county. We need to notify the next of kin. That would be you, Connie, and any grandparents, aunts or uncles. And we need to arrange for someone to take care of you, Connie," Deputy Smith answered.

Connie said, "I have lots of aunts and uncles. At church." Connie frowned, then continued, "I don't have any grandparents; I wish I did."

Deputy Michelle Smith saw Barbara could barely hold back her tears. She stood and held out her hand to Connie as she asked, "Do you know where your Mom keeps her list of your aunts and uncles at church? Could you show it to me?"

Connie nodded, "It's on the fridge." Connie slid off the couch and went with Michelle into the kitchen, where she pointed at the list held to the fridge by a magnet.

In the living room, Barbara's tears made trails down her face. She asked Deputy Johnson, "What happens now? What am I supposed to do?"

"We have to find a blood relative who can take Connie. If we don't, we need to put her in emergency foster care. We have to make sure she has someone to take care of her," Deputy Johnson replied. "Did the Daily's give you someone to contact if Connie has an emergency while they are out?"

"Yes, I'm supposed to call them on Dr. Daily's cell phone. I know the number," Barbara sighed, "But, like, in this case, I guess that wouldn't help."

Barbara sat back on the couch, pulled her feet up onto the cushions, and wiped her face with her sleeve, and said, "I can't do this. I don't know of any blood relatives. I know the Dailys from church. Connie refers to my parents as Aunt Claire and Uncle Howard, even though we aren't blood relatives." Barbara began to breathe quickly. "Oh, my God! I don't know what to do! I need to call my parents!" Barbara started to sob and grabbed a throw pillow to cover her mouth and stifle her blubbering, as she tried to conceal her distress from Connie.

Deputy Johnson moved and sat next to Barbara on the couch. He put a supportive hand on her shoulder, "Don't panic. There are systems in place to handle this. Do your parents live nearby?"

"Yes, the next street over, they can be here in, like, five minutes. I need my parents!"

"Go ahead, and call them. Deputy Smith will keep Connie busy a little longer in the kitchen."

Barbara picked up the phone on the end table next to the couch and called home.

Minutes after Barbara had made the call, the Sullivan's front door suddenly flew open, and Barbara's parents rushed in to aid their daughter. Claire went to the distraught Barbara on the couch and consoled her. Howard introduced himself and his wife to Deputy Johnson.

"So, what's going on? How can we help?" asked Howard.

In the kitchen, Connie heard the commotion created by the new arrivals when the front door banged open and then slammed shut. Deputy Smith quickly redirected her attention.

"We have the church list. Does your mom also have a personal phone book? Might it be in a drawer? Maybe near the phone?" Deputy Smith asked.

"She carries that one in her purse," Connie said.

In the living room, Deputy Johnson informed Barbara's parents, "We need to find a blood relative or designated guardian for Connie. Her parents were in a car accident. Otherwise, we need to arrange emergency foster care."

Howard said, "As far as I know, she only has Brian and Lisa. Brian grew up raised by his grandparents, and they have both passed. Lisa just inherited this house from her mother, who passed away last year. Lisa's dad died in Vietnam. I don't think either of those kids had siblings, just a tough start in life."

Claire continued to console Barbara, who wouldn't settle down. Claire finally said, "You can't upset Connie with your hysterics. Let your dad deal with the chaos. We can wait in the car for your dad."

Barbara quickly nodded her agreement as she cried, and they went outside to wait for Howard.

Howard led Deputy Johnson to the home office. He helped Deputy Johnson with a quick search. Deputy Johnson searched the desk. Howard did a quick review of the folders in the file cabinet. None of the papers divulged a will or a trust.

They found no documents of any kind to guide Connie's care in case of an emergency. An expanded search of the house revealed a fireproof safe in the parents' bedroom closet. It was locked tight. Before they left the bedroom, Howard asked, "So what happened?"

"A drunk ran a red light. The Dailys are both critical and not expected to make it. Poor kid," Deputy Johnson replied as he shook his head sympathetically.

"That's awful," Howard said. "Since I can't be any more help here and I don't want to get in the way, I'm taking my family home. If you need to ask me anything else let me know." He gave Deputy Johnson his contact information, then left.

Finding no helpful information in the kitchen. Deputy Smith asked, "Connie, can I see your bedroom?"

Connie shrugged and said, "Okay." She led the way upstairs to her room. Once there, Deputy Smith asked Connie, "If you couldn't come home again for a long time, what would you take with you?"

"You mean like on a fun trip or something else? Why wouldn't I come home again?" Connie asked. She jumped onto her full-sized bed with a lavender-colored comforter. She sat on the mattress and faced Deputy Smith, who then sat down on the bed next to her.

Deputy Johnson leaned into the room to ask, "Do you know the combination to the safe in your parents' room?"

"Nope," replied Connie. "Why?"

"There might be some papers in there to tell us who to call for you when your parents can't come home right away," Deputy Johnson said.

"When my parents aren't home, Barbara looks after me, and she just left. So where are my parents?" Connie demanded. "You aren't babysitters. You're cops."

Deputy Johnson stepped back out of the room. He contacted dispatch from the phone in the kitchen to arrange emergency foster care for Connie.

"Why can't they just come home?" Connie asked.

Deputy Smith explained, "Sweetie, your mom and dad were in an accident. They have to be in the hospital for a while. Someone other than Barbara needs to look after you. An adult. She's a teenager, so she's too young."

"No, they were fine. Mom's a safe driver. So is Dad. They wouldn't get in an accident. They're too careful," Connie said.

"It wasn't their fault. But your parents were hurt bad, and they can't leave the hospital, so someone else has to look after you."

Connie began to cry. "Who will look after Mac?" Connie asked as tears ran down her face.

The question startled Deputy Smith. "Who is Mac, Honey?" she asked.

"My dog."

"Where is he?"

"In his kennel. Dad said he had to be there when Barbara's here; she's intimidated by him. I think it's because she doesn't know German."

"Well, Barbara left with her parents. What does German have to do with anything? What kind of dog is Mac, Honey?" Deputy Smith asked.

"He's my father's retired bomb dog. My dad got to keep him when he got out of the Army after they both got hurt in Somalia."

"If you got dressed to go outside, put on shoes and a coat, could I see Mac?" Deputy Smith asked.

"I'm not supposed to take anyone to see Mac without my mom or dad with me."

"I'll make it okay with your parents, but I do need to see Mac," said Deputy Smith.

"No! Why? I don't understand," Connie cried. "I'm not supposed to show Mac to anyone! My father said so! Why can't I wait for my parents here? I promise to go to school and do my homework and feed Mac and clean up after him. I know how to fix meals; Dad taught me. I'll be good. I promise," Connie pleaded.

Deputy Johnson stepped into the room and locked eyes with Deputy Smith. Deputy Johnson gave his head a slight shake.

Deputy Smith asked him, "Both?"

Deputy Johnson responded, "Yes, and no relatives."

Deputy Smith said, "Okay. We've got a retired Army bomb dog in a kennel in back, Mac. Only knows German commands, according to Connie. She's not allowed to show Mac to anyone without a parent present, and since we don't have that, she's not moving. So, we need to make arrangements for him too."

Deputy Johnson forced a tiny smile for Connie's benefit, then said, "Swell. I'll handle it."

Connie was scared. She was also cranky. It was hours past her bedtime. After she looked at her bedside clock on the nightstand, she demanded, "Where's my dad! I want my dad! Now! I want my mom! They promised to be home by now!" and then she began to weep.

Deputy Smith gathered Connie carefully into her arms so as not to stab her with the badge pinned to her shirt or the pens in her shirt pocket and said, "I'm sorry Honey, but your parents can't come home. They're in heaven now."

"No!" Connie screamed. "They can't be in heaven! God lives there! My parents live here! They promised to come home! It's not right! I want Mac!"

With that statement, Connie leaped off the bed and thundered barefoot down the stairs. She raced out the back door, without a coat, and ran to the dog kennel.

Mac waited at the kennel gate. He was a big black male German Shepherd who was missing his right back leg.

Connie let herself into his kennel and crawled into his dog house. He followed and licked her face as he tried to soothe the distress of his young mistress.

The deputies followed Connie's flight. When they got into the backyard, in the beam of their flashlights, they saw a sizable German Shepherd move to stand in the entrance to his dog house. He filled the space, lifted his lip at them, and growled a low warning.

"Shit!" Deputy Johnson muttered, "This just gets better and better."

"You got that right," Deputy Smith said. She spoke into her portable radio. "Dispatch, we're gonna need a canine handler who speaks German. If not, ask the city. We need the handler to meet us in the back yard at our current location. Access through the gate next to the garage."

"Dispatch copies. Will advise, twenty-three nineteen, (11:19 p.m.)."

K-9 handler, Deputy Mike Nelson, finally arrived in the backyard. He met with Deputy Smith and asked, "What gives? Radio was kind of cryptic."

Deputy Smith pointed. Mac had exited his huge dog house to take in the newest arrival. "He's protecting a kid we need to hand over to child services. Her parents were killed in a car accident tonight. She's in his dog house. That dog is a retired Army bomb dog, dad's dog. Only knows German commands according to the kid."

When he observed the dog's protective posture and mildly agitated attitude towards the deputies, Deputy Mike Nelson said, "You don't want much, do you?"

S . GUETTER

"A small miracle will do. I would hate to have to tranquilize or shoot the dog in front of the kid, just to get her out of the dog house. She's had a crappy enough night as it is."

Deputy Johnson stepped away from the other two deputies to answer his radio.

"That's not going to be our only problem," Deputy Nelson replied. He saw Deputy Smith's confused look. Deputy Nelson continued, "That dog will find her, wherever she is, and protect her from any threat or die trying."

"Shit!" said Deputy Smith.

"There's no way to have someone stay here with the kid until he calms down? I know it's unorthodox, but it's the safest for everyone if we let him calm down, get used to us and let him relax a bit."

Mac backed into his dog house, looked at the deputies, then retreated out of sight into his doghouse.

"Fantastic," Deputy Smith said sarcastically. "Who's going to stay all night?"

Silence weighed the air for a while as none of the deputies volunteered.

Mike Nelson blew out a breath, "I will," he said. "Just let me get Vera out here. Let's see how Mac responds to her. She might help diffuse things." Deputy Nelson went to his patrol vehicle. He snapped a long line on Vera, his female Belgian Malinois. Leashed, he let her out of his K-9 modified patrol car. From Vera's area of the patrol car, he grabbed a folded blanket Vera lay on in the back while waiting to work.

Deputy Smith watched Deputy Nelson settle himself and Vera on the ground next to the kennel.

When Deputy Johnson returned, he said, "I've got to back up Deputy Anderson on a domestic violence call. I locked the front door, and I left the back door unlocked. You guys gonna be all right?"

"Yeah, go," Deputy Smith responded.

Deputy Johnson loped to the gate that led to the front of the house. He made sure the gate latched when he let himself out. In moments, the deputies in the back yard heard the roar of Deputy Johnson's patrol truck as it sped down the street. The reflection of the flashing blue and red lights faded as he raced out of the neighborhood.

"You gonna need anything before I take off?" Deputy Smith asked Deputy Nelson.

"Could you run to the Kum and Go and get me a super-size hot coffee? Just black. I think this'll take a while," Deputy Nelson replied.

- 8 -

"Sure, Mike, I'll be right back." Deputy Smith left on the coffee run.

Deputy Mike Nelson and Vera sat next to the kennel, partly sheltered from the cool nighttime breeze by the large dog house Connie and Mac were occupying. Deputy Nelson called out, "Connie, my name is Mike. Do you want to come out and see my dog? Her name is Vera. Mac likes her."

"No! I want my dad! I want my dad now! And my mom! I want my mom!" Connie sobbed.

Deputy Smith returned and handed Deputy Nelson his coffee. She also gave him a sleeping bag.

"Where'd you get this?" Mike Nelson asked.

"I also work search and rescue. I have all kinds of stuff in the back of my truck. The weather report is saying overnight low around 40 degrees or so at the airport, so it probably will be colder here. I thought you might want the sleeping bag to wrap up in."

Deputy Nelson took the large coffee in one hand, as he gestured to Deputy Smith to drop the sleeping bag next to him, "I appreciate it. Thanks," he said.

Deputy Smith looked at the K-9 deputy and tipped her head in inquiry. Deputy Nelson shook his head in reply. "Thanks for the coffee," he said as he took an appreciative sip. "Go. You have other things to do tonight. Tell dispatch not to notify children's services. I'll call them as soon as I get her out. If we try to speed this up, it will make the kid more stressed than she is already."

Deputy Smith nodded and left Deputy Nelson to his task of getting the stubborn child out of the dog house.

Deputy Nelson tried to talk with Connie again a little later, "Connie, Sweetie, aren't you getting cold in Mac's dog house?"

"No." came the defiant response.

"Why not, I'm getting chilly out here, and I'm cuddled with Vera on her blanket."

"I have Mac. He keeps me warm. Mac and I have our sleeping bags on our cot. Daddy made them for us," a much more subdued Connie replied, she still wept, just not as hard as before.

"Jesus, Lord, how much longer can this kid last?" Deputy Nelson asked his dog as if she had the answer. Connie was breaking his heart.

MAY 13, 1994
CASPER, WYOMING

DEPUTY MIKE NELSON AND VERA STAYED WITH MAC AND CONNIE ALL night. They sat on Vera's car blanket, wrapped together in the unzipped sleeping bag. Occasionally Mike talked to Connie. Most of the time, without any response, other than the sounds of her despair.

Mac had taken to Vera, which was good. He would come to check on Vera, touch noses with her through his kennel fence, then return to Connie.

Mike wanted to save the dog for the little girl he hadn't yet seen. He knew where she was, just not how to get her out of the big canine's doghouse.

The sounds of Connie as she cried off and on, all night, stabbed Mike in the heart. The thought of his twin girls going through what this kid was, just made his heart hurt for her. Her whole life as she had known it had been torn away by the ringing of a doorbell.

Sunrise brightened the eastern horizon. Connie was finally ready to talk with him. Negotiations for Mac's care began.

"What about if I promise to adopt Mac as soon as he gets to animal control?" Mike asked.

"No!" bellowed Connie. "Adopt him now! From here straight to your house. And you have to take his dog house and his special cot and his sleeping bag and his special food, so he will know your house is his home."

"Deal. You drive a hard bargain. Now, will you come out? I'm cold," Deputy Nelson replied, then stifled a yawn.

Connie crawled to the dog house entrance, stopped and poked her head out the flap. She surveyed the deputy and Vera as she leaned on her elbows in the dog house entrance. Connie took in how Vera leaned against Mike, tongue slightly out. The dog looked happy to be with him. That was important. And he has his arm around the dog as if he liked Vera and she mattered to him. Sitting down like he was, Connie couldn't tell how tall he was.

The deputy had a friendly face, wire-framed glasses, dark hair going by the mustache, and his face looked like he wasn't fat. He wore a dark knit cap and a sheriff's department uniform like the other deputies that had first come to her house.

The deputy had a sleeping bag over his shoulders and the dog. It hung open in front so she could see his uniform, and he had Vera cuddled next to him, inside the sleeping bag, too. She was pretty, Connie liked the black on her face. Connie left her sanctuary and neared the gate to the fenced enclosure. Mac was at her side once she cleared the entrance to the dog house. Vera stretched her head out, nose raised to catch scents.

While still inside, Connie knelt and held her hand out for Vera to sniff through the chain-link fence of the kennel.

Mike finally got a look at the kid he had been negotiating with all night. The tear-stained face, swollen red eyes, mussed brown hair to her shoulders, long-sleeved t-shirt, and jeans; she looked small. But she had negotiated the safety of Mac before coming out, so she was smart, and she cared about her dog.

"Hi, nice to meet you in person. I'm Deputy Nelson. You can call me Mike. You must be Connie." His vigil over, he got up from the ground. His knees and vertebrae popped as he stood and reached his hands over his head. He leaned left, then right to stretch out his back.

Vera stood and stretched, chest high, back legs extended out behind her, as Mike gathered up the sleeping bag and blanket.

Connie watched undecided. She still stood inside the kennel gate, not yet leaving her place of sanctuary, Mac beside her.

"You are one tough negotiator, Connie," Mike told the ten-year-old. "I promise Mac will live at my house and play with Vera. You can come to visit anytime you want, as long as your foster parents say it's okay." Mike wanted to be cautious about making promises. He didn't want to lie to this little girl. "So, will you come out now? I don't know about you, but I could use some breakfast. Aren't you even a little bit hungry?" Connie nodded.

Once Deputy Mike Nelson had Connie, Mac, and Vera in the house, he raided the fridge. He decided to make bacon, eggs, hashbrowns, and toast. Before he started cooking, Mike contacted his dispatcher using the kitchen's wall phone.

He told dispatch, "I've got Connie in the house, with her dog. He's very protective of her. I promised to take the dog and look after him for her, so we don't need animal control. I'm going to feed her breakfast. If you could get someone from child protective services over here in about an hour to take her, I can take the dog and make adoption arrangements for him. Please notify my sergeant I'm still here, and I plan to take tonight off as flex time."

After they had eaten, Mike helped Connie put the used breakfast dishes in the dishwasher. Then the doorbell rang. When he glanced at the wall clock in the kitchen, Mike saw it was just after six in the morning.

Mac went to the front door with Vera. He woofed once, loudly. Mike and Connie followed the dogs. To ensure the dogs would stay when he opened the door, Mike told the dogs, *"Blibe."* Confident the dogs would stay, and wouldn't rush the CPS worker; he opened it for the child protective services representative.

The stout brown-haired lady was nervous about the two dogs beside the deputy when he opened the door. She took a step back as the unmoving dogs gave her the once over while she stood on the porch.

Connie peeked around Mike at the stranger on her porch. "Who are you?" Connie demanded.

Deputy Nelson said, "Connie, first tell your dog she is okay and can come in the house, okay?"

"Mac, *Sicher.*" Connie instructed her dog to let him know the woman was 'safe.' Mike gave his dog Vera her command as well and then invited the CPS worker into the house.

Connie moved with Mike. She kept him between her and the woman as the CPS employee entered the house. The CPS worker leaned down to talk around Mike to Connie, who instead, bolted to her room. The CPS worker never got a word out. Mac and Vera followed on her heels. Moments later, a door slammed.

"That went well," she sighed as she straightened, then held her hand out to Mike. "I'm Samantha Anderson. I saw your unit outside. How did a K-9 officer get this call? I thought this was an emergency placement after a fatal car crash."

"It was, the complication being the German Shepherd. He knows only German commands. From what Connie tells me that dog served in Somalia with her dad and saved his life. The same mortar blast injured both of them. Her dad petitioned the Army and got to keep him. I use German commands with my K-9, so here I am. She spent the night in his dog house with him," Mike Nelson explained.

"It was in the 40's last night. How is she not frozen?" Samantha Anderson asked.

"More like, how am I not frozen? I've been here since last night. It took me all night, negotiating with Connie to get her to come out. She was toasty in the dog house with her dog. I finally got her talked out about an hour ago. You know, I'm going to need Connie to tell her dog to get in my patrol car with Vera before you take her anywhere, so Mac will know it is okay to go," Deputy Nelson said.

"Crap! Why me? Why do I always get complicated ones?" Ms. Anderson complained. She heaved a deep sigh then started up the stairs Connie had fled up earlier.

Deputy Nelson quickly followed, and put a restraining hand on her arm, "Let me go first. She's upset, and the dogs may get protective," he warned.

That stopped Ms. Anderson in her tracks on the stairs. She flattened against the wall to let the deputy pass her.

"Honey, it's Mike, can I come in?" Deputy Nelson asked at Connie's bedroom door.

Connie weakly said, "Ohh-kaay." Once in the bedroom, Mike took in Connie on her bed, curled in a ball, her head on her pillow. She clutched a teddy bear to her chest. Mac and Vera were on the bed with her. A dog on each side. Vera at her back, Mac in front of her, between Connie and the door.

Samantha stood in the doorway to the bedroom. She looked in but didn't enter. She told Connie, "I need you to pack some clothes and pick a few things you want to have with you. You're going to be staying with foster parents until we find someone to look after you."

Mike sat down on a corner of the bed. He reached out to Connie and gently stroked her back as he pacified her. "Come on, Connie. You negotiated a safe place for Mac. I'll look after him. You need a safe place too. If you want, I can help you," he said.

Connie, head still on her pillow, nodded. She finally rose to pack. She picked a few outfits and a picture of her parents with her taken on a camping trip. Then she got her piggy bank. She sat on the bed with her teddy bear and the bank.

Mike was about to say something when she opened her bank and took out bills. She left the change. He watched as she opened the back of the teddy bear, removed the music box, and put the paper money into the opening.

"How much money do you have?" Mike asked as he watched her stuff the teddy bear.

"Two hundred and eighteen dollars," Connie responded. "But I never spend more than twenty dollars at any one time."

"That's a lot of money," Mike replied.

"That's why I'm taking it with me and not leaving it here," Connie said as she checked the inside of the bear after putting the tightly rolled bills into the spot the music box had occupied. She felt there was room, so Connie added the loose change from her bank, quarters first, then dimes until the bear couldn't hold any more change.

When she was ready to go, Connie had a backpack with school books and a small rolling suitcase with her clothes and personal items, and her teddy bear clutched to her chest.

Tears rolled down Connie's cheeks when she ordered Mac into the back of Mike's patrol car with Vera. Ms. Anderson kept a hand on Connie's shoulder as Mike drove away with her dog. When the patrol car was out of sight, Ms. Anderson steered Connie to the car that would take her to the Child Protective Services office.

It took a couple of hours for Samantha to finally deliver Connie to an emergency placement foster home. She said, "Remember, this is a temporary placement for you. I'll set up a permanent foster home for you soon." Connie nodded her acknowledgment. "You'll get to go to your regular school and see your friends, just like before. You'll see, it'll be fine," Ms. Anderson assured Connie.

Ms. Anderson got back to her office after she had dropped off Connie to find a message from Deputy Mike Nelson. He wanted to know the contact information for the foster home where Connie was. Samantha wondered about the request, but he had spent all night with the kid. When she had time, she'd think about it.

That night Connie wept herself into an exhausted sleep. She was devastated by all the changes that had happened. The other girls in the foster home were older and wanted her to be quiet. They didn't have any family to stay with either, what was the big deal? Every night Connie cried herself to sleep; she just did it quietly, so as not to bring the wrath of the other girls she shared the room with down upon her.

MAY 20, 1994
CASPER WYOMING

WHEN MIKE NELSON HADN'T HEARD ANYTHING FROM CHILD PROTECTIVE services about how to contact Connie, he dropped by her school, with Mac in his SUV. He timed it to be there right when school was letting out.

He saw Connie as she exited the building. She dragged her feet as she came out of school. Her fire and brightness he had seen the night he had met her were gone. She was a sad shell of her former self, head down, back curved, shoulders slumped, as she dragged her backpack along beside her down the sidewalk as she left the school.

"Connie!" he called.

Her head snapped up. She looked around.

"Connie!" he called again.

When she saw him, she lit up, smiled, dropped her backpack on the sidewalk, and ran to him. "Deputy Mike!" She staggered him when she slammed into him at a run and wrapped her arms around his waist.

Mac yipped through the open window of Mike's SUV.

"Mac! You brought Mac!" She lit up even more. She ran to the SUV and held her hands out to Mac, who had stuck his head out the partially open window. The happy dog licked her face as she stood on the running board.

Not to be ignored, Vera shoved Mac sideways to get in a few licks, then backed away so Mac could continue to wash Connie's face with his tongue.

Mike walked up behind her, "I told you I would make sure you could see Mac. Finding your school took me a while. Mac's doing okay. He and Vera are good friends."

At her name, Vera stuck her head out the window beside Mac and gave Connie another lick on the face. Connie reached to open the SUV door, but Mike stopped her. "I can't let you in; I could get in trouble."

"Can't I come live with you, Deputy Mike? I would behave. I would clean my room, do my homework, feed and clean up after Mac, and Vera, I could help with housework. I'd be good, I promise." The tears slowly trailed down her face. "I hate where I live now. The other girls don't like me. And school will be out soon so I won't see my friends. I can't even sign up for softball this summer. I have to stay in my room all the time, and it isn't even mine. I have to share with three other girls. There's nowhere for quiet time."

Mike said, "I wish I could Honey, but I would get in trouble and Mac would get taken away from me and so would Vera. Your life has been through a big change. You need to give yourself time to adjust."

"I don't want to adjust," Connie snarled and lightly kicked her toe against the side of Mike's SUV tire. "I want to go home! To my home, not foster care. Or your home, I could live with Mac! There's room in his dog house for me!"

"Talk to Samantha. Maybe she can get you someplace different," Mike advised.

"Can you tell me where Mac lives so I can send him presents?" Connie asked.

"I don't see why not. Give me a piece of paper from your backpack. I'll give you my address." Deputy Mike Nelson wrote his address and home phone number on the paper for Connie. "I need to let you keep going home now, so we both stay out of trouble, okay kiddo? I have to go to work tonight, but I need to take Mac home and put on my uniform first."

"Okay," Connie agreed. She stepped off the running board and stuffed the paper with Mike's address in her pocket. She watched as Mike got into his SUV and drove away with the last surviving member of her family.

MAY 25, 1994
CASPER, WYOMING

IT WAS LATE MORNING WHEN MIKE WENT OUT TO FEED MAC AND VERA. Vera met him at her kennel gate for her breakfast. Mac didn't come out of the dog house in his kennel. Mike shook the metal food bowl to make the dry kibble rattle. "Breakfast," Mike announced. Still no response. His heart sank. "Mac?" he called. "Crap," muttered Mike, "He didn't get out somehow and go look for Connie, did he?" He entered the kennel and on hands and knees crawled into the dog house.

"It's okay Mac. *Sicher*," Mike told Mac quietly as he crawled partway into the dog house, and peered around the wind partition inside the dog house.

"Oh, shit," Mike muttered. Curled up against the big dog was Connie, sound asleep, wrapped in her coat and Mac's sleeping bag, her head on the big dog's flank. Mac stared at him steadily, not moving, his upper lip twitching. From the looks of things, she had come here from school yesterday. Mike swore quietly.

"Mike!" his wife Donna yelled out the back door of the house. "My water just broke! I called our parents! Time to go!"

"Shit!" Mike muttered to himself as he backed out of the dog house. He left Mac and Connie undisturbed.

Once he had his wife checked into her room in the maternity ward, he took the hands of his twin girls and led them to the waiting room. There he used a waiting room courtesy phone, and he called his boss, Sergeant Amy Lochwood. He told her, "Connie probably spent the night in the kennel at my house with Mac, and she's still there."

"Wow," said Sergeant Lochwood.

"I'm at the hospital with Donna, her water just broke, and she's ready to pop according to her doctor. New topic. About Connie, can you find out if there has been a missing kid report or runaway juvenile report out on Connie for me?" Mike asked.

"I can, why?" his sergeant asked.

"Please, I need to know someone is looking out for her at CPS. Because as soon as Stephen is born and Donna is okay, I plan to call CPS and tear some hide off of someone. It isn't right!" he said.

Sergeant Lockwood said, "Let me handle it; you focus on your wife and son, Mike."

Mike's parents arrived from Evansville and took the twins off his hands. They took the girls back home so he could focus on his wife as she labored to give birth to his son, Stephen.

Donna's parents would go to the house as soon as their plane landed at the Natrona County airport in Casper, and they had rented a car.

CPS supervisor Ted Rose strode up to Mike Nelson in the hospital outside Donna Nelson's room. "I got a call from your Sergeant, Amy Lochwood. I am confused about what has you all worked up Deputy Nelson," he said.

"There's a ten-year-old girl, Connie Daily, who your department is supposed to be responsible for and looking after. She was supposed to be in a good foster home. Instead, I found her in my back-yard sleeping in a dog house this morning! I'm pretty sure she spent the night! That's what has me all worked up!" Mike's voice increased in volume the longer he talked. He took a breath and let it out slowly; he continued, "She's a bright, intelligent, helpful kid. She has done nothing wrong, and neither did her parents. A drunk driver killed them on their way home from supper. Connie has no living relatives. I'm not a foster parent, and my wife is about to have a baby, or I would have taken her in myself, but right now, I can't," Mike said.

"You seem awful invested in the welfare of this kid; why is that?" asked the CPS supervisor.

"That's what has you worried? My investment in this kid? What about your investment? Aren't you supposed to be invested in the welfare of this kid? According to my Sergeant, there isn't even a missing report on her, either as a missing child or a runaway. From the looks of things, she got in my yard sometime yesterday. Maybe look in your backyard before worrying about mine!" Mike snapped. "Now get her a new case manager and find her some decent people to be her foster parents."

"Sure. I'll just run by your house, pick her up, and take her to a group home until I find her a new foster home. What's your address?" Ted Rose asked.

Mike worked to tamp down his increasing agitation, as he said, "Not gonna happen, it's too dangerous. As soon as my wife has the baby, and everything is fine, I'll pick Connie up and bring her to the substation. I'll call you when we get there. Then you and the new case manager can meet us. I'll go with them to pick up her belongings from the last foster home and follow them to the new one so I can make sure she'll stay."

A nurse poked her head out of the delivery room into the hall, "Mike, it's time."

"But," said Ted Rose. He was talking to thin air. Mike had walked into the delivery room. "That's not how we do things deputy," he called out to the door as it closed behind Mike. He dropped into a chair and called Mike's supervisor, thinking he could get the address that way.

Sergeant Lochwood told him, "Are you out of your fricking mind?! No way in hell! Do you have any idea of the liability involved if I did that? Not without Deputy Nelson at the house will you set one foot on his property. His work dog is a trained attack dog! The other dog is an Army trained attack and bomb dog! These dogs are not family pets! But they will both protect Connie. She's safe right now, don't mess that up. Do you understand me?"

"Yes. You haven't heard the end of this sergeant," Ted Rose snapped.

MAY 26, 1994
CASPER, WYOMING

CONNIE HATED THE NEW FOSTER HOME. YES, SHE HAD A ROOM TO herself now. The lady was very nice but had cats. Lots of cats! Inside cats! The kind of cats that never went outside. Not even to pee or poop. Yuck!

The place stank like cat pee and poop, and no one noticed but her. The smell almost made her gag. She was a dog person, but for some reason, two of the cats liked her and wouldn't leave her alone.

By bedtime, she wasn't feeling good, and it was a kind of not feeling good she had never felt before. Her skin felt itchy and too tight. When she had put on her pajamas that night, she noticed she had welts all over her stomach, chest, arms, and legs. She lay down on the bed, which was nice and soft and should have been comfy, but she was uncomfortable. She itched all over and couldn't stop scratching. Then the coughing and wheezing started, and it got harder to breathe. She got out of bed and went to find Mrs. Jones, the foster mom.

"I don't know what's wrong, but I feel funny. Like funny - peculiar, not funny ha-ha," Connie told her.

Mrs. Jones looked up from her book, saw Connie's bloated face, and puffed up lips, and said, "Get your coat honey; we need to get you to the emergency room."

Connie asked, almost hopeful, "Am I gonna die like my mom and dad did?"

"No, Honey, not if we get you there soon enough," Mrs. Jones said, wasting no time bundling Connie into the car and speeding to the hospital.

Clutching her teddy bear, Connie let the silent tears roll down her cheeks as Mrs. Jones drove to the emergency room. She wanted to be with her parents. How else was the pain in her chest from missing them going to ease?

In the emergency room, shots stopped the allergic reaction. The only thing the doctors could figure out was Connie was allergic to Mrs. Jones's cats. Since she had never been around cats, she hadn't known she was allergic.

Mrs. Jones said, "I'll call your case manager and let her know they need to find a new place for you to stay."

Connie shrugged in her hospital bed. She asked, "Okay, but what about my clothes?" as she clutched her teddy bear to her chest.

"I'll wash them at the Laundromat and drop them off at your new foster home. I don't think it would be safe to wash them at home. Oh, Honey, I am so sorry this happened to you. I was looking forward to having you stay with me."

Politely lying, Connie replied, "I was too. Thank you for having me in your home, even if it was only for an afternoon."

MAY 27, 1994
CASPER, WYOMING

CONNIE SPENT THE NIGHT IN THE HOSPITAL FOR OBSERVATION TO MAKE sure the allergic reaction had entirely subsided before she was taken to school by a new CPS caseworker, Mrs. Patricia Butler.

After school, Mrs. Butler met her and drove her to the new foster home. "If you run away from this one, you'll have used up all your chances and go to a group home," Mrs. Butler threatened Connie. "Understand me?" Connie nodded.

The long ride worried Connie. "Do I have to change schools now?" she asked.

"No, you're still in the same school district, a bus will pick you up and drop you off here," said Mrs. Butler. This foster home was far away from Mike Nelson's house, and Mac and Vera.

Connie had Mike's address and planned to send him a letter to let him know where she was now so he could make sure she saw Mac again. And Vera. She liked Vera too.

The long ride ended when Mrs. Butler turned in at a sign that read, "Farm Fresh eggs for sale," with a phone number. The car bumped up the rough dirt driveway to a large run-down mobile home.

Connie looked around. She was way out in the country. There were no nearby neighbors. Nope, this wasn't good. It didn't feel right, Connie thought.

The new foster parents, Mr. & Mrs. Specter, greeted her and her caseworker at the door. They were old and fat. At least in their sixties, Connie thought. When he walked, she noticed the man had boobs that jiggled along with his gelatinous gut. He needed a bra, Connie thought.

His enormous belly hung over his stressed belt. He had suspenders attached to his belt to help keep his pants up. He had an unkempt gray beard streaked with some dark brown. His hair was just like a ruffled bed skirt, ear high and gray. The top of his head was completely shiny bald. The way he looked at her made Connie uneasy.

Connie wanted away from here. The wife was skinny but still icky. She wore her hair in a loose, greasy grey ponytail down the back of her bleached out dress. No makeup and she had dark circles under her eyes. Her glasses were big, round, and thick. Connie noted that the house smelled funny, but not like cats. It was a weird, almost chemical smell.

"Now you said you had no cats on the property, correct?" Mrs. Butler asked Mr. Specter.

"We don't own any cats, but I'm not going to be responsible for any stray or feral cats that cross my property. I'm just not. Can't control everything you know," said Mr. Specter. This reply satisfied the caseworker, but not Connie.

In the kitchen, Connie paid close attention while Mrs. Butler explained to the Specters how the Epi-pens worked. "If Connie comes in contact with any cats, use the Epi-pens immediately and get her to a hospital emergency room, promptly," instructed Mrs. Butler.

Mrs. Specter asked, "Now when do the checks for her care start to come?"

Mrs. Butler replied, "As soon as I get her paperwork filed, it will take about thirty days to get through the system. The funds are released at the end of the first complete month she is with you. The days from the partial month will be prorated and added to the first check."

Connie was not impressed by Mr. & Mrs. Specter. They showed the caseworker and Connie her room. It was bigger than a breadbox, but not by much. She would be the only kid there. The Specters had no house pets. In the barn out back, they had forty chickens. They sold the eggs from them.

When the caseworker left, Mr. Specter gave Connie a list of chores she was expected to 'help' with around the place. Meaning; she did the tasks while the Specters watched. Dishes, dusting, mopping the floors, vacuuming, laundry, and outside, she was to pull weeds and all the chicken stuff.

JUNE 2, 1994
CASPER, WYOMING

A WEEK WAS ALL IT TOOK FOR CONNIE TO DECIDE THERE HAD TO BE better places to live than at the chicken farm. Like a horse barn. No matter how much she cleaned, she couldn't keep up with the trash the Specters generated every day. The chicken pens in the barn smelled worse. She was tired of places that smelled bad.

She stank from having to clean out the chicken pens, and she hated getting the eggs. The chickens didn't want to give them up and pecked at her hands, hard. When she cleaned the pens, the stench was so strong, her eyes watered.

She held her breath when she shoveled out the pens. Not long enough to prevent breathing in the stink that came from chicken poop. Each morning she had to rake out the pine chips and put them in a wheelbarrow and dump them into a compost pile behind the barn. Then she had to spread new pine chips for the chickens, then collect eggs. And eggs had to be gathered in the evening too. "Birds! I hate birds," she told a hen as she took its egg. The chicken pecked her hand.

She used one set of clothes just for her chores, so she didn't stink too bad at school. At least at school, she could shower every day after her first class of the day, gym class, without an audience. She hated showering in the evening at the Specters; they watched. Mr. Specter was adamant; it was only to make sure she got completely clean. As if! Connie thought. She knew it was an excuse to look at a naked, young girl.

When she got home from school, she asked about doing all her chores, except the chickens. The question enraged the Specters, and both Mr. and Mrs. Specter hit her. "That's why you're here! You ungrateful brat!" Mr. Specter yelled as he hit her with his fists. "You have to earn your keep!"

"No one wants you, or you wouldn't be here," Mrs. Specter snapped, then whipped her across her back with a strap. It tore her shirt. After they beat her, she was sent out to do the chores she hated. Mr. Specter followed her and watched Connie, to ensure she completed her tasks, then ordered her to bed without a shower or dinner.

That night she made her plans to run away. She was getting pretty good at leaving places. She would never have thought of running away from her parents. They wanted her. They loved her. Here, she was just a paycheck and slave labor. She knew she could find a better family, one who wanted her, all on her own. Tomorrow she planned to be out of here!

The TV in the living room was cranked up as always. The sound filled the house. Tonight, this let her listen to the weather report before she fell asleep. Tomorrow would be her last day here, she decided. She planned to run away after school. She'd miss the bus home and start walking. There had to be maps in the school library, and she could find herself a place to live.

JUNE 3, 1994
CASPER WYOMING

AFTER SCHOOL LET OUT, SHE EMPTIED EVERYTHING EXCEPT HER TEDDY bear from her backpack into her school locker. Then she walked to the nearby grocery store and bought the same things she and Dad had always bought when they went camping. Non-perishables Dad had called them. Jerky, dried fruit, and trail-mix. As a treat, she included one bag of almond M&Ms.

Also, she bought two 20-ounce bottles of water to stay hydrated. Dad always had said it was the most important thing other than not getting hurt. You had to stay hydrated.

The water bottles were heavy, but she had to have water. When she left the store, she loaded her purchases into her backpack. Ready for a new life, she headed towards the interstate. She followed it while she walked along on the frontage road, east to Glenrock.

Since she was afraid of being caught, she hid in the roadside ditch whenever she heard a car approach. She had walked for hours and was tired. It was after dark when she found an abandoned house, or at least it seemed deserted, and she hid behind some wooden pallets stacked in the garage for the night. She used her backpack for a pillow as she clutched her teddy bear to her chest while she slept.

JUNE 4, 1994
ALONG INTERSTATE 25

The next morning, sunrise woke her. She continued east, eating just enough to keep her going. That night she hid in another garage, detached from the house. She hadn't seen any other buildings for a while, so she planned to take her chances here. The idea of sleeping outside made her uncomfortable. She could be spotted while she slept.

She waited until after dark again. There were two cars parked in the driveway in front of the garage. She went to the door and tried the knob. It opened. Inside was a boat on a trailer, with a cover over it. Yippee. She crawled inside, and after a light snack, she slept on the padded seat along the back of the boat.

JUNE 5, 1994
ALONG INTERSTATE 25

She was exhausted when the sounds of people starting their cars woke her. She was tired but knew she had to keep moving. She waited until she heard both cars drive away. It was light out as she stayed hidden. She waited until all was quiet again before she crawled out of the boat and left the garage. She filled up her water bottles from a water spigot on the side of the house. She continued to walk east as she nibbled on trail-mix. She knew there was another little town somewhere this way that was called Glenrock. She just had to keep walking.

GLENROCK, WYOMING

Towards evening lightning lit the distant sky as she walked. She watched, and it kept flashing closer. When she heard thunder rumble in the clouds, she looked for shelter. She hid in a barn. She was exhausted and wanted someplace that felt safe for the night. The storm moved closer. She could smell the moisture in the air. It was getting ready to rain.

A horse nickered at her when she came into the barn, his head poked over his stall gate. He was a nice horse. He nuzzled her hand and face when she approached him. The horse was big, but seemed gentle; he let Connie pet him before she entered his stall.

In the stall, she petted and stroked the horse as she poured out her troubles to him. When she finished her tale of woe, the horse let her sleep in a clean corner of his stall. He was careful as he moved around her. Connie felt safe with the horse as the thunderstorm roared and raged outside.

JUNE 6, 1994
GLENROCK WYOMING

IN THE MORNING, THE HORSE OWNER, ART MILLER, CAME OUT TO TURN the horses loose to run in the pasture so he could clean out their stalls. He'd kept them in the barn since the storm had been predicted to be severe.

"It would have been nice to get more than a tenth of an inch of rain with the wind, thunder, and lightning last night," Art grumbled after he checked the rain gauge mounted on the pasture fence.

In the barn, Nanny ran out into the pasture as soon as he opened her stall door. He noticed something was up with Rebel. The horse wouldn't leave his stall and go out into the paddock. Usually, he couldn't run outside fast enough.

Art looked around him, but Rebel kept standing between him and something brown, but not horse droppings, a piece of dark brown fabric maybe? "Where did you get that?" Art asked Rebel. When Rebel finally moved, he saw the brown fabric was a brown sweatshirt worn by a sleeping kid.

"Oh, shit!" Art ran from the barn to get his wife, Belle. He was a big man, he wasn't graceful when he ran, but his fifty-two years old legs got him to the kitchen in record time.

"Belle!" Art yelled, a little winded as he slammed into the kitchen, "Come quick! There's a kid in Rebel's stall, back in the corner. I don't know if he hurt her or not."

Belle dropped the laundry she had pulled from the washer back into the machine. She grabbed a couple of carrots from the refrigerator. She snatched her coat from the hook by the backdoor and raced with Art back to the barn.

Outside the barn, they stopped to catch their breath and calm themselves before going inside to Rebel. Having been abused before Art bought him, Rebel was super sensitive to emotions, and being calm was the only way to deal with the horse. Belle had to deal with Rebel, as men scared him most of the time. Art wanted to save that kid if the kid was still alive.

Once in the barn, Belle saw Rebel in his stall, he stood near the kid. Art stood back and let Belle sweet talk Rebel out of his stall with the carrots.

After some coaxing, Rebel decided that the carrots were more enticing than his new stall-mate. He followed the carrots Belle held out as she led him out of his stall. With Rebel in his pasture, Art checked on the kid.

The kid moved, not much, but enough for Art to see a blackened eye and swollen cheek. Art froze and backed out of the stall. He waited for Belle.

When Belle joined him, Art pointed and quietly said, "Black eye and swollen cheek. It doesn't look fresh, but I don't know if it was Rebel."

Belle said, "I'll look. Go to the house. Bring me some ice in a towel for..." she pointed at the kid in the stall. "I'll see if I can talk them into coming to the house, but don't wait for us, bring the ice right away."

The voices woke Connie. Discovered, Connie lay still and pretended to be sleeping.

Belle spoke softly, "I saw that."

"I know that you know I found you sleeping in my barn," Belle said.

At that, Connie sat up stiffly. "I'll leave. Right now. I didn't mean to make trouble." Connie stood and gathered up her backpack she had used as a pillow and clutched her teddy-bear to her chest. Belle watched the disheveled kid gather her things.

"Honey, that's not what I meant. Why don't you come up to the house? I'll fix you some breakfast, and you can tell me about your adventures," Belle coaxed.

Connie thought a moment, looked Belle straight in the eye and said, "Call the cops or anyone else, and I'm gone. No more group homes. No more foster homes. No more cats!" Tears rolled slowly down her cheeks. Connie dropped her head and stood, her shoulders convulsed as she wept. "I want my dad! I want my mom! Why did they have to go to heaven without me?"

The sobs tore at Belle. She moved to the kid and gently stroked her hair as she cried her heart out.

Art had returned with the ice pack in time to hear Connie's last comments before the sobs started. When he peeked into the stall at Belle, she nodded.

He said, "Kid, listen to me." The sobs quieted to tears that rolled down cheeks as the small bruised face looked up at him. "We promise no phone calls without asking you first. But only if it has something to do with you. If I need a vet for a horse or cow, I'm making the call. I will not tell you first. You have my word."

Belle chimed in right after Art, "I make you the same promise, Honey. So, you feel like telling us your name?"

Connie mutely shook her head.

"Okay, what's this about cats?" asked Belle.

"In foster home number two, the lady had six cats. In the house type cats," Connie said.

Belle glanced at Art; he was as appalled as she was.

"I didn't know I'm allergic. I had to go to the hospital. I hate the hospital," Connie paused. "Dad and Mom died at the hospital," she whimpered.

"We don't have any cats, dear. The coyotes around here make sure of that," Belle continued, "Are you hungry? We usually eat after letting the horses out. I know Art is hungry," Belle said.

Connie nodded.

"I fix a tasty country breakfast. You know what that is?" Belle asked.

Connie shook her head.

"Bacon, eggs, toast, hash browns, and coffee, or in your case, milk or iced tea. Does that sound good to you?"

Connie nodded.

"Let's head up to the house then. Art has a couple of other things to do before he comes in for breakfast. I can make you something to eat, and you can tell me about yourself. But only as much as you want. Deal?"

Connie nodded again and followed Belle into the house. Once inside, Belle asked the girl, "What do you want me to call you?"

"My name is Connie," Connie answered.

"Okay, Connie, how much do you want for breakfast?" Belle asked as she pulled the fixings from the fridge to feed her husband and guest.

"If you don't mind, just the bacon, scrambled eggs and hash browns, please. Oh, and iced tea."

"You got it," Belle replied. She placed a frying pan on the stove to warm for making bacon. "I fry eggs in the bacon grease. I do the same with the hash browns. That going to be okay?" Belle asked.

"Fine. May I be excused to use the bathroom to wash up before eating?" Connie asked.

Belle gave her the directions and watched as the kid moved carefully towards the bathroom.

Art came in. "Was it Rebel who hurt her?"

"I don't know yet, but she is hurt. Her name's Connie. When she went to the bathroom, she was walking funny, as if she's protecting her back or ribs maybe? And she is very polite. Someone raised her right at some point."

Belle placed strips of bacon into the heated frying pan. Art prepped the drip coffee maker on the counter and started it. He then put the iced tea pitcher, plates, and silverware on the table. He had just finished when Connie reappeared, hands and face washed and stood behind a chair at the table.

Art leaned his butt against the counter next to where Belle worked at the stove. "Belle tells me your name is Connie, is that right?" Connie nodded her head. "Did Rebel hurt you at all last night?"

Connie asked, "Who's Rebel?"

"That big brown horse you were sleeping with this morning."

"No, he was nice. I felt safe with him so that I could get some sleep."

Art released the tension he had been holding in his shoulders and neck. "Thank you for telling me that. Bad people hurt him before I got him away from them. I just wanted to make sure he hadn't hurt you by accident," Art explained.

When it was ready, Belle put breakfast on the table. There was a big spoon in the bowl of scrambled eggs, a big fork in the bacon and a spatula in the hash browns. "Sit down and dig in everybody," Belle instructed. "Connie, you go first."

Belle watched Connie load her plate high enough to feed a working cowboy just in from branding. Then she watched the large meal disappear into the small child at an astonishing rate.

"Slow down, Honey," Belled coaxed. "I won't take your plate until you say you're done eating." Connie slowed down but kept eating.

As soon as Connie finished her breakfast, she cleared the breakfast dishes. Belle and Art watched as she rinsed the dishes, then placed them in the dishwasher. Connie scrubbed the silverware before she placed it in the basket in the dishwasher for such implements. She took a dishrag that hung over the sink faucet and dampened it. Connie used the rag to wash off the stovetop, then came and wiped down the table.

Belle finally found her voice, "Thank you so much for doing that, Connie, but you didn't have to."

"It's my job, what I did at home with dad, before....," she began to cry.

Belle and Art both went to her to comfort her. "Is it okay if I give you a hug?" Belle asked before touching her.

Art patted her gently on her back before she had time to respond to Belle. The contact made her yelp and pull away.

"What is it?" Belle asked, "What's wrong with your back?"

Connie pulled further away and mumbled, "Nothing."

"That's no nothing little girl," Art said gently. "Let Belle take a look. She used to help in a doctor's office."

Connie studied the couple. They both had some gray hair at the temples and some gray mixed in with the rest of their hair. They both wore glasses with the funny line through the lenses, but they had kind faces. They had been kind to her. They were clean, and their house was clean, it looked clean and smelled fresh. "Only if you don't," she instructed Art.

Art turned to look out the kitchen window. "Tell me when I can turn around," he said.

When Art had faced away, Connie let Belle lift the back of her shirt. Belle's sudden indrawn breath told Art everything he needed to know.

"Connie, I need to call a friend of mine so we can make sure you can stay with us. He's a guy I fish with. His name's Roger, and he's a lawyer," Art said.

"No! We had a deal!" Connie yelled.

"Cover her back up, Belle; I need to make a phone call. Don't let her shower until I call Roger. We need to get her some protection."

"Don't you get it? You can't protect me! No one can!" Connie yelled, frustrated. She stomped her foot.

Mutely, Belle dropped Connie's shirt back into place. "Okay, Art, you can turn around," Belle growled. When Art turned back to face Belle, he saw her lips pressed together, and her face white with fury.

Connie continued, "If you think I'm going into a group home or another foster home, I'm not. I'll run away again!" Tears streamed down her face. "I want to be in heaven with my parents," she cried, her whole body shook as she sobbed.

"No, Honey, you're too young to go to heaven. What we want is for you to stay with us, to be safe and clean, and not have to worry. We'll do it in a way that no one can take you away. That's why I need to make a phone call. It's the only way I can make sure you stay with us, but only if you want to stay with us," Art said.

"You need to see a doctor about your back. It's infected. We need a way to take you to the doctor and not let anyone take you away from us when we do," Belle added. "And if you don't want to stay with us, I still think you need someone who will look out for you and what you need, right?"

Connie sniffled, "Okay, I do want to stay with you, but I need to meet and talk to whoever you call."

"I'm calling Roger," Art said.

Art used the kitchen phone, so Connie heard everything he said. Art told Roger everything he knew up to this point. When he finished, he instructed Roger, "I want emergency foster parent rights, guardianship or whatever. We need to protect this kid. I don't know it all, but she was raised right before she entered foster care. Someone has to look out for her. The system isn't. Where ever she was last, they hurt her. She needs a doctor."

Roger directed, "Don't let her shower or wash up. I'll be right there with my wife. Dena's going to need to photograph the injuries. I'll bring some boilerplate documents we can adjust to fit her needs that we can take to any Superior Court Judge, although I do have one in mind." With the details worked out, Art hung up the phone.

"You okay with everything you heard?" Art asked. Connie nodded soberly. Belle handed Connie a couple of tissues to wipe her tear-streaked face and blow her nose.

"Will I ever get to see my parents again? I know they're dead. On TV, they show people get to see their relatives before they get buried. Where are they going to be buried? Will I be able to visit them?" Connie rattled off her questions.

"You weren't taken to the funeral, honey?" Belle choked out past the lump in her throat.

Connie shook her head, "I don't know where they are. The last time I saw them was before...," she replied in a quiet voice.

Art said, "When we get custody sorted out, I'll make sure that happens, today, if possible. Then we'll find out where your parents are, so you can see them and know where they are buried. I promise you that."

Art went to Connie and squatted down in front of her. He said, "Now this is gonna be strange, it normally happens in court, but I have some friends coming over. One is a lawyer, and he is going to talk to you about custody, and if you would want us to be your foster parents. His wife, Dena, is an evidence tech for the sheriff's department. Do you know what that means?"

"Yes, I watch Law and Order with, I mean I used to watch Law and Order with my parents."

"Then you know what an evidence tech does? She's going to need to photograph the injuries on your back, your cuts, and bruises and take your clothes," Art said.

Belle added, "I have some clean clothes for you to wear after you take a shower, but we have to wait for that until after Roger and Dena arrive and take whatever photos they need. Doing this will help us keep you with us."

"Okay," Connie agreed.

When Roger and Dena arrived, Connie and Dena went into the master bathroom for Dena to collect clothes and photograph injuries.

In the kitchen, Roger and Art worked on the emergency foster parent petition.

Belle went through her "donation bag" of clothes that she kept in her sewing room. It contained still usable clothes that had shrunk after numerous washings. She picked out some things for Connie to wear temporarily.

Dena pulled on latex gloves to take Connie's clothes away. Each garment was placed into a separate paper bag as Connie handed them over. Dena gave Connie a towel to wrap around herself. Then she took photos of the injuries Connie had, her infected cuts, and nasty bruises. When Dena had everything documented, she told Connie she could shower.

Connie leaned into the shower, started the water running, and adjusted the temperature. When the water was a comfortable temperature, Connie prepared to step into the shower. When she saw Dena leaving the bathroom, she asked, "You aren't going to watch me shower? To make sure I get clean?"

"Why do you ask, sweetheart?" Dena asked, puzzled.

"Cuz at the last foster home, they'd both watch me shower. They said it was to make sure I washed everywhere when I showered."

Dena replied, "No, Honey, I trust you to know how to wash. I'm going to take all your clothes for evidence. Belle has some clean clothes that you can wear until she can take you shopping for clothes for you, okay?"

Belle tapped on the bathroom door, "I have clothes for Connie to wear. Can I come in?"

Connie stepped into the shower and pulled the curtain closed to hide behind before she said, "Yes if you are alone, you can come in."

"I am, the boys are in the kitchen doing paperwork," Belle responded.

Belle entered as Dena left with her bags of clothes and her camera. Belle placed the clean garments on the closed toilet lid. "Any questions before I leave?"

"Is there a time limit on my shower?"

"The only limit is how long there is hot water. Other than that, take all the time you want."

"Thank you. I may need to wash twice. I feel so icky."

"That's fine, Sweetie. We'll be in the kitchen when you finish with your showering," Belle said as she hung a towel on the back of the bathroom door on a hook. "There's a fresh towel for you on the hook on the back of the door." With that, Belle left Connie to shower and dress.

When Belle got to the kitchen and heard Dena's report to Roger and Art, she snarled, "Tell me where they live; I'll kill them myself!"

Connie washed from hair to toes three times. The last time she enjoyed the feeling of being clean. She felt completely clean for the first time in days. Out of the shower, Connie dried off with the large fluffy towel Belle had left her. Once dry, she put on the too large for her sweatshirt and sweat pants. Belle had also supplied a belt for Connie to keep the elastic waisted sweat pants up. She finger-combed her damp hair, heaved a sigh and, barefoot, left the sanctuary of the bathroom.

Refreshed and tired, Connie returned to the kitchen and agreed to let Roger record her as she described her life since her parents had died. Dena, Art, and Belle silently listened as she spoke, then answered Roger's questions.

When he had completed his interview with Connie, Roger asked, "Where's a phone I can use?"

"My office or the one on the wall here," Art said and pointed behind Roger.

Roger said, "Art, I don't know if you've kept up with Harry since he moved to Douglas, but he's now a Superior Court Judge. We need him here for Connie. Then we need to get the folks Dena works with involved."

"I haven't," Art acknowledged, "Call him. Whatever we need to do to keep Connie safe first, and here with us second, but a very close second."

Roger called Superior Court Judge Harry Phillips and explained the situation. Judge Harry said, "I'll be there in thirty to forty minutes. I'm in Douglas right now."

While they waited for Harry, Connie began to yawn. And rub her eyes, and yawn, and yawn some more.

Belle asked Connie, "Would you like to take a nap in the guest room? I'll wake you when Harry gets here."

Connie nodded and followed Belle to the spare room. It was huge. The bed was big too; Queen-sized. When she climbed on, she noticed it was so soft. She was sound asleep on top of the bed as soon as she stretched out. Belle grabbed a light blanket from the bedroom closet to cover her and left, closing the door behind her.

Connie slept through Harry's arrival and the discussions the adults had as they figured out how to keep her safe and make it legal for her to stay with Art and Belle. Art wasn't surprised when Belle added, "I want to adopt her if she has no one else."

Judge Harry Phillips reviewed the documents Roger had prepared. He listened to the recording Roger had made when he interviewed the little girl. "Where is she? Connie Doe," the Judge asked.

"Sleeping in the guest room," Belle replied. "Do you want me to get her?"

"No, from what I've just heard you are now her foster parents." Judge Harry Phillips signed the forms Roger had adapted for Connie's care. "Keep her safe, I'll be checking up on you, and next time I come out here, I want to talk with her. That'll be tomorrow," Harry said. He continued to give orders, "Dena I want copies of all the photos you took that detail her lack of care. Tomorrow. Roger, get those documents filed with the county clerk today. That means leave now. I don't want any screw-ups. That kid has had enough of them to last her lifetime and then some."

Dena said, "Yes, sir. I work tonight. I can drop them off at your office first thing before I go home in the morning."

Roger scooped up the signed documents and hurried to the door with Dena.

Harry stayed a little bit longer to visit with Art and Belle before he left. He told Art and Belle, "You need to consider what you are committing to, today and for the next who knows how many years."

"Harry, you know we've always wanted kids," Art said.

Belle added, "This may be an unconventional way to get one, but we'll take her."

Connie slept all day. After supper, Belle checked on Connie. She went quietly into the guest room. Belle stood near the bed and listened, satisfied, as she heard Connie's steady breathing and crept back out.

CASPER, WYOMING

MIKE NELSON WENT OUT TO FEED VERA AND MAC. AS USUAL, VERA WAS at her kennel door, waiting for food; today, Mac wasn't.

"Mac, time to eat," Mike called out as he had every day since Mac had come to live with him. Still no sign of the big dog. "Crap," Mike muttered.

He gave Vera her food, then went into Mac's kennel through the gate. On his knees, he crawled into Mac's dog house. "Mac, are you hiding a fugitive again?" he asked the dog. When he got inside, he saw Mac on his sleeping bag, head on his paws, watching him. Alive and dejected.

"I know you miss her, big guy," Mike soothed, "But you gotta eat. Aren't you a little hungry?"

Mac groaned and flopped onto his side.

"I'll call today to find out where she is so we can go visit, okay? Just eat something for me so you will be strong and healthy when she sees you."

Mike exited the dog house with Mac's bowl. He took it into the house and added a whipped raw egg to the dog's kibble and brought it back to him in hopes that would entice him to eat. When he put the food bowl in Mac's kennel Mike called, "Mac, it's gourmet dog food now, come out and eat."

Mac refused to eat. Mike went into the house and called child protection services to locate Connie. While on the phone he watched out the window to see if Mac came out to eat. Mike left a message with the office secretary for the CPS supervisor he had met the last time he had seen Connie. After lunch, he left a second message for Ted Rose, followed by a third message late that afternoon. The messages went unanswered.

After he began his shift at 2000 (8:00 p.m.), he asked his dispatcher to query the National Crime Information Center (NCIC) database to see if Connie Daily was listed as missing or as a runaway juvenile. Nothing. "Well, Vera, I bet she slipped by CPS again, and that's why no one'll call me back. Where should we look for Connie?" he asked his patrol dog. She licked his right ear through the open panel to her part of the car. He went by Connie's parents' house to make sure she wasn't there somewhere. It was empty.

At midnight he went home for lunch and visited with his wife and new son, then looked in on his sleeping twin girls. Before leaving to go back on shift, he checked Mac's kennel to make sure he wasn't harboring a runaway. Mac was alone, and Mac hadn't eaten his food.

Back on patrol after his lunch break, he met up with his Sergeant, Amy Lockwood. "Connie is missing again. I know it. And her dog isn't eating," Mike worried at his Sergeant.

"Give it time, Mike. The dog will eat when he gets hungry enough," Sergeant Lochwood said.

JUNE 7 1994
GLENROCK, WYOMING

THE SOUND OF CRYING WOKE BELLE AFTER MIDNIGHT. SHE FOLLOWED the sound to Connie's room and tapped on the door before she entered the room. Belle sat on the edge of the bed and stroked Connie's back to comfort her. "What is it, Honey?"

"I want Mac," sobbed Connie.

"Who is Mac?" asked Belle

"My dog. I made Deputy Mike take him when my parents died, but I want him back."

"It's the middle of the night. He's probably home sleeping, how about we work on that in the morning? Are you hungry? You slept all day."

"You mean it? We can find Mac? And yes, please. I am hungry," Connie said as she pulled her knees under her, sat on her feet, and wiped the tears from her eyes.

"We can try to find Mac after breakfast," Belle corrected. "I don't know yet who deputy Mike is or how to find him."

"I know where he lives if we start at my old house. I can show you. And his patrol dog is named Vera," Connie said.

"That should help. Come on, let's get you a snack. Then back to bed," Belle said as she led the way to the kitchen.

While she fixed Connie a snack, Belle told Connie, "The Judge is coming back to talk to you after breakfast. He gave us temporary emergency foster parent status, just for you, but there are other things he needs to talk to you about."

Belle pulled a small plate and a glass from the cabinet for Connie's snack. She pulled a blueberry muffin from a Tupperware container in the fridge, along with a carton of milk. The muffin went on a plate and in the microwave to warm while she poured Connie's milk. "I don't want you to worry. Sleep well tonight, in the morning after we talk to Judge Harry, we can run into Douglas and do some clothes shopping."

"What about finding Mac?" Connie asked.

"We have to give Art something to do other than shopping for clothes. He'd like finding Mac for you," Belle said as she placed the snack on the table in front of Connie and sat down across the table from her. "You need clothes that fit. Shopping for clothes isn't fun for him," she said.

Connie wolfed down the blueberry muffin in front of her, then quickly drank her milk.

After breakfast, Connie watched out the window for Judge Harry to arrive. She watched as someone drove up in a shiny black pickup truck, then came to the door carrying a battered brown briefcase. He was tall, not skinny but not fat, and had a slight limp, like her father. When he knocked twice against the door, then opened it, Connie looked over to Belle and Art on the couch.

"It's okay Honey," Art said. "We know who it is."

Once everyone settled at the table, Belle served coffee to Judge Harry Phillips, Art and herself and milk to Connie.

"Do you know why I want to talk to you this morning, Connie?" Judge Harry asked.

"No."

"I need to know your whole name for the paperwork to let Art and Belle look after you; otherwise, child protective services can take you away from them."

"My full name is Connie Suzanne Daily. Not Constance, Connie. My great grandmother was Constance. And mister Judge, please don't let child protective services take me away. With Mr. Art and Mrs. Belle, it's the best place I've lived since my parents died."

Connie paused, tears filled her eyes, "Please, can I see them? I know they're dead. Don't I get to see them before they get buried? That's what happened when Grandma Margaret died." She continued, "Mister Judge, Mr. Art, and Mrs. Belle, can I have Mac here? Please? I want my dog." Connie's tears began to roll down her cheeks.

Belle informed the two men at the table about her discussion with Connie during the night when Connie's crying had wakened her. She learned of the dog when she had gone to Connie's room to console her.

Harry ordered, "Art, call the Natrona County Sheriff's Department. See if they can track down the dog handler, Deputy Mike. In the meantime, Belle, I need to talk to Connie alone for a little bit."

Art and Belle left the kitchen. Before Harry could get a word in, Connie asked, "Did you lose your leg in a war the same as my father did?"

"How did you know I lost a leg?"

"You walk the way my father does, I mean, did," Connie corrected herself as she wiped teardrops from her face. "What war were you in?"

"It wasn't a war, Connie, it was a driver not paying attention. I was riding a motorcycle. The people who hit me didn't see me and drove right into me. What war was your daddy in?"

"Somalia. He and Mac both got hurt there before they came home." Connie rubbed the last of the tears from her face. "What did you want to ask me?"

"Would you like it if I made Art and Belle your legal guardians? You would live with them permanently, and child protective services couldn't take you away. Having a permanent home will also help with getting your dog back. Art and Belle will do whatever it takes to make sure you see where your parents are. I know they would enjoy helping you grow up into the wonderful young lady I know you will one day be."

"I'm okay with that as long as if things go bad, I can tell you and you'll fix it. Promise?" Connie asked.

"I promise," Harry said. He pulled a business card from his wallet and wrote on the back. The front of the card said Judge Harry Phillips and listed a couple of phone numbers. Handing Connie the card, he said, "If you ever need my help, on the front is my work number, on the back is my home phone number and pager number. Keep this somewhere safe, so you have it if you need me. Now for serious things, was everything you told Roger yesterday when he recorded you the truth?"

Connie nodded, whispered, "Yes, I wish it wasn't."

"Okay, then I need to make a phone call. We need this documented, so those people never have foster kids again, wouldn't you agree?" Judge Harry asked.

"Yes! They're bad people. And chickens stink!" Connie wrinkled her nose as she described the chickens and their behavior.

After Harry left, Art drove Belle and Connie into Douglas for shopping. They ate lunch out before they headed back home. Connie was drooping by the time they left the restaurant. She was asleep in the backseat of the pickup when they got home. She shuffled to her room on her own to finish her nap.

"Is it crazy I love her already?" Belle asked Art as they watched Connie go down the hall. Art pulled Belle against his side in a one-armed hug.

"No crazier than me loving that kid. Let's let things calm down a little. Let her get to know us. Then we can talk to her about us adopting her. I don't want to scare her with how much it would mean to both of us to adopt her," Art suggested.

JUNE 9, 1994
GLENROCK, WYOMING

CONNIE WAS ELEVEN YEARS OLD TODAY. SHE DIDN'T TELL ANYONE IT WAS her birthday. She didn't feel like celebrating. No parents. No Mac. The Millers were friendly, and she liked them, she just wasn't ready to do any celebrating with them yet.

CASPER WYOMING

DEPUTY MIKE NELSON ARRIVED AT THE SUBSTATION WITH VERA AFTER his Tuesday and Wednesday weekend to find a message slip in his inbox. He read the phone message: *Contact Converse County Superior Court Judge Harry Phillips immediately, any time as soon as this message is received.*

Included were a pager number, a home, and an office phone number. He muttered, "What the hell? I haven't done anything in Converse County. I wonder what he wants?"

He placed the call while he monitored dispatch on his portable radio. Vera lay at his feet as he talked to the Judge. "I'm glad she's safe and with people who care about her," Mike said.

"You understand this little girl wants her dog back? That won't be a problem, will it?" Judge Harry Phillips asked.

"No, Sir, it won't. He stopped eating a couple of days ago. I've been trying to find her and CPS hasn't been getting back to me. I'm glad to know she's safe and I can get Mac back to her. Where do I drop him off? I want to meet these people." Mike gave the Superior Court Judge his home phone number, his pager number, and the number to the Natrona County Sheriff's Department dispatch center.

"I'll arrange something. I'll need you to bring a case report form with you when you bring the dog out to Connie. Tomorrow morning work for you?" asked Judge Harry Phillips.

"Um, yeah, late morning? I don't get off work until four a.m.," Mike replied hesitantly. "Bring a case report form?"

"Documentation about the dog, to show chain of custody," the Judge explained. "Have a safe shift."

Mike sat back in his desk chair when the call ended, relieved. Connie was safe and had someone to watch out for her. Now he just had to get Mac back to her and eating again. Then he could focus on his family and job and worry about Connie wouldn't lurk in the back of his mind.

As he sat at his desk, his portable radio squawked, his Sergeant needed to meet with him. He picked up his handheld radio, acknowledged the request, and left with Vera.

At his meeting with Sergeant Amy Lochwood, he filled her in on what was going on with Connie and Mac. When he finished briefing her, Sergeant Lochwood thought for a moment.

"Keep me up to date on this. I don't want any surprises later. And if you need backing up, I don't want you or me hanging in the breeze because you didn't keep me informed. Get me?" Sergeant Lochwood asked.

"Yes, Ma'am!" Mike replied, grateful for her support.

When Mike stopped by his house at midnight on his lunch break, he checked on Mac. "Hey, big guy, I found Connie. We're going to see her tomorrow, so hang in there, buddy, okay?"

After his chat with Mac, he went into the house for lunch. He slapped together a sandwich and ate while he filled Donna in on his day so far. When it was time to leave, he gave his wife and new son a kiss each. He went down the hall, and he peeked in on his twin girls as they slept before going back to work.

JUNE 10, 1994
GLENROCK, WYOMING

CONNIE DRESSED IN HER FRESHLY WASHED NEW CLOTHES AND SHOES that fit, yeah! In the morning after breakfast, she went out to the barn with Art and Belle. She watched as they turned out the horses from their stalls in the barn into their paddocks for the day.

Rebel came out and sniffed the air intently. He caught Connie's scent and went right over to her at the paddock fence. Rebel reached his head over the fence and nuzzled her hair, making Connie laugh. She reached up and stroked his head. "You're just a big dog in a different shape, aren't you, dude?" she asked.

Art watched to ensure Rebel didn't hurt Connie. The imp had stolen his heart.

Belle came up beside Connie, "Made yourself a new friend, didn't you?"

"I think so. But it would be hard to have Rebel cuddle in bed at night when you feel lonely," Connie replied.

"Are you happy with the new clothes? Does the jacket fit? Now that you have worn them a little longer than at the store, do the shoes fit okay? Did we miss anything?" Belle asked question after question.

"I like them a lot. I think we got everything I need for now, except. . ."

"Except what, Honey?"

"Well, do you have a computer connected to the internet?"

"Yes, why?"

Connie stepped down from the fence. "I have pictures I took in the cloud, online. Of me and mom and dad from before they died." Connie sniffed, stepped back onto the bottom rail of the paddock fence and rubbed Rebel's forehead before she said, "I want to see them. I want you to see them." She sniffed a little, "When we bury my parents, can they be buried nearby so I can visit them?"

"We'll do what we can. Your parents may have already made funeral arrangements. They may have already chosen a spot for their burial. That's something we'll work on tomorrow," Belle said. "The computer in Art's office has internet so that you can show us pictures from there. We have a surprise for you later that I want you to be ready for."

Connie brightened, "Another surprise for me? Thank you, Mrs. Belle!"

After lunch, dishes had been loaded into the dishwasher when Judge Harry showed up in his shiny black pickup truck. Connie heard the vehicle on the crushed gravel driveway, and she met him at the door and let him into the house.

"I need to ask you some more questions, but that can wait a little bit. I need to talk to Art and Belle. About adult stuff, okay?" the Judge told Connie as he gently ruffled her hair as he came into the house.

"Okay, can I play outside? I won't go far."

"Ask Art or Belle, that's not my area of jurisdiction."

While Connie ran to do that, a Converse County deputy pulled up next to the Judge's pickup in his marked patrol car. The judge let the deputy into the house. He shook hands with Deputy Jerry Byrnes.

"Jerry, thanks for coming. I'm gonna warn you; this is a crappy one," Judge Phillips said.

Deputy Byrnes said, "I can handle it, Sir. From the little you told me already, I'm glad it's me and not some of the other guys taking the report." He shook hands with the Judge.

"Remember, the deputy from Natrona County thinks he's coming to deliver her dog and creating a report for a chain of evidence regarding the dog and his associated property. He has no idea about the abuse. We need to take it easy on him; he got invested in this kid. For that, we can only thank God."

Connie had just gone outside when she saw the dark green SUV coming up the long driveway to the ranch house. Mike's SUV, and it towed a trailer that had things under a huge blue tarp. She ran back inside and announced, "Company!"

Mike Nelson had arrived with Mac. Mike had taken in the well-kept ranch house, fences, buildings and yard as he eased up the driveway. He thought the horses looked well cared for; they were curious about the new arrivals. That was a good sign to him.

He took a minute, to just let himself get a feel for the place before he got out of the SUV. The place had a good feel to it. The Converse County patrol car was an unexpected sight. "I wonder what that's all about?" he asked Mac in the backseat.

When Mike exited the SUV, Mac had his nose out the partially opened rear window. He was taking in deep breaths of air through his nose. He began to whine, then whined louder and bounced slightly on his front feet.

Connie came out on the porch with two adults. "*Einfach*, Mac. Easy, big guy." He tried to soothe the excited dog — Mac was having none of it.

Mac had eyes and nose only for his girl, Connie. It was obvious he smelled her.

Connie saw Mike and Mac, and ran to the SUV, "Mac! Oh, Mac!" Happy tears ran down her cheeks as she climbed up on the running board to reach through the window to her dog. Mac reached his tongue through the window to swipe at Connie's face.

The adults approached Mike and his SUV at a walk, letting Connie have a little time with Mac while they talked.

Connie turned to Mike, "Can I get in with him if he can't get out yet? Please?!"

"Sure, Honey." Mike opened the front passenger door for her to climb into the SUV. She immediately went over the console into the back with Mac for a proper reunion.

Mike turned to the two adults who had come out with Connie. The man looked vaguely familiar. Going to the man, Mike asked, "Do I know you from somewhere?"

Art replied, "Art Miller, I may have spoken to your academy class about arson right before I left the department to help my mother care for my dad and to run the ranch." Left-arm around his wife as he held out his right hand to shake Mike's hand. "Thanks for coming all this way."

Belle smiled at Mike and said, "I'm Belle. It's nice to meet you, Mike. Thank you so much for bringing Mac to Connie. She's been missing him."

"He's been missing her too." Mike lowered his voice. "He quit eating a couple of days ago. They need to be together."

The door to the house opened. A man with a slight limp came out on the porch and approached the group of adults. He stuck out his hand to Mike and said, "Judge Harry Phillips. I'm glad you could make it out here. So, other than the dog, what else have you got for us?" He gestured at the loaded trailer.

Turning to the judge, he answered, "I have Mac's dog house and disassembled kennel. I also brought bags of cement, a roll of chain link fencing and posts to set up a fenced area for him near the house. Mac knows how to use a doggie door. He's accustomed to going in and out of the house into a fenced yard. I hope that will work here. Do you know where you want me to unload this stuff?"

The judge interrupted Mike's planning, "If you think it's safe, why don't we let Mac and Connie out of your truck, and give Art and Belle a chance to look around to decide where they want the kennel and yard fenced. Do you have the blank case report form I asked you to bring?"

"Yes, Sir, I'll get it and turn the kids loose." Mike went back to his vehicle, let Connie and Mac out and retrieved his case report form.

A hyper excited Mac danced circles around Connie. She kneeled to Mac's level as they celebrated their reunion in the yard. Mac knocked Connie on her back with a head-butt to the chest and lay down next to her. His whole-body wriggled in delight. He washed her face and neck, and anywhere else he could reach with his tongue, his wagging tail swept the ground.

Belle said, "I don't think I've ever seen her that happy."

Connie smiled and laughed being with the big dog. Her face lit with joy at the tongue attack. "Oh, Mac, I missed you so much! What a *guter hund*, Mac. I'm so glad you're here," Connie told the dog as she stroked and petted what she could reach of the wriggling, happy dog.

When Mac had settled down, Connie led him to Art and Belle. "Hold out your hands, palms down, in a loose fist," she instructed, as she demonstrated with her small hand. When the adults complied, Connie held Belle's hand for Mac to sniff.

"*Sicher*, Mac." Mac sniffed Belle's fist then gave Belle a small lick with the tip of his tongue. Connie repeated the command with Art and brought Mac to smell his hand. Art was also accepted. "*Guter hund*, Mac!" Connie enthusiastically told her canine friend. She gave him a two-handed fur ruffle around his head and ears. "Mac, *freunde finden*," Connie then instructed the dog.

He walked around Belle and Art, sniffing. "I'm going to hug you but don't hug me back. I need Mac to see you're safe for me, okay?" she told Art and Belle. They nodded, and Connie showed Mac the two adults were safe for her, and Mac was to accept them. "We may have to do this every morning for a few times until he is sure about you. Daddy introduced Mac to me this way when they got home from the hospital after getting blown up in Somalia. Mac can stay, can't he?"

"Yes, Honey, that's why Mike brought his dog house. We need to see where to set up his kennel and yard. You want to help us pick out a spot?" Art asked.

"Yes!" They wandered around the house. Mac was velcroed to Connie's side as she surveyed the shade trees, yard porches, and doors before saying, "Here would be best. Especially if you allow Mac to have a doggie door."

In the house, Judge Harry Phillips sat Mike Nelson down at the kitchen table with Deputy Jerry Byrnes and made introductions. Then he said, "You aren't going to like what I have to say, Mike, but it needs to be documented. You've been part of this from the start."

Mike felt his stomach knot.

"Coffee?" the judge asked Mike and Jerry.

"Water is fine," Mike said.

"I'll have the same," said Jerry.

Mike squared up his case report forms. Harry helped himself to coffee from the pot on the counter, then, playing host, brought Mike and Jerry their water before he joined them at the table, with his coffee.

Harry took a sip of his coffee, pulled a small tape recorder from his briefcase, and placed it on the table.

"I'm recording our conversation and will give you both a copy for your reports," Judge Harry Phillips said as he started the recorder. He spoke the time, date, and listed the parties present. Then he detailed everything he knew about Connie's last few weeks since her parents died.

Listening, Mike felt angry and sick; so did Jerry.

The Judge ended his part of the report with, "I want you to fill me in on anything you know that I don't. I want to keep the custody stuff in Converse county, that's why Jerry's here. But, since the CPS foul-ups and abuse at the chicken farm happened in Natrona county, Mike, I want you to take a case report on that. I have copies of photos taken by a Converse County evidence tech, and recordings of interviews with Connie. I'll give you both copies to include in your case reports. Any questions?"

Mike nodded, "How was this allowed to happen? She's a good kid. I know this shouldn't surprise me, but sometimes, man. . ." Mike shook his head. The men went to work on their respective case reports, Jerry interviewed Mike about all his contacts with Connie and with CPS, getting names where Mike knew them.

Mike stayed and listened to the instructions Judge Harry gave Jerry before he left, his case report finished. Mike went out to his SUV and secured the case report, with the photographs, and the recordings Judge Harry had given him. That done, he found Art and helped him with laying out the fence posts where Mac's yard was going to be set up behind the house.

Mike considered where the new dog yard would go. It was a good place and included a large shade tree for hot summer days, and access to the back porch and the door into the mudroom.

Art and Belle had agreed a doggie door would go into the mudroom. Mac's fenced dog yard would be about forty feet by sixty feet.

Mike was thrilled when Art drove a tractor with the fence post hole attachment out of the barn. No digging fence post holes by hand! He had been willing if it had been necessary.

Mike got the kennel fence panels laid out for the smaller kennel area that would be inside the fenced yard. He consulted with Belle about the local winds through the yard and set up Mac's dog house within the kennel so that it would be shielded as much as possible from the constant wind that always seemed to blow in Wyoming.

Art used the tractor and post hole digger to quickly dig out all the holes needed for the dog yard fence posts. Turning the tractor around, he used the bucket of the tractor for a wheelbarrow. He mixed water and cement in the bucket. He and Mike used shovels to put cement around each fence post that Belle held straight in each hole. The chain-link fence would go up tomorrow after the posts had time to set in the cement.

Connie and Mac watched the progress from the porch. Connie and Mac sat on the chaise lounge, with Mac lying next to her outstretched legs on the chair.

After they cemented all the fence posts into place, Belle announced, "Time for a break" As they stepped onto the porch, Mike confided, "Mac sleeps with her. I hope that'll be alright. I know some folks don't let dogs in the house."

"He's a war hero. Who are we to tell Mac he can't sleep in the house with Connie if he wants to?" Belle replied as a grin lit her face.

Break over, everyone helped Mike unload Mac's remaining stuff from his SUV. While he opened the rear cargo doors to his SUV, Mike asked, "Where do you want these in the house? In the kitchen or the mudroom?"

Belle responded, "Kitchen is fine. We can sort it out from there. Thanks, Mike, you have been such a great help."

Connie and Mac raced ahead to open the door to the house to let Mike carry Mac's large sack of food into the house. Belle carried his bowls. Art brought Mac's dog bed into the house after he closed up the now empty SUV.

Mike smiled back at Belle, "He's a good dog. Even at my house, he was great with my twin girls, and they're only five years old. He just missed Connie so much. We need to make sure he eats today. I plan on coming back to help set up the kennel panels and the chain-link fence for the dog yard tomorrow. It's heavy work alone."

"We appreciate all you have done for Connie, and Mac," Belle said. "Thank you."

In the house, Connie held out some food for Mac in her hands. It was a small amount of food. "*Essen*," Connie ordered the dog, instructing him to eat. He slowly ate the food, as if savoring each piece of kibble.

"Thank goodness," Mike said. "I don't think there'll be anything to worry about with Mac, as long as he's with Connie."

"I appreciate all you did for her," Art replied. He held out his hand to shake Mike's. "We're so grateful to have her."

"You're lucky to have her. If my wife hadn't just had a new baby, we would have tried to take her in," Mike said. He looked around and continued, "She'll do well here with you. I'm glad you found each other." Mike clapped Art on the shoulder.

"Get yourself home to your wife and kids. Be safe," Art replied.

While Belle continued to supervise Connie and Mac outside, Art went back into the house for iced tea and saw Harry was still there, sitting at Art's desk in his office. "How bad was it?" Art asked.

"Bad," Judge Harry replied. "Be glad you didn't hear it. I got a little more detail from Mike about what happened. Her dad was Army. He lost a leg in Somalia as did Mac in the same mortar attack. That's why they got to keep him. Mom was an ER doctor at Wyoming Medical Center in Casper. Her folks were on date night. Can you believe it? They were still going on dates after being married well over a decade."

Harry shook his head, then continued, "They were coming home from the restaurant when they got hit by some stoned out of his mind jackass. The idiot stole a loaded dump truck and drove it in the dark without lights, and went the wrong way down the street. They never saw it coming. The minivan they were driving never had a chance; it got crushed like an aluminum can." Harry heaved a sigh and scrubbed his face with his hands. "Anyway, that is how you are foster parents to this kid and her dog. Once the paperwork goes through and you have had some time as Connie's foster parents, we can work on making you her legal guardians until she is eighteen," Harry finished.

"Belle and I were talking last night. What if we want to adopt her?" Art asked.

"I would still become her legal guardian first." Judge Harry explained, "That way any possible contentions will have already been eliminated through the courts before you apply to adopt her and you will have the added benefit of already being her foster parents, then her legal guardians before filing for adoption. Make sense?"

"Yeah, it does," Art said.

"That's a special kid," Harry said and grinned at Art. "You hit the jackpot with her." Harry shoved back from the desk, "Time for me to go before you put me to work."

Art and Connie assembled Mac's doghouse. "Your dad designed and built this dog house after getting hurt?" Art asked.

"Yes, he called it constructive therapy," Connie replied.

"It sure was thoughtful of your dad to assemble it with bolts and nuts so it could be taken apart and put back together easily," Art said.

"He told me he did it that way so if we ever moved, we could take it with us," Connie said. "Then he said he wasn't planning on moving any time soon."

Mac supervised the assembly of his dog house very closely.

Connie was happy. She had Mac. She was the most relaxed Art, and Belle had seen; she just glowed. Mac pranced at her side, his joy at being with Connie evident to anyone.

When Belle called Connie and Art in from outside for supper, Mac came along. When Connie sat at the table, Mac lay down behind her chair.

"Is Mac going to mind if I walk around behind your chair while I put food on the table?" Belle asked.

"No, Mrs. Belle. He'll be good. He knows house rules," Connie replied.

Supper went off without a hitch. Art, Belle, and Connie ate at the table. Mac stayed behind Connie's chair during the meal. Connie fed Mac after the supper dishes were rinsed and in the dishwasher.

After supper, Connie and Mac went out to play and burn off more of their excited energy so they would be able to settle down and sleep at bedtime.

While they watched Connie and Mac through the kitchen window, Art told Belle what he had discussed with Harry about guardianship and adoption. "I think we need to talk it over with Connie before we go further than guardianship. We need to let her have a say in this, so she feels like she has some control over her life," Belle said.

"I agree, but let's let things calm down before we bring that up to her," Art said. When he went out to do barn chores, Belle went out to spend more time with Connie and Mac.

At bedtime, Connie was tired but happy. She had Mac again!

Belle didn't even have to tell her when it was time for bed. At 8:30 p.m., Connie took Mac outside to take care of his business for the night. That done they went up and got ready for bed without being told. By nine, the two reunited best friends were cuddled together in Connie's bed.

Connie was sound asleep when Belle opened the door. From the light in the hall, she saw Mac looking back at her. He had positioned himself on the bed between the door and Connie. Satisfied that everything was as it should be, Belle gently closed the door and returned to the living room and her recliner, which sat next to Art's recliner.

"They're tucked in, and I pity anyone who tries to go after that little girl," Belle said.

Art smiled, then said, "I don't doubt it. Tomorrow I plan to go into Casper to get a doggie door for Mac and find out about her parents, her house and take care of anything else that needs attention. Afterwards, I'm also going to stop by in Douglas and see Harry, about what we need to do to file for permanent guardianship as soon as possible. Then I'll see Roger. That way, we can look after her parents' estate and put everything in a trust for her."

"Good plan, I'll talk to her about school while you're gone and spend time with her. Find out what she likes to do, who she is when she isn't scared to death about what's going to happen next."

JUNE 11, 1994
DOUGLAS, WYOMING

AFTER BREAKFAST THE NEXT MORNING, ART LEFT ON HIS ERRANDS. He met Harry in Douglas in his courthouse office. In Judge Harry's office, he asked, "Any word on the location of the bodies of Connie's parents?"

"Not yet. I finally tracked down the trustee appointed by the courts in Natrona County. Tyler Brown. I haven't had a chance to talk to him yet. That is next on the agenda, although trying to find him on a Saturday may be asking a bit much..." Harry said.

"I wanted to get that settled for her, soon," Art said.

Nodding, Harry replied, "I understand. I'll call you as soon as I have something."

"Connie wants to go visit her parents' graves, then her house and get more clothes and some photos of her parents."

"I'll arrange that when I talk to Tyler. What day are you free to go to Casper?"

"Any time," Art said, "I want to get this done for Connie."

"I'll call you. Now get out. I have things to do," Harry smiled as he banished Art from his office.

GLENROCK, WYOMING

AT THE RANCH, BELLE TOLD CONNIE SHE WOULD NEED TO BE REGISTERED in the Glenrock school district soon. The school district would then have Connie tested to see what grade she belonged in.

Connie asked, "Can we pretend you and Mr. Art are my parents instead of everyone knowing my parents got killed in a car accident? I don't like how everyone treated me at my old school after that happened."

"Any way you want to do it, Honey, whatever makes you comfortable."

"It makes me comfortable to stay with you and Mr. Art."

"Connie, it's okay for you to call us Art and Belle. Those are our names, after all," Belle reminded Connie.

"But you're grownups. I have to be respectful of grownups. Dad always said so."

Mike arrived in the afternoon, followed by Art as he returned from his errands. Mike and Art quickly assembled Mac's kennel. Then they tackled the chain-link dog yard fence. While Mike hung the gate, Art installed the doggie door into the mudroom door. By nightfall, it was finished. Mac had a safe and secure yard with access to the house through a doggie door.

"We couldn't have done it without your help, Mike. I appreciate it," Art said as he shook Mike's hand after Mac's dog yard was completely set up. "If there's ever any way we can return the favor, please let me know."

JUNE 12, 1994
GLENROCK, WYOMING

IT WAS SUNDAY, AND CONNIE WAS WORRIED. "I HAVEN'T BEEN TO CHURCH since Mom and Dad died. Is God going to be mad at me?" Connie asked Belle after breakfast while she helped do dishes.

"No Honey, it was up to the adults who were looking after you to make sure you went to church. God doesn't care what religion you are as long as you want to do what is good and right and kind," Belle answered. "God only wants you to love God and yourself and the world he made. He would want you to treat all the people, plants, and animals He made with respect." Belle handed Connie the last dish for the dishwasher. Belle directed, "Now run and get Mac ready to stay home while we go to church. Then come in and wash your hands and face before we leave."

Connie and Mac headed out for his kennel and dog house. "You be a *guter hund*," She pointed into the enclosure. "Kennel," Connie ordered as she gave him the hand signal to enter his fenced kennel area inside his dog yard.

Mac acted dejected as he followed Connie's orders. He had his head, tail, and ears down as he went into his new kennel. He lay down in the shady spot created by the nearby tree. From where Mac lay, he could see the back door and the place where the pickup was parked.

Connie then gave Mac the hand signal to stay. "*Bleib*, I promise to come home from church for you. I promise!" Connie told her dog.

At church, Connie was relieved to see Art and Belle's church routines were just like where she had gone to church with her parents. She was grateful they allowed her to sit with them in the adult section. Maybe in a few weeks, Connie would feel ready for going to the kid classes, but right now she needed the security of staying with Art and Belle. She tried to follow everything the pastor was saying.

Belle felt Connie jerk and put an arm around her. Belle bent over and whispered, "It's all right to miss them." Church seemed to go on forever before finally ending. Connie stayed glued to Belle and Art, as they visited with some other churchgoers out in the parking lot before going home.

When they got home, Connie's first stop out of the truck was Mac's kennel. "See, I told you I would come back. I promised," She said as she turned him loose.

Mac danced around Connie. His one back leg working like a piston as he jumped and danced around her. She bent down for some enthusiastic face licks and a couple of gentle head butts to the chest, followed by more happy circles in front of and around his favorite person.

"Connie, lunchtime," Belle called out as she and Art entered the house.

JUNE 13, 1994
CASPER, WYOMING

THE FIRST CALL TYLER BROWN RETURNED AFTER GETTING IN TO WORK that Monday morning, was the one that said it was about Connie Daily. When he dialed the number on the message slip, he got the Converse County Courthouse switchboard. He hung up and dialed again. This time when the woman answered, "Converse County Courthouse, how may I direct your call?" he stayed on the line.

"I'm trying to reach Harry Phillips. My name is Tyler Brown. I'm calling the number that was left for me to call. It's about a kid named Connie Daily."

"One moment please, I'll transfer you," the woman said, and Tyler heard the ringing of a transferred call. On the third ring, a man answered, "Judge's chambers, how may I help you?"

Tyler explained again. "Hang on. I'll get the Judge for you, one moment please." Tyler was put on hold.

"Superior Court Judge Harry Phillips here, who's calling?" a deep male voice said into Tyler's ear.

Tyler swallowed past the sudden constriction in his throat, "Tyler Brown, with the Natrona County Courts returning your call, sir, about Connie Daily."

"It's about time! What's going on with her? Why wasn't she at her parent's funeral?" Harry demanded.

"There hasn't been one sir; I haven't been able to find her. Every time CPS tells me she is with a certain foster parent, when I contact them, she isn't there anymore. It's like trying to catch smoke," Tyler responded.

"I have appointed foster parents for Connie Daily here in Converse County as Natrona County hasn't done well by her. Will you have any problem working with them to get Connie's affairs sorted out?"

"No, sir. No problem at all," Tyler responded.

"Will you have a problem detailing your attempts to find Connie Daily to a deputy for a case report? Have you documented your efforts to find Connie Daily since you became her court-appointed trustee?" Judge Harry Phillips asked.

"No, Sir! Yes, Sir!" Tyler answered the questions in the same order as the Judge had asked them. "I'd be happy to talk to someone. This is the first time I've had trouble finding a juvenile I was a trustee for."

"Give me your contact information. I'll have a deputy call you this evening, so I need your home number. Deputy Nelson will be the one to call you, and he works evenings."

"Yes, sir. I look forward to talking to him. Thank you, sir. May I ask. Is Connie alright? Do you want me to set up a funeral for her parents?" Tyler asked before he provided the Judge with his contact information.

"No, I've talked with Connie. She wants to plan it with her current foster parents who are going to be her permanent legal guardians until she is eighteen," Harry said. "And she's doing much better now. She has her dog with her. She's settling in well where she is; in Converse County. I'll have her new foster parents, Art and Belle Miller contact you. Connie wants some things from her house," Harry told Tyler.

"Not a problem, Sir. Can I have Art Miller's number? I can call him," Tyler offered. "I don't know what happened with Connie Daily. I have never had a child slip through the cracks like this before," Tyler explained, "I always get to meet the kids assigned to me."

"We will find out. Thank you for your time, Tyler. Stay in touch as you feel it's necessary. I'm due in court," Judge Harry Phillips said and terminated the call.

He had his court clerk leave a message for Deputy Nelson to call Tyler Brown when he got on shift.

GLENROCK, WYOMING

Shortly before lunch, the phone rang at the Miller's Ranch. Art answered the phone.

"Mr. Miller, my name is Tyler Brown. I am Connie's court-appointed trustee in Natrona County since her parents died. I've been talking with Judge Harry Phillips. I understand he is the judge handling your case to be Connie's permanent legal guardian. How can I help?" Tyler asked.

"I have a list. First, I need to know where the bodies of Connie's parents are so she can see them before the funeral. Second, I need to make arrangements for burial here in Glenrock. After that, I need to work on setting up a trust, if you haven't already. Fourth, I need to take her to her house to let her take whatever she wants," Art said.

He continued, "Then I need to set up an estate sale and after that sell the house. I want to put all the profits into a trust for Connie. I want to set it up so she can't touch any money from the trust until she is twenty-one, so she can go to college without worrying about money."

Art finally asked, "You willing to work with me on this, son, or do I need to get a lawyer?"

"I am more than willing to help in any way I can. I can refer you to a good trust and estate attorney. But, about her parents. They were injured so badly; no person in their right mind would have let her see the bodies. Better she remembers them as she last saw them."

"That bad?" Art asked.

"Worse. It was awful, and I've seen car accident victims before. Minivans don't stand a chance against a fully loaded speeding dump truck," Tyler said.

"I had them cremated. I have the Dailys' ashes so they can be buried or scattered where ever Connie wants. As for the rest, I am at your disposal. Anything I can help with, please, call me."

"I think we'll work well together," Art said. "Looking at my calendar, I have tomorrow morning open, will that work for you?"

"Yes," Tyler replied and provided Art directions to his office.

After lunch, Art sat down with Connie and Belle in the living room. He explained what he had learned after speaking with Tyler Brown. "Connie, he's your court-appointed trustee," Art finished.

"Can you and Mrs. Belle be my trustee?" Connie asked. "Then I would know who to ask for stuff."

"Art and I'll talk to Judge Harry, and find out what we need to do to make that happen, as soon as we get your trust set up," Belle stated.

"Now, do you understand about your parents' cremation?" Art asked.

"Yes, I think so. But . . ." a few tears slipped down Connie's cheeks. "Did they hurt much before they died? I don't want them to have hurt," Connie said and sniffed.

Belle went and sat with Connie in the large recliner she where she had curled up, Mac on the floor next to her. Pulling Connie against her, Belle explained about the body going into shock when there was a severe injury. "Most likely, your parents wouldn't have been aware of how badly they were hurt," Belle explained.

Connie wiped her eyes and nose on the sleeve of her sweatshirt after the explanation, not happy, but understanding a bit better what had happened to her parents.

Art called Mike Nelson at home. He left a message with Mike's wife, Donna, asking Mike to call when he had time. Art told Donna it was about the accident that took the lives of Connie's parents.

When Mike called Art back, Mike filled in Art on all the details he knew without looking at the case report. Mike promised to call that evening after he got in to work so that he could give Art the case report number. With the number, Art could get a copy of the report for Connie.

"But maybe save it until she's older, it's pretty gruesome. There will be photos of the accident and the aftermath," Mike told Art.

"Understood," Art assured Mike. "I just want to be able to answer when Connie has questions."

JUNE 14, 1994
CASPER, WYOMING

ART'S MEETING WITH TYLER WENT WELL. HE LIKED THE YOUNG MAN.

"Here are Connie's clothes from her last two foster homes," Tyler said. He handed Art two plastic trash bags, each containing some clothes belonging to Connie that she had left behind. At the look on Art's face, Tyler apologized, "Sorry, it's just we can't buy the children suitcases, it's too expensive."

Together, Art and Tyler set up a schedule to get Connie into her parents' house, then the estate sale, followed by the house sale. They went together to set up the account at the bank for Connie's trust to be administered by Tyler and Art jointly for now, and later by Art and Belle.

With the trust account set up, the money from Brian and Lisa Daily's life insurance policies finally had a place to go. Tyler handled providing the insurance companies with the account information.

After concluding his business with Tyler, Art went to the Casper Police Department to get a copy of the accident report with photos. Taking Mike Nelson's advice, he never looked at the pictures, just made sure the suspect's name and information were not blacked out.

Task completed; he drove by the address of Connie's house. It was in a nice neighborhood, but the yard needed work. He would bring a lawnmower and gas-powered weed-whacker and clean up the yard while Belle and Connie figured out what she wanted from the house to bring to the ranch.

JUNE 15, 1994
CASPER, WYOMING

ART PULLED INTO THE DRIVEWAY OF CONNIE'S HOUSE. BELLE SAT NEXT to him in the front seat of the pickup. Connie and Mac were in the back seat. Art didn't know what he had been expecting from Connie, but the sobs she was trying to suppress from the back seat of his four-door pickup wasn't it. He put the truck in park and looked at Belle. She had tears in her eyes, too. When he looked in the rearview mirror, he saw Mac as he tried to console Connie by licking her face. Connie hugged the big dog as if she was hanging on for dear life.

Art got out of the truck and checked his watch. "We're a few minutes early. Tyler should be showing up soon with keys to the house," Art said.

Belle stayed in the truck with Connie and Mac. "They're really gone, aren't they?" Connie whimpered as she wiped tears from her face.

"Yes, Sweetie. I'm so sorry. I wish I could make it better, but that will only happen with time, and it will never go away completely. It's just that with time eventually, it doesn't hurt so much all the time. And by time, I mean it could be months or even years before you can think of your parents and remember the good times with them and not the bad time you're having now," Belle said.

Connie nodded and buried her face back in Mac's neck.

Tyler arrived in his car and got out to shake hands with Art. "Is she here? I wanted to apologize for not touching base with her before I cremated her parents. I couldn't find her. The morgue had a time limit for unclaimed remains," Tyler explained.

Art indicated his truck with a tip of his head. "She's here, but taking it hard. It's the first time she's been back since child protective services, an oxymoron if I ever heard one, took her away from here," Art said.

Art and Tyler peered in the truck and saw Connie weeping, her arms wrapped around Mac's neck as she cried into his fur.

Belle got out to talk to them. "Let me have the house keys. I can take her in when she's ready. In the meantime, Art, that grass won't cut itself," Belle said, as she smiled at Art.

Belle turned to Tyler. She said, "Hi, I'm Belle Miller, Art's wife, and we plan to take very good care of Connie and make her parents proud when they look down from Heaven and see how well she grows up. No need for you to hang around."

"I wanted to apologize to Connie for missing her at all the different foster homes. I cleaned out the perishables in the refrigerator. There are still staples and frozen foods that will need decisions," Tyler said.

"That can wait. Connie has enough on her plate today," Belle said. "She doesn't need to deal with any more strangers in her business right now."

"Yes, ma'am," Tyler replied and gave Belle the keys.

Going to the back of the pickup, Tyler helped Art unload a walk-behind lawnmower and a five-gallon gas can. He said, "Keep in touch and let me know if there is anything I can do to help, anything at all."

The men shook hands. Tyler got in his car and left.

When Connie finally stopped crying, Belle took her and Mac into the house and helped Connie wash her face. "I wish I could take your pain away but I can't, only time can. Any time you need a hug, you tell me, and I'll give you all the hugs you need. So will Art, okay, Sweetie?" Belle asked.

The roaring lawnmower went by outside, just under the bathroom window as Connie nodded. Belle continued, "So where do you want to start?"

Connie led the way to her room. Once there, Mac hopped up on the bed to watch the goings-on. "How much of my things can I bring? When that lady came last time, it was only one small suitcase and my backpack with school books. I don't even know where my suitcase is anymore," Connie said.

"That's not important. Show me what you want. If we can't get it in the truck this time, we'll hire movers. That goes for the whole house. We're going to take everything you want to keep."

"What happens to the rest?" Connie asked, "You know, the stuff I don't want?"

"There will be an estate sale. All the money from that will go into a special bank account for you that will pay for college. After that, we will put the house up for sale. That money will go in the same account."

"What about the cars? Mom has a minivan. The night they never came home, they were in Mom's minivan. Dad's new pickup is in the garage."

"The van didn't make it, Honey. I'll let Art know about your Dad's truck. You two can decide together about what to do with it, okay? Our job right now is to get the stuff you want to take to the house," Belle said.

In a small voice, Connie asked, "Can I bring everything in my room and have it at your house? Can I have my room at your house, and give back the guest room?"

"Yes, Honey, that's why we came today. To find out what you want to take to the ranch."

Half an hour later, Art came into the house for a glass of cold water. After he drank it down, he walked through the house to find Connie and Belle in the master bedroom. "Any progress?" he asked.

"She wants to take her whole bedroom. We found the photo albums. We're taking those. She wants the computer and computer desk, and some other odds and ends," Belle replied.

"She wants to take her whole bedroom? Or just all the stuff in it?" Art asked as he smiled at Connie.

"Just everything in it," Connie answered.

"We'll come back with the horse trailer tomorrow and load up the things you want to take. Sound okay to you?" Art asked.

"Yes, thank you, Mr. Art."

"Just Art."

"Okay, thank you, just Art." Connie smiled at him; her smile warmed his heart.

"Well, keep at it, I have weed-whacking to do. When I finish, we'll go home. Then we can get everything ready at the house to come back tomorrow to pick up everything you want," Art said, then went back outside. Soon the weed-whacker was buzzing around the house.

Inside, Connie and Belle picked out the towels, sheets, and blankets Connie wanted. Belle also decided to take the fine china she found in the kitchen. She would save it for Connie when she was older. She would bring some boxes tomorrow to pack it safely.

Connie held a photo album to her chest as she and Mac shared the back seat of the pickup on the drive back to Glenrock. It was the album her mother had made of the courtship her parents had shared before getting married. There were lots of photos of them in different places doing things. And in every picture, her Dad had both legs. Her parents were smiling, happy — the way she wanted to remember them.

GLENROCK, WYOMING

CONNIE PLAYED OUTSIDE WITH MAC, WHILE BELLE AND ART SURVEYED the sewing room.

"I don't know, Belle; I think it may be best to build a room and bathroom on for her. A room big enough for her to grow into as she gets older and accumulates more stuff. I don't think there is going to be enough room in here. And where would you sew?"

Heaving a sigh, Belle agreed, "I think you're right. Her bedroom in the house in Casper was bigger."

After they finished supper, and the dishes were taken care of, Art and Belle sat down with Connie. "Connie, we looked at everything you have and the space we have in this house. We want to build on a new bedroom and bathroom for you. Do you think you can stand to live in the guest room for a few more months? We're still going back to Casper for everything you want to bring here. We'll store it in the barn until construction on your room is done," Art explained.

Connie thought about this for a few moments, "Can I help design the addition?"

Art nodded.

"Awesome, I'll start right now!" Connie jumped out of her chair and went to her room for paper and a pencil. Back at the kitchen table, she asked, "Where would I find a ruler?"

Belle pulled one from a drawer at the phone nook and handed it to Connie, "There you go kiddo."

"Thank you," Connie said. She took it, sat at the kitchen table, and went to work.

Art smiled at her determination. He watched her as she carefully measured out her design on the notebook paper she had gotten to draw out her plans.

Much later, Connie brought her room plan into the living room and said, "Finished, I hope it isn't too big."

"Bring it here and let me look at it," Art said from his recliner as he placed his book face down on the arm.

When she presented it to Art, he saw she had included a bathroom with shower and linen closet, a desk alcove with bookshelves and a large walk-in closet as well as a labeled "dog nook" next to where she figured her bed would be. She had drawn in all her furniture. He took in the dimensions she had listed. The overall the space she had drawn was 340 square feet.

Art figured he would round it up to 400 square feet, but didn't tell Connie. It would be a surprise when completed — a pleasant surprise. Art smiled. "Well done. I think we can do this. I'll start making arrangements after we get your things from Casper. In the meantime, take Mac out for his last trip of the night and get ready for bed. Tomorrow is going to be busy. Then get some sleep," Art said.

Connie nodded, leaned in, and gave him a big hug, then went to Belle for a hug before she took Mac outside.

"I like the hugs at bedtime," Belle commented.

Art smiled and said, "I do too."

Half an hour later she was in bed with Mac, still discussing with him what she should take from the house in Casper and what she should let go to the estate sale. Connie fell asleep, still pondering the different choices she had to make in the morning.

JUNE 16, 1994
GLENROCK, WYOMING

Art, Belle, and Connie were finishing an early breakfast when the phone rang. Art was surprised to be talking with Tyler. "Art, I finally got the parents safe drilled last night, I had to wait for a court order to go through to do that. Documents in the safe indicate Connie's parents had already set up a trust, and it owns everything. You're going to have to get a lawyer involved to handle the sale of the house, the truck, and the personal property. I've made a copy of the trust for you. The original needs to go to the lawyer. Are you planning on being in Casper any time soon or should I mail you the documents?" Tyler asked.

"We're going back today, to the house to get the stuff Connie wants to keep. Can you meet us there in a few hours?" Art asked.

"Sure, call me when you get there. I'll run over with everything. I'll also bring the names of a couple estate sale and auction places depending on how you want to dispose of the personal property of her parents."

"That sounds good, see you then," Art said, and ended the call. Art called his lawyer, Roger, and briefed him on what he had learned from Tyler. "Roger, I also want you to redo my will, and Belle's so that we have Connie as our beneficiary after we both pass on. Can you do that?" Art asked. "I'll stop by this afternoon with the trust documents for Connie's trust."

"Swing by at four o'clock, I have an opening in my schedule then," Roger said.

While Art was on the phone, Connie cleared the breakfast dishes, and Belle put together a cooler full of lunch items.

CASPER, WYOMING

ONCE IN CASPER, ART STOPPED AT THE U-HAUL STORE TO PICK UP boxes, tape, bubble wrap, and packing paper. Belle waited in the truck with Connie and Mac. Art loaded all the supplies into the horse trailer he was towing before continuing to Connie's house.

At the house, Belle and Connie packed her room while Mac supervised. Art tackled the garage, scavenging anything that looked useful among the impressive tool collection her dad had accumulated. He picked out a few tools he didn't have that he planned to take home. He looked over the pickup. It was so new, when he opened the door, it still smelled new, and it was loaded.

Garage finished; Art packed the fancy dishes in the kitchen. Belle had told him they needed to save those for Connie for when she got married.

Art was packing the dishes when Tyler showed up with all the documents about Connie he needed to give to Art. Tyler volunteered, "I can stay and help pack. Just tell me where to start."

"Thank you, young man. You can start over here. If it has a yellow posty note on it, it needs to be packed, if not, ignore it," Art instructed and put him to work in the living room.

When everything Connie wanted or the adults thought she might want in the future had been boxed, Art went out and backed the horse trailer up to the porch right across the front yard. They loaded the heavy boxes first and then furniture.

Once loaded, Art said, "Thanks, Tyler. Belle packed lunch. Do you want to stay and eat?"

Tyler watched as Belle removed food from the cooler. She removed thick roast beef sandwiches, a quart jar of homemade pickles, and iced tea in a half-gallon jar from the cooler. Then, Belle took a large bag of potato chips, homemade chocolate chip cookies, paper plates, napkins, and plastic drinking cups from a paper bag. Once Tyler knew the menu, he couldn't say no. When lunch was over, they thanked Tyler for his help and said goodbye when he left.

Connie took Mac into the back yard to make sure none of his toys got left behind. Connie returned with a chewed up frisbee and a rawhide bone. Prancing, Mac carried his chewed-up Jolly ball by the rope back into the house. She dropped those off in the 'to go in the truck' pile, then Connie took Mac to make another sweep of the back yard and came back with a nylon dog bone. Sure she had everything, Connie and Mac went back into the house and helped clean up after lunch. With everything done, they left.

GLENROCK, WYOMING

At the ranch, Art pulled the loaded horse trailer into the barn and covered it with several tarps to keep the hay out of the furniture. He then set mouse traps around the trailer to keep mice out of the boxes and furniture. He planned to set up proper storage tomorrow. He had decided to rent a truck trailer. He could safely leave in the barn for several months without having to worry about rodents getting at the furniture and boxes. Connie's room would take a few months to add to the house.

When he had first seen Connie in Rebel's stall, he had just wanted to protect her. Now he couldn't imagine life without her — "Time to quit gathering wool and get over to Roger's office with everything Tyler gave me," Art reminded himself.

At Roger's office, Art handed over the documents Tyler had given him. Roger riffled through the documents and immediately saw that Connie's parents had listed three different couples to look after Connie if anything happened to them. "What about these folks?" asked Roger.

Art shrugged. "Don't know. I don't think she would have been in foster care if they could have found any of them. It's been a month now," he said.

"I'll need to look into this further before we file for permanent legal guardianship," Roger said. "Is Connie seeing anyone, professionally, about losing her parents?"

"No, but she does spend a great deal of time talking it over, with Mac. She talks to Belle and me as well," Art said. "We'll do whatever it takes, just please don't break my bank account," Art requested.

JUNE 17, 1994 TO JULY 3, 1994
GLENROCK, WYOMING

OVER TIME, ART, BELLE, CONNIE, AND MAC SETTLED INTO THEIR NEW routines. Construction began on Connie's bedroom and bathroom addition. There were still nights where either Art or Belle had to go into Connie's room to console her while she cried for her deceased parents.

One day while Connie was outside with Mac, Belle commented to Art, "We are so lucky. Connie is such a delightful, helpful, kind, and energetic kid. Her parents would be so proud of her." Belle continued to dust the living room as Art sat in his recliner, reading the Casper Star-Tribune.

"And with Mac always at her side when she helps with chores," Art said.

"She's a gift from God," Belle replied. "I never told you but, I never felt complete when we couldn't have children. It's like God's giving us a second chance. I am so grateful."

JULY 4, 1994
GLENROCK, WYOMING

ON JULY 4TH, ART AND BELLE PLANNED TO TAKE CONNIE INTO TOWN FOR the parade, then a picnic at church, followed by that evening's fireworks. Connie declined, she said, "I need to stay with Mac. Fireworks could scare him. They might sound too much like bombs and mortars going off."

"What about if we just go to the parade and picnic?" Belle asked.

"Is it a noisy parade? I don't want to have him get hurt or lost because he got scared," Connie worried. "I'll stay home with Mac, and you can go. I'll be alright. I promise."

"You're a very responsible young lady. I don't see why not. Belle and I'll see the parade. When we come back, we'll all go to the picnic at church, together, including Mac. You and Mac can stay home tonight during the fireworks," Art decided. "Sound like a plan?"

"Yes! Thank you!" Connie said and rushed to hug Art. "Mac's all I have left of my old family. You're my new family, but I want to keep Mac, too." Her eyes were shiny with unshed tears.

AUGUST 1, 1994
GLENROCK, WYOMING

"CONNIE," CALLED BELLE OUT THE BACK DOOR AN HOUR AFTER BREAKFAST, "We need to get going to the school. Today's registration."

"Coming," replied Connie, running up from the barn, Mac at her heels. Connie directed Mac into his kennel. "*Bleib.* You stay here. I'll come back; I promise. It's just too hot to let you wait in the truck at school," Connie told her dog.

Mac flopped with a groan in the shade of the tree near his dog house. Coming into the house, Connie asked, "Do I need to change from play clothes for registration?"

Belle looked her over, and said, "Nope, you look clean enough to me. Let's get going so we can do some school clothes shopping after we get you set up at school. If things go fast enough, we can eat in town before we come back."

Connie responded, "Let's see about eating out when we get done with all the 'we have to' stuff."

"Okay, let me know," Belle replied. They climbed into the truck, waved to Art by the barn and headed into town and the school.

AUGUST 11, 1994
GLENROCK, WYOMING

THE FOUNDATION FOR CONNIE'S ROOM WAS FINISHED AND CURED. THE framing was complete. The addition was roofed, shingled, and sided. The work was all on the inside. Every morning Connie checked on the job, from a pre-approved spot so she could look without getting in the way of the contractors doing the work.

After lunch, Connie loaded the dishwasher. The phone rang. Belle answered it and found Roger on the other end of the call. "Belle, just to let you and Art know, I finished tracking down all the folks Connie's parents listed as legal guardians. She has no one. So as far as I can see, the application for permanent legal guardianship should go through without a hitch," he said.

"Oh, thank the Lord!" Belle responded. "I don't know how Art or I would survive without our little ray of sunshine. We can go ahead and start the paperwork through the courts?"

Roger's voice conveyed his smile as he answered Belle's question, "I see no problem with getting that going. I'll start it today."

"Thank you, Roger. You don't know how much this means to us," Belle said.

"Oh, I think I have a suspicion," Roger said.

After the call, Belle had Connie go with her out to the barn where Art worked repairing tack. She told them both the good news at the same time.

AUGUST 15, 1994
GLENROCK, WYOMING

ART DROVE AS HE AND BELLE TOOK CONNIE TO SCHOOL FOR HER FIRST day. Mac was in the backseat with Connie. When he glanced in the rearview mirror at Connie, he could see the pensive expression on her face as she leaned against Mac and whispered her fears to the big dog. That was Art's best guess at the conversation as he couldn't hear it.

At the school student drop off area Art told Connie, "I will be right here to pick you up after school, so stay here and wait for me. I shouldn't be late, but just in case, you wait for me, okay?"

Connie nodded, then released her seatbelt and got out of the truck and stood staring at the school building. Art and Belle watched as Connie took a few steps from the pickup, then stopped.

"You can do this," Belle called out her open truck window. "You just need to find room 10."

Connie walked into the building. When she found room 10, she went in and found a desk. Some of the other desks already had kids sitting at them. They all seemed to be having first-day jitters, Connie observed, so she wasn't the only one.

Back home, Mac stayed on the shady back porch and watched the truck from inside his dog yard. Belle called the panting dog in for lunch and to cool off. When he came in, she closed the doggie door. Belle didn't want him to overheat, waiting outside for Connie.

After lunch, Belle gave Mac a small plate with a few cold roast beef bits. Mac had stayed on his throw-rug, his designated spot during meals. It wasn't much, just enough to keep him interested in staying in the house with Belle as she cleaned up the dishes, and he cooled down.

As she did the dishes, Belle talked to Mac, "You'll come with us when we go get her from school. Just know, this is the new routine until school is out in the spring. You're going to have to adapt, boy. Maybe you could hang out with me. Or maybe Art if he is doing something interesting."

Mac watched Belle intently as she talked to him. "You're a smart boy, aren't you, Mac?" Belle asked the dog. Mac did the German Shepherd head tilt, while he thumped his tail hesitantly on the floor.

Belle dried her hands after she finished loading the dishwasher. She went to the big dog and stroked his head. "Why don't you come with me while I work on Connie's quilt for a while. Now you can't tell her about it, it's for her Christmas present, but you can help me. Come on, Mac."

Belle used the hand signal she had seen Connie use for the command 'come.' They headed down the hall to her sewing room. She sat at the considerable quilt frame that held the work in progress. Mac followed her. "Yes." Belle murmured, "You listened."

Once she got into the rhythm of sewing, she also chatted with Mac. It seemed mere minutes had passed when Art came in and asked, "How's it going?"

"Good. I think I'll have it finished in plenty of time for Christmas. And Mac has promised not to tell." Belle smiled at her husband.

"Are you coming with me to pick up Connie? If you are, we need to leave in about ten minutes," Art said.

Belle tucked her needle into the fabric where she stopped working and stood, "Of course we're coming, aren't we Mac?"

Belle led the dog from the room and shut the door. Outside, Belle used one of the few English commands she had heard Connie use with Mac. She said, "Take a break, Mac."

The dog looked at her, then went and watered the nearest tree and came back to Belle.

"Good boy, Mac!" Belle praised him enthusiastically, then led him to the truck where Art was waiting. "You want to go for a ride?" Belle asked. Mac danced in circles at her feet for two spins then ran to the back door he always used to get in the truck. Once everyone was in, they drove to the school to pick up Connie.

AUGUST 16, 1994
GLENROCK, WYOMING

ART SIPPED HIS FIRST CUP OF COFFEE BEFORE BREAKFAST WHEN MAC barked ferociously at the doggie door. "What's wrong, dog?" Art asked. He got up from the kitchen table.

Mac was at the open doggie door, but he wouldn't go out. Art watched Mac dance around the doggie door flap barking at it.

When Art moved to open the door, Mac blocked him. Art picked up the panel that locked the doggie door closed and slid it in place. Then he ordered Mac, "Back up," in English.

Even though it was the wrong language, Mac seemed to know what Art needed him to do and got out of the way.

Doggie door locked; Art looked out the window. He saw a large rattlesnake comfortably curled up in the morning sun on the porch right outside the door. "Good boy, Mac," Art praised the German Shepherd.

Art made a large pitcher of ice water. Mac's barking had awakened Belle and Connie, who both came into the kitchen. Belle had dressed for the day, but Connie was still in her pajamas.

Leaving his half-gallon pitcher of ice water on the counter, Art got his homemade snake catcher and a large paper bag from the broom cupboard. The snake catcher was an old broom handle with eye-bolts running up the side with a rope through the eye-bolts, so a loop formed at the end. He could tighten the loop to the needed circumference to trap a snake.

"Keep Mac back from the door, we got a rattler on the porch," Art told Belle. "I'm gonna ice water him so I can relocate him away from the house," Art explained.

With everything he needed close at hand, Art picked up the pitcher of ice water, opened the door and dumped the ice water on the slumbering snake.

While the snake was still in shock from the cold water, Art grabbed it just behind the arrow-shaped head with his snake catcher, picked it up, and carefully put it in the paper bag.

He carried the bag out to the alfalfa field opposite the barn and threw it, with the snake still inside, out into the long grass, and returned to the house. "We'll give it a few hours. When the bag moves in the breeze, I'll check on it. You ladies leave that to me," Art ordered once he was back in the kitchen. He poured a second cup of coffee.

Belle turned to Connie and said, "Better go, get dressed. I'll get breakfast going. We don't want you to be late for school on your second day."

Connie nodded, rubbed her eyes, and headed back to her bedroom.

Mac scratched at the closed doggie door and stared at Art. Mac said, "woof."

Art looked over at the dog. "Sorry Mac, I guess you want to go out, don't you?"

"Woof," repeated Mac, with a little more intensity.

Art opened the doggie door, and Mac went out to take care of his business before he returned to Connie's room. Mac had to supervise her as she got dressed for school.

SEPTEMBER 10, 1994
GLENROCK, WYOMING

AFTER BREAKFAST, BELLE HAD CONNIE WITH HER IN THE GARDEN. THEY were picking all the vegetables that wouldn't survive the coming night's predicted freeze.

The tomato plants were pulled up by the roots and piled in a plastic swimming pool in the barn. That way the tomatoes would continue to ripen for canning.

The cabbage, squash, green beans and cucumbers were also picked to be canned.

The carrots were left in the ground to let the freeze sweeten them. As they were needed, Connie or Belle could dig them up.

The potatoes were dug up and put in burlap bags, with the dirt on them, to sit in the root cellar until Belle was ready to use them, then they would be cleaned up.

It was hard work. Connie enjoyed helping in the garden. Belle's garden was much bigger than any her mother had ever planted.

They began right after lunch. The process started with the squash, Connie diced it, and Belle put it in quart bags that went into the chest freezer in the basement. They then blanched the green beans in boiling water before it was put under cold water, drained and placed in pint freezer bags.

Next, Connie and Belle hauled empty quart jars up from the basement to make pickles. Connie rinsed the cucumbers, Belle sliced them lengthwise and stuffed them into the quart jars. She made sure to leave enough room at the top of each jar for half of a Vidalia onion.

Connie's job was to cut the onions. Belle heated a canning solution on the stove that was a mix of water, vinegar, salt, and sugar. After the jars had the canning solution in them, Connie capped the jars and Belle put them into the hot water bath for thirty minutes.

Canning was hard work that Connie enjoyed immensely. She liked that at the end of the day, there was proof of all your hard work in the bags in the freezer and jars on the shelves.

The cabbage was going to wait to become sauerkraut. It wouldn't mind sitting on the counter for a day or two.

OCTOBER 25, 1994
GLENROCK, WYOMING

IT WAS AFTER SCHOOL WHEN MAC'S BARK ANNOUNCED A VEHICLE approaching the house. Art looked out the window of the living room and recognized the truck. Harry was coming for a surprise visit.

"Connie, tell Mac it's okay, please," Art said. Connie complied, and Mac quieted.

After Harry got parked, he came up onto the porch, knocked twice then turned the doorknob to let himself in.

Mac growled a warning as Harry began to open the door. Harry promptly pulled the door shut and shouted, "Permission to enter?"

Connie told Mac, "*Sicher.* Safe."

Mac quieted, then she opened the door for Harry.

Once he entered, Harry glanced at Mac, then at Connie. Mac was right beside her, not bristling, but alert.

"It's been a while since you've been here. I know bending down is hard, so go sit in a chair and I can re-do introductions," Connie told the judge.

Harry went to the nearest chair in the living room and sat. Connie approached with Mac at her side. "Mac, *Sicher*," she pointed at Harry.

"Stay still while he checks you out," Connie instructed Harry. Mac went to the Judge and gave him a thorough sniff then returned to Connie's side.

"You should be fine now, as long as you don't do anything that Mac thinks means you want to hurt me," Connie said. Then she headed to the kitchen.

Art had watched the whole exchange from the doorway of his office. He commented, "Harry, this is a surprise."

"Surprise visit to check on Connie and see how things are going. I had to. I made the ruling that you were her foster parents. Due diligence and all that," Harry said. "She's doing okay? You and Belle are doing okay?"

Art came into the living room and sat on the couch, facing Harry. "We're all doing fine. Belle and I couldn't be happier. Connie still has days where she misses her parents, but I think that's normal. Mac is a huge help when she needs consoling, but she comes to us as well. We've told her if she ever wants to talk to someone other than us, tell us and we'll set it up," Art said.

"Good, I'm glad to hear that. Reinforces that I made the right choice." Harry smiled at Art. "Although how you and Belle could have been a bad choice is beyond me."

The men settled in to talk about an upcoming fishing trip they planned to make with Roger once the ice froze thick enough for a fish house to sit on this year's lake of choice.

NOVEMBER 12, 1994
GLENROCK, WYOMING

TODAY CONNIE WOULD GET TO MOVE INTO HER NEW BEDROOM. Anticipation made Connie think breakfast took much too long. Even though breakfast today was the same as every other day on the ranch. When breakfast was finally over, the dishes rinsed, and in the dishwasher, Connie ran to her room with Mac at her side. There she waited for her furniture.

While she was in her room, Roger and Dena, and Harry arrived to help with the furniture wrangling. Today she could use her things again. She was so excited she bounced on her toes.

The weather outside was beautiful. Sunny, with a gentle, crisp breeze. The yard between the barn where her furniture was stored, and the house was dry. The move wouldn't track lots of mud into the house or her bedroom. Mac circled Connie, having caught her excitement.

Belle came in and asked, "Is this worse than waiting to open Christmas presents?"

"Almost," Connie replied.

When everything was in the house, Connie directed the placement of the furniture in her room. She wanted it arranged the same as her room in Casper. Then she sat on the bed with Mac and surveyed her room.

After giving the furniture placement much consideration, Connie decided she needed to rearrange it. The current arrangement didn't feel right.

Belle called out, "Connie, lunch." Connie rose from her bed and went to the kitchen with Mac. After she sat at the kitchen table, Mac flopped on the floor behind her.

Belle served Art, Dena, and Roger, followed by Harry, and Connie before sitting at the table and helping herself to pot roast, salad, and coffee.

After taking a few bites of her lunch, Connie asked in a quiet voice, "Would it be okay to rearrange the furniture in my room? The way I asked to have it arranged makes me feel sad. I want to redo it." When she looked up from her plate, Belle saw tears in Connie's eyes.

Belle rose from her chair and went to hug Connie in her chair. "Of course, it's okay. After lunch, why don't you, Dena and I go up and look at things and figure out a new way to arrange your room. When we're ready, we'll have the men come to move the furniture, okay?" Belle asked as she comforted Connie.

Connie nodded, satisfied, and smiled at Belle before she resumed eating her lunch.

After lunch, the ladies went to Connie's room and surveyed the furniture situation. Mac went along to supervise. It took only a few minutes, with suggestions from both Belle and Dena to come up with an arrangement that suited Connie.

Then the men were invited into Connie's room to move the furniture, into the new arrangement. Satisfied, Connie asked, "Can I have a corkboard wall? Or some shelves to put my pictures on?" She pointed at the stack of photos from her previous life in Casper that were in a box on her desk. "I want to put some of those up, so I don't forget what they look like."

"I think a cork wall is doable," Art said. "We'll go to the hardware store on Monday after I pick you up from school. How's that sound?"

"Good!" Connie brightened, jumped off the bed to give first Belle and then Art a hug.

NOVEMBER 19, 1994
GLENROCK, WYOMING

THE WEEKEND WAS SPENT PUTTING UP THE LIGHT-COLORED CORK ON Connie's bedroom wall. She put a few photos of Mac and her parents on the cork wall with thumbtacks. She asked, "Is there a picture of you both I can have to put on my wall?"

"I'm sure we have something. After supper we can look through the photo albums," Belle said.

NOVEMBER 28, 1994
DOUGLAS, WYOMING

IN THE COURTROOM OF THE CONVERSE COUNTY SUPERIOR COURT, Connie tried to sit still in her assigned chair. She was dressed in her Sunday go to church clothes. So were Art and Belle who sat on either side of Connie. Roger sat at a table on the other side of the waist-high barrier.

Dark-colored paneling covered the walls of the courtroom. There was a raised area with a tall desk and chair, with lower desks on either side. Flags were behind the big raised desk.

Connie started when a door behind and beside one of the low desks opened, and two people came out. A lady, who carried a weird thing on a stand and a man in a uniform like deputy Mike wore.

The deputy ordered, "All rise." Everyone in the courtroom stood.

Connie saw another door open behind the desks, and Judge Harry came out in his black robes. Once he sat, the man in uniform said, "You may be seated," and everyone sat.

The lady with the strange gadget sat. Connie watched her. Whenever anyone spoke, the lady typed on the machine, and paper came out and piled into a small basket attached to the thing.

Judge Harry read aloud a bunch of stuff that had Connie wondering how she was going to stay awake. It was boring stuff about some estate and dispensations. Her mind wandered but snapped back to what the judge said when she heard her parents' names and her name.

Connie tried to follow what was going on, but the strange language defeated her. Individually, they were words she knew, but the way the lawyers used the words was difficult to follow. To Connie, it almost sounded like a new language.

When Judge Harry finished talking, Roger stood and spoke more incomprehensible English back to Judge Harry. The lady with the gadget typed away, and the paper flowed out.

A man at the desk next to Roger said he represented someone in Natrona County. Connie didn't hear the name or office served. This man jumped up and said, "I object!" Many times, after Judge Harry spoke and after Roger spoke, he jumped up behind his table to say, "I object," in varying volumes.

Connie watched Judge Harry. She could tell he was getting quite irritated. Connie had no idea what the man was objecting to, other than it had something to do with "jurisdiction," whatever that was. Connie tuned out again.

A few minutes later, she heard Judge Harry call her name and ask her to sit in the big empty chair next to his desk. Almost panicked, she looked at Art while she grabbed Belle's hand. "Don't make me go!" she whispered to them.

"It's okay honey; this will be okay. Harry needs you to sit in the "truth chair" while he asks you some questions. Tell the truth to whatever he asks. That's why you sit in a special chair. You'll go home with us. You have to. Remember, Mac is waiting for you," Belle reminded her. "I'll walk up with you, okay?" Connie nodded and walked to the witness chair with Belle.

Once in the "truth chair," Connie was sworn in.

The man at the desk next to Roger's jumped up and said, "I object! I can't stress that strongly enough."

"Noted," Judge Harry said, "Now sit down and don't interrupt her." Judge Harry then had Connie detail her life. She got through her first day being an orphan when objection man jumped to his feet and yelled, "I object!"

"Sit!" Judge Harry bellowed. More quietly, he told Connie, "Continue."

She detailed from the time she left her parents' home in Casper until Art found her in his barn with Rebel. Objection-man began to rise from his chair several times as Connie explained her journey from a happy home to the courtroom. Judge Harry stared him back into his chair.

The next time the "objection-man," as Connie thought of him, rose from his chair, Judge Harry reprimanded him, "Let the witness finish. You weren't there. You don't know what she experienced. You have no reason to object to her summary of her life. So, sit down!"

Objection-man was unhappy. One more time, he rose completely from his chair.

Judge Harry ordered, "Sit down! Or be held in contempt!"

Connie watched Objection-man fidget at his table, and then she looked at Roger, who was relaxed.

After Connie got off the truth chair, it was Art's turn, then Belle's turn to describe finding Connie in their barn and her condition.

Connie was bored. She was sure today would never end. She would never see Mac again. They were never getting out of here. She was daydreaming when the crack of Judge Harry's gavel brought her back to the present.

"I am ordering that Art and Belle Miller are to be Connie Daily's permanent legal guardians until she reaches her majority. They will have all the legal rights to act and make decisions as her legal guardians; they will also act as her trustee until she is twenty-one years of age and make decisions with her best interests in mind regarding the Daily Revocable Family Trust," said Judge Harry.

"Objection!" exploded out of objection-man's mouth.

"You do not get to object! Your county did not take care of the welfare of this child!" roared Judge Harry at the man. He smacked his gavel down on his desk. "Thirty days for contempt! You will be reimbursing Converse County for the cost of your incarceration as it was completely avoidable! All you had to do was follow instructions. My courtroom is not television, Mr. Jones," Judge Harry said and slammed down his gavel again. "Bailiff, escort Mr. Jones to the holding cells, and let his office know he won't be available for the next thirty days!"

The bailiff took a silent but agitated Mr. Jones by the elbow and led him out a door in the wall. Connie hadn't seen anyone use that door yet. She had thought it must be a coat closet.

Another man in a deputy's uniform came in and announced, "All rise." Everyone stood. Harry stood and left his big desk to disappear through the same door he had used to enter the courtroom.

Connie looked at Art and Belle. "What does all that mean?" she asked.

"It means we are not your parents, but we have the same responsibilities to look after you that your parents had. It means that no one can take you away from us, as long as we are as good as your parents were at looking after you," Art explained.

"It means," Belle cut into Art's explanation, "We are a family now. I hope that makes you happy?"

"Yes! It does. I am. I didn't want to leave you," Connie said. She hugged them both around the waist at the same time.

They went out to lunch to celebrate before the ride back to Glenrock. Roger joined them at lunch to congratulate Connie and explained to her that in any legal matter, he was her legal representative. If Art or Belle needed legal representation in anything involving her, they would have to find another lawyer.

GLENROCK, WYOMING

ONCE IN GLENROCK, CONNIE QUICKLY CHANGED INTO HER PLAY CLOTHES and went out to tell Mac the wonderful news. They had a family again. "No one could take us from Art and Belle, except if they die," Connie told Mac. "I didn't think of that in court! We need to go ask Mr. Art what happens if he or Mrs. Belle dies!"

Connie raced back into the house, Mac at her heels. She was out of breath from running when she found Art. Panting, she asked him, "If you and Mrs. Belle die, what happens to Mac and me?"

"Roger and I are already working on that. Would you be okay with Roger and his wife Dena looking out for you if anything bad ever happened to Belle and me?" Art asked. Connie nodded. Mac sat at her side.

"What if something happened to Roger and Dena? Then what?" Connie asked.

"I was thinking of Judge Harry and his wife, just in case. You do like Judge Harry and trust him, right?" Art asked.

"Judge Harry, yes, his wife…" Connie shrugged her shoulders, "I would have to meet her first."

Belle had wandered in during the discussion about alternative guardianships. Belle said, "I'll invite Harry and his wife to the Christmas party. That way, you can meet Dorothy, and visit with Harry out of the courtroom. After you visit with everyone at the Christmas party, we can discuss things again if you are uncomfortable with any of the arrangements for guardianship. Sound good?"

Connie agreed and went back out to play.

"Tough kid," Art said to Belle once Connie was outside. "How many kids think that far ahead and worry that much at her age? I know I sure didn't."

DECEMBER 23, 1994
GLENROCK, WYOMING

TO MINIMIZE MAC'S BARKING AS HE ANNOUNCED EACH ARRIVING VEHICLE, Mac was in Connie's room for the duration of the party.

The Christmas party the Miller's held annually was underway. Connie helped Belle set the table with fancy dishes and glasses. Then, she was in charge of answering the door and putting coats away.

Most of the people coming she knew, but there were a few couples she still didn't know. They made her a little nervous. She didn't want to have to talk about why she now lived with Art and Belle. Her stomach ached from her parents' deaths. She had felt close to tears all day. She missed them so much.

It was her first Christmas without her mom and dad. For as long as they had been dead, this hurt a lot more than she had expected.

Belle noticed Connie was distressed and motioned Connie into the kitchen. Once there, Belle asked, "Would you feel better if you stayed in your room and I brought you a tray? Is it just too soon for Christmas after losing your parents? If it is, I do understand."

Connie nodded and with tears running down her face, hugged Belle. "I want to be with Mac," Connie wept. "It's just too much celebrating and I don't feel like celebrating. I just hurt, here," she put her hand over her heart and stomach. "It hurts so much."

Belle hugged Connie to her and said, "It's all right to feel that way. Go to your room. I'll bring up a tray after supper, okay?"

Connie nodded, ran to her room, closed the door, and crawled into bed. Mac hopped up with her and washed the tears from her face.

"Art, you're in charge of the front door," Belle called from the kitchen.

As Belle walked back through the dining room and living room, making one last pass to ensure was in place. Art gave her a look, and shoulder shrug from across the living room, where tables end to end went from the kitchen through the dining room and into the living room to accommodate all the guests. Belle gave him a quick, slight headshake in response.

Just then, Harry and his wife Dorothy arrived. Once Art took their coats, Harry asked, "Where're Connie, and Mac? I wanted them to meet my beautiful bride."

"Celebrating got to be too much for her, so we're giving her the night off. She's staying in her room, and she'll get a tray later," Art told him. "If she feels better, she might come out of her room. We're leaving it up to her and what she feels she can handle."

"That makes sense. I didn't mean to be insensitive. If I went to Connie's room, do you think she'd talk to me?"

"No idea, Harry. She was in tears when she left. You can try, but don't push, please, Harry."

Harry held his wife's hand as he led her to Connie's room. He said, "You have got to meet this kid, she's amazing. She's only eleven years old now, but she is a born negotiator, and whip-smart."

"Honey, remember what Art said. Today is tough for her, with losing her family and all," Dorothy reminded her husband.

At Connie's door, Harry tapped with a knuckle and said, "Connie? It's Harry. I just came to check up on you."

"I'm okay, now go away," Connie yelled through the door. "Leave me alone! Please!"

"Okay, I will. Can I check on you before I leave?"

"No! Now go away!" Mac added a low warning rumble to Connie's last statement that Harry heard clearly through the closed door.

After a pleasant feast with friends, Harry and Dorothy stayed behind to help clean up. Art and Harry collapsed each of the extra tables used to extend the small regular dining table after Dorothy cleared the dishes. Belle manned the sink and dishwasher.

Dorothy brought another pile of plates to the kitchen sink for Belle. "So how are things really going with Connie?" Dorothy asked.

"This is the first time I have felt completely inadequate. But nothing can heal the hurt except time. And patience and love," Belle said as she continued rinsing plates and loading the dishwasher.

"When do you think I should meet her. Harry is over the moon about her. He says I have to meet this kid who took on Natrona County and won."

"I think I would give her until after New Year's Day myself. It hasn't even been six months since she lost her parents, home and everything she knew. I think once we get through all the important dates, the next time will be easier," Belle said as she finished loading plates and started loading the silverware lying in the bottom of the sink.

Belle sighed and said, "Don't get me wrong. I love that kid. We always wanted kids, but couldn't make it happen. We had given up, years ago, and then one day, there she was — a gift from God. A kid who wanted and needed us. It turns out we needed her, more than we knew. We may be old enough to be her grandparents, but she's keeping us young. It's been a blessing all around. We give her space when she asks for it. As long as she has Mac to talk to, I think she will be alright."

"Who is this Mac I keep hearing about?" Dorothy asked as she handed over several coffee cups that Belle loaded into the dishwasher.

"Her dog, I should say, her Army dog," Belle corrected herself.

"How in the world did she end up with an Army dog? Who would give a highly trained dog like that to a kid?" Dorothy was shocked. "It takes years and loads of money, some of that money being my tax dollars, to get those dogs trained."

"It's not like that. Connie's dad was Mac's handler in Somalia when mortar fire hit them. Her dad wasn't hit directly, but close enough, he lost a leg and had some head injuries. Mac was injured too. Mac lost a leg and was medically retired. The Army was going to euthanize Mac from what Connie told me. That's when her dad stepped in and asked to adopt him. The Army let him. So, she has a three-legged dog that's also her shrink as far as I can tell," Belle said.

"Oh," Dorothy said softly, "I didn't know."

"No, you didn't," Belle said tartly. She released a quiet sigh to vent her frustrations. "It helps to know the facts before jumping to a conclusion," Belle explained. Finished loading the dishwasher, Belle added the detergent and started it.

DECEMBER 25, 1994
GLENROCK, WYOMING

NOISES THE HORSE TRAILER MADE AS IT RUMBLED PAST THE HOUSE TO the barn woke Connie. She was used to Art being awake before she was, but he usually kept things quiet until she and Belle were up. Today was Christmas morning, but somehow it didn't feel the same as it used to. The skin-tingling anticipation wasn't there this year.

Since she was awake, she got up and dressed. When she let Mac out for his morning potty break, she was surprised to see a Wyoming Highway Patrol cruiser had followed the horse trailer to the barn. She could see Art and Belle out there. Curious, she put on her coat and went out to see what was going on.

At the barn, Art unloaded a young horse, a foal that was a couple of months old at most. As Belle held the halter, Art checked the young horse's legs.

The highway patrolman took pictures of the horse from all angles. Staying out of the way, Connie kept Mac at her side. Connie didn't want Mac's presence to scare the foal. Except the young horse seemed very interested in Mac. It kept reaching out towards him, so Connie brought him closer. "Be nice," she told him in a soothing voice. "*Sicher.*"

Belle was the first to see her and Mac watching.

"What happened?" Connie asked.

"Accident on I-25. The horse trailer got hit by a semi that slid on black ice," said Art. "The owner of this filly and the momma horse died. We're going to look after this little girl until she makes a full recovery."

Tears immediately streamed down Connie's face. Mac whined, distressed because Connie was distressed.

"You want to help her get better and grow up?" Art asked Connie.

"Yes," she choked out, "How do I help?"

"Dry your eyes, then come over here real slow. Bring Mac with you," Art directed. "If she acts afraid of Mac, back him off, okay?"

"Yes," Connie replied. She followed Art's directions. She used the sleeves of her coat to dry her eyes before she slowly approached with Mac. She stayed where the filly could see her and Mac the whole time as she and Mac got closer.

The filly wasn't afraid of Mac. She reached out further to touch Mac with her nose and smelled Mac. After Mac, the foal smelled Connie's outstretched hand.

"Here, you hold her," Belle said, and motioned for Connie to hold the halter.

Belle went back into the house to put the presents they had for Connie under the tree and start breakfast.

The horse vet pulled up in his pickup, exited with his medical bag, saw Mac and froze. "Art, when the hell did you get a dog? You didn't tell me you had a freaking dog," Henry accused.

"Sorry, Henry, slipped my mind. He came with the kid," Art said.

"What kid? When did you get a kid? I don't see a goat," Dr. Henry Potter said, as he looked for a young goat.

"Yup, she's right here," Art said as he turned and pointed at Connie. To Connie, he said, "Make sure Mac knows Henry is okay. Henry's a bit nervous around dogs; bulls, horses, not a bit, but dogs, yes he is afraid of them."

"Mac, *sicher*," Connie said to the dog. To the vet, she said, "It's okay now."

Dr. Potter approached the filly and began his exam. Connie watched everything he did with interest.

Once the highway patrol officer had everything he needed, he gave the vet and Art his card with the case number on it. "Art, Henry, thanks for giving this little critter a place to stay and medical care. I appreciate it," he said.

His radio crackled with another accident on Interstate 25. "Gotta run. If I find an owner, I'll let you know. Let me know if you need anything," he said as he ran for his cruiser. As soon as he drove by the house, he accelerated rapidly to the road. Once on the street, the siren could be heard at the horse barn as the patrolman raced his car to the accident.

When Henry Potter finished his exam, he said, "This little filly was very lucky. Some bumps and scrapes, but nothing serious. As young as she is, she will need to be bottle-fed but get her on some foal feed, too. She should be ready to dig into some solid food." With that, the vet packed up his medical kit and walked back to his truck.

Once he left, Connie asked, "Now what? Where will she stay?"

Art led the way to a stall and at the door whistled sharply. A few moments later, a golden horse with a white mane came into the barn and stuck her head over her stall door. "You remember Nanny, don't you?" Art asked as he stroked the nose of the mare.

'Yes. You said that next spring I could learn to ride on Nanny," Connie said.

"Bring Baby over here. Let's get them acquainted," Art said.

Connie led the foal to Nanny and let them smell each other. After they had given each other a good smelling, Art reached for the halter on the filly. "Let me have her," he directed.

Connie released the foal and stepped back, Mac at her side. Art led the foal into Nanny's stall that was open to her paddock. He supervised them as they got to know each other better. Art asked, "You remember why we named her Nanny?"

"You told me she is your foster mom horse. She takes care of the foals if they need a new mom," Connie replied.

"That's right. See, Nanny doesn't even mind getting poked in the belly when babies look for food," Art said as the foal he had christened Baby was poking her nose in Nanny's belly looking for a snack.

"Get a pail of foal feed from the tack room and a couple of flakes of hay and bring them here. I can't leave them alone yet," Art instructed.

Connie did as she Art directed. When the feed was in the stall, the horses ate companionably. Art was satisfied all would be well with the new horse pairing, and he let himself out of the stall.

As they headed to the house for a late breakfast, Art commented to Connie, "Not how you expected Christmas morning to start, was it?"

"No, but I'm glad we could help her. How did you know her name was Baby?" Connie asked.

"I didn't, but we had to call her something. I don't know her real name. We have to wait for the highway patrol to get back to us on who owns her."

"What if there is no other owner, what happens to her then? Who will look after her?" Connie worried.

"We will. We'll become the filly's legal guardian just like we did with you," Art said.

"Good," Connie replied.

Christmas night when Mac was sent out for his last potty break of the night, he barked loudly and vigorously at the horse barn from the corner of his fenced yard.

"What in creation set him off?" Art wondered as he put on his coat and took the rifle out of the closet. He grabbed a flashlight before he went out. In the beam of the light, he saw what he first thought was a coyote, a huge coyote. But it didn't act like one. Instead, it sat and looked at him, the eyes reflecting green in the beam of his flashlight.

When he got very close, he saw it was a young German Shepherd, and hurt. Art got down on one knee and softly called the dog to him, "Come on, dog, come to me. Let's see how bad you're hurt." He was surprised how quickly the dog came to him.

He could see the dog was a female, and she was limping on her front right leg. She also looked unsteady on her feet as she walked to him. "Let's get you up to the house and see how bad off you are, come on," Art said to the dog. She stayed right with him, limping as he slowly led the way to the house.

On the porch, Art called to Belle, "Go have Connie tell Mac this dog is safe so we can look at her in the house. It's dark and too damn cold for my hands to work right out here. She's hurt, and I wonder if she didn't come from that accident this morning. It didn't happen too far away."

Connie put a leash on Mac to keep him calm, and Art brought the new dog into the house. It was a cream and black German Shepherd female, a young one, not filled out. It had a collar with two tags. One tag was the rabies vaccination tag. The other was a decorative metal tag with the name Caycee, but no helpful information on it. Time and the wear from the tags rubbing together had made the veterinarian's office information on the rabies tag unreadable. The vaccination was good for another year, that was still legible.

"So, Caycee, tell me what happened to you," Belle crooned to the injured dog as she continued to look over the dog for apparent injuries. Connie kept Mac back until she was sure he would be nice to the new dog.

"*Sicher. Freunde finden,*" Connie told Mac then let go of his leash. He slowly walked up to the new arrival, gave her a thorough sniffing, licked her face, and lay down next to the new dog. Mac's company helped calm the injured dog as Connie and Belle sat down near the pup. They cleaned the dog of dirt and grime with damp paper towels to better see its injuries.

Belle got up and called the small animal vet, Dr. Ellen Gunther. Belle asked Dr. Gunther to come out for an emergency visit for an injured dog.

Connie talked to Caycee in a constant low conversation, in English and some German as she gently stroked the dog.

Art and Belle had no idea what she was telling the dog, but she kept it calm. After a few minutes of listening to Connie talk to the dog, Art asked, "Just how many languages do you speak anyway?"

"English, German, some French, very little Italian, and American. At least that is what dad said," Connie replied, as she continued to wipe down the injured dog with gentle strokes with the damp paper towel.

"And English is different than American?" Art asked.

"Yes, same words but different meanings. Some words you can say here, and it isn't a bad word, but in England, it is a bad word. Some words, you can say there, and they aren't bad words but are considered bad words here. It took a lot of getting used to when we first moved here," Connie said.

It took about an hour before the modified motor home; now, a mobile vet clinic came to a stop in front of the house. Dr. Gunther let herself into the house after a quick knock on the door. Connie jumped for and grabbed Mac's collar, commanding "*Sicher!*" as the veterinarian walked into the kitchen to her newest patient.

"What have we got here? The Miller's Christmas Animal Rescue?" Dr. Gunther asked. She set her medical bag down on the floor. Then she sat on the floor near the newest arrival. "Come on, sweetie, let me have a look at you."

She slid on the tile floor closer to the injured German Shepherd. "I'm just here to help." She slid her stethoscope from around her neck and put the earpieces in, then held the other end out for the injured dog to sniff along with her hands. Dr. Gunther glanced at the dog's tags then listened to the dogs breathing. After that, she ran her hands over the dog's body and legs, noting all the places that caused flinching as she murmured calm words to Caycee. Then she fished a small flashlight from her pocket and shined it into the dog's eyes, nose, and ears.

Exam finished, she said, "Well definitely a concussion. Bring Caycee in tomorrow for x-rays at my office. The road rash on her paws and shoulder I can take care of here unless you want me to take her back with me tonight?"

"No!" The word exploded from Connie. More quietly, she asked, "What happens to Caycee if you take her?"

"I check her out, make sure she's healthy, then put her up for adoption. If no one takes her in five days, she gets put to sleep," Dr. Gunther answered.

"I'll take her; I have money!" Connie ran to her room, Mac on her heels. She came back to the kitchen with her teddy bear.

Art and Belle watched with as much amazement as the vet when Connie unzipped the back and removed bills, then coins.

When Connie had emptied the bear onto the kitchen table, she had just less than two hundred dollars. "Is that enough to adopt her?" Connie asked as she handed all the money to Dr. Gunther.

Dr. Gunther quickly glanced at Art and Belle, who both nodded.

"It's more than enough. I may even have to give you some money back tomorrow after I get a look at Caycee's x-rays. She should be okay overnight, though she'll probably be very thirsty from all the adrenaline so she'll need to go out during the night," Dr. Gunther said.

"I'll look after her, me and Mac will," Connie volunteered.

"We all will," Art said.

"Okay, then, I'm going to clean and bandage Caycee's paws. You need to keep them dry, so when she needs to go out, you'll need to put plastic bags on her feet over the bandages. Think you can handle that?" the vet asked Connie.

"Yes, I can do whatever she needs," Connie said. Connie watched as Dr. Gunther cleaned grit, dirt, and dried blood from each paw, put medicated cream on each paw and bandaged it.

When she finished, Dr. Gunther stood, stretched her back, and said to Art and Belle, "I think you have a private vet in your future, if her grades are good enough."

Connie kept Caycee calm with Mac's help. Mac stayed close to Caycee and washed her face, then her ears with his long pink tongue which soothed the injured pup. Other than potty breaks followed by drinking more water, the injured dog, had an uneventful night.

DECEMBER 26, 1994
GLENROCK, WYOMING

THE DARK CIRCLES UNDER CONNIE'S EYES TESTIFIED SHE HAD KEPT watch over Caycee all night. The new dog had spent the night in Connie's room with Mac, except for necessary outside excursions during the night. Connie had written down all of Caycee's activities during the night for the vet and left the note on the kitchen table.

When she came in from outside with the dogs, Connie met Art in the kitchen. He had made coffee and sipped from his cup. Belle bustled into the kitchen to start breakfast. Knowing the adults were awake and could look after Caycee and Mac, Connie allowed herself to sleep.

Mac heard Art open the doggie door panel. He led Caycee out of the open door from Connie's room to the doggie door. Mac hopped through. Art watched to see if Caycee knew how to use it.

The new dog sniffed around the doggie door after Mac hopped through. She poked at it with her nose, then followed Mac outside into the yard.

When the dogs came back in, Mac wanted to go back to Connie, who had left her bedroom door ajar when she went to sleep. Caycee wanted to be with Mac.

Art figured he would know where to find Caycee when it was time to go to the vet for x-rays and a more thorough check-up.

After lunch, Belle woke Connie to see if she still wanted to go along to the vet for Caycee's checkup. She did, and in minutes, Connie was dressed and ready to go.

Mac went along with Caycee as well. The back seat of the truck was full of one kid and two dogs. Art felt more content than he had in years when he saw them in the rear-view mirror. He pointed into the back. Belle turned to see that Connie had fallen asleep, leaning against Mac's side. At the vet's office, Connie roused, when the vehicle stopped moving.

Caycee was checked over and had no broken bones, so she was sent home with the Millers after getting up to date on her vaccinations. Art told the vet they planned to keep Caycee if no one claimed her. The vet found Caycee had no tattoos and hadn't gotten one of those new microchips. The dog had no identifying information of any kind, and the local rancher and driver of the truck in the horse accident had no living relatives according to the highway patrol. Of course, the dog might not have been his. The German Shepherd might be a stray.

Connie self-appointed herself night nurse and trainer for Caycee as the dog learned the routines of the ranch. The few times Caycee had a problem with a command, Connie had Mac show her the correct response, and the pup got it. Connie also used Caycee to train Mac in English commands.

Art and Belle were no longer surprised at their eleven-year-old. Their kid wasn't an average kid. Her report card spoke to that. They were going to have to decide whether or not to let her jump ahead a grade in the new school year.

JANUARY 1, 1995
GLENROCK, WYOMING

IT WAS LATE MORNING. BELLE SAT ON THE COUCH, HOLDING THE PHOTO album that contained the pictures that detailed the courtship and marriage of Connie's parents.

"Do you feel up to looking through this with me? I thought it might give you some idea of how you wanted to take care of your parents' ashes," Belle suggested.

"I don't know," Connie said as she reluctantly sat next to Belle.

"Why don't we try and see how far we get?" Belle asked, opening the photo album.

When Connie sat on the couch, the whap-whap of the doggie door as each dog came through announced the arrival of her canine support team.

Mac hopped onto the sofa next to Connie and put his head in her lap. Caycee hopped up next to Mac and rested her head on his hip. Connie absently stroked Mac's head as Belle held the photo album so they could both look at it.

"Can you tell me anything about this picture?" Belle asked.

"That's where they met, the campground in Tingle Creek. It's in Arizona."

"What were they doing in Arizona?" Belle asked.

"Dad was stationed at Fort Huachuca in Sierra Vista, and mom was finishing med school at the University of Arizona in Tucson. They were hiking near Tingle Creek with their dogs. Dad's dog got away and went to mom's dog. They were both camped at the same campground. Their dogs liked each other."

Belle flipped the page. "What can you tell me about this picture?"

"I think that's in Saguaro National Monument."

"Is that in Arizona, too?" Belle asked.

"I think so. Tucson, maybe? I know I was born in Arizona, but I don't remember it," Connie said.

"Would you like to go back someday?"

"I don't know, maybe, if it isn't too hot," Connie said as she fidgeted. Belle closed the photo album.

"Well, that's enough for today. I need to start making lunch. Want to help?"

"Sure," Connie said. She gave Mac a hand gesture, and he lifted his head from her lap and allowed her to get up from the couch. Mac groaned as he dropped his head to the couch pillows and Caycee, who took her cues from Mac, put her head back on his hip, and nodded off. Mac watched Connie in the kitchen from his vantage point on the couch. He had become accustomed to the routines of the ranch. As long as he could see Connie, he was content.

JANUARY 9, 1995
GLENROCK, WYOMING

CONNIE ROUTINELY TOOK THE BUS TO SCHOOL AND HOME AGAIN. SHE had begun to make friends at school. She sat with the same group of kids at lunch every day. When the school bus dropped her off in the afternoon, Mac and Caycee waited for her at their designated point on the driveway. They were not to pass that point onto the road, ever. They greeted her enthusiastically and walked home with her every day, no matter the weather.

Art and Belle stood at the living room picture window and watched Connie and the dogs walk towards the house from the school bus. Art said, "I'm going to have to build those dogs a shelter of some kind to protect them from the weather. They wait out there for Connie every afternoon. I don't think we could stop them, either."

In the house, Connie saw papers on the kitchen table with her name on them written on school stationery. Connie was curious and looked at the papers. She saw recommendations for her to be in higher grades for math, science, language arts, and English. She was behind in American history. She shrugged and went and changed into play clothes.

Outside again with the dogs, she headed to the barn and the still healing filly, Baby. That Baby was healing well, according to the last visit from the vet, made Connie happy.

Caycee was also healing well. No owner had been found for her, and Connie was happy to have Caycee adopted by Art and Belle.

At supper, Art and Belle discussed the school letter about advancing Connie. Connie said, "I'd rather stick with the kids my age so that I can make friends. I can take the other classes during summer school. Is that okay?"

Belle answered, "Whatever makes you happy. We didn't want you to be bored out of your skull in school."

"I'm not, at least not yet. If I decide I want to advance, I'll tell you."

MAY 12, 1995
GLENROCK, WYOMING

BELLE CAME INTO THE KITCHEN TO MAKE BREAKFAST. ART WAS THERE, sipping his first coffee of the day. Belle looked around, "Where's Connie?"

"I haven't seen her this morning," Art replied.

"That's odd," Belle said. "Art, go look for Connie outside. I'll check her room. This isn't like her."

When Belle looked into Connie's room, she didn't see her. She did see the black tail of one of the dogs sticking out under the closed door of the walk-in closet. Standing at the door to the closet, she listened and heard Connie crying softly.

Belle left Connie and went looking for Art. When she found him, she told him where she had found Connie. "What should we do? Leave her alone or make her tell us what's going on?" Belle asked.

"I think we ask her and find out," Art said.

At Connie's closet door, Art knocked gently. "Connie," he called through the door. "Can we help?"

"Is there anything we can do for you?" Belle asked.

"No, Nobody can help me," Connie wept.

"Can you at least tell us what's wrong? We're worried," Belle said.

"Last year, today, my parents were killed," Connie sobbed.

"I understand, we're here for you, whatever you need, Sweetie," Art said. "I'll call the school and tell them you are sick today."

JUNE 6, 1995
GLENROCK, WYOMING

BELLE GOT UP EXTRA EARLY TO MAKE A SPECIAL BREAKFAST TO CELEBRATE Connie being with them for one year. "Art," Belle said, "Connie's been with us for a year now, and we haven't celebrated a birthday for her."

"Make your blueberry waffles," Art suggested.

"I have a better idea," Belle said. She smiled as she got the ingredients out of the cupboard. "Connie has mentioned in passing that she missed the waffles her dad used to make for special occasions. I have the recipe."

"I'm going out to the barn to turn the horses loose," Art said.

It had taken Belle quite some time to find the Mesquite flour listed in Brian Daily's recipe. She had finally found it in a health food store in Casper. But it was what Connie missed, and she didn't ask for much.

Connie followed her nose into the kitchen, as always accompanied by her furry shadows, Mac and Caycee. "What do I smell? Cuz it smells good!" Connie announced. She had gotten into the kitchen without Belle seeing her.

"A surprise. Now go call Art in for breakfast, and I'll tell you," Belle replied.

Connie went to the door, put on her jacket as it was still a bit chilly out and ran to the barn. The dogs raced at her side as she went in search of Art to tell him Belle had breakfast ready.

Back in the kitchen, Connie set the table, put out the syrup, butter and a pitcher of iced tea as they waited for Art to finish washing up. They sat down to a breakfast of waffles, bacon, and hash browns.

Connie prepared her waffles, with butter and syrup, salted her hash browns and then proceeded to dig in. Belle watched as she took her first bite of waffles. Connie looked at Belle in wonderment. Connie, the bite of waffle shoved into her cheek like a chipmunk, asked, "Dad's waffles? Did you make Dad's waffles? How? And thank you!"

"I found the recipe in one of the cookbooks I kept from your parents' house. I had to find all the ingredients; that took some doing," Belle replied, smiling. "You like them?"

"I love them. Thank you so much!" Connie replied as she went back to eating.

"Slow down kiddo," Art said as he watched Connie all but vacuum her plate. "You'll get indigestion if you keep eating like that. Chew your food please, then swallow."

Connie slowed, taking time to chew. "It's so good!" she mumbled with food in her mouth.

"Don't talk with your mouth full," Belle ordered. "Now after breakfast, but before you run off, we have some things we need to talk about, Connie, okay?"

Connie nodded her head in acknowledgment; concern marred her happy smile.

After breakfast, the dishes were rinsed and put in the dishwasher, the condiments put away, and the table wiped off, they sat back at the table.

Art began, "As of today, you have been with us for one year. We wanted to do something to celebrate that. We want to know when you want to celebrate your birthday, and have you made any decisions regarding your parents' ashes."

Connie looked at her hands in her lap. Then looked up at Art then Belle. "I think I want to spread their ashes in the place the picture shows they got engaged. But that's in Arizona, and it's far away. I guess I could miss some of the classes in summer school," Connie said.

"Well, let's get out a map and have a look," Art said.

JUNE 9, 1995
GLENROCK, WYOMING

"Today's my birthday, and I'm twelve," Connie told Mac and Caycee as she dressed.

At breakfast, she announced, "I want to go to summer school and make the Arizona trip over fall break or spring break. I want to take chemistry with the teacher they have for summer school this year; she's supposed to be good."

Belle looked up from cooking bacon, "How good is good?"

"Well, most kids don't want her class because they say she's too hard, so that's good. She'll make me work," Connie replied, as she set the breakfast table.

Belle nodded, pulled the bacon pan from the stove, and placed the bacon onto a plate, "When you finish setting the table, go find Art, and tell him breakfast is ready."

Table set, Connie and dogs, went out to the barn in search of Art.

Breakfast finished, Art suggested to Connie, "What if we took a plane down to Arizona, rented a car and stayed just for a few days, and then came back? We could go after summer school is done, but before the fall session starts. What do you think?"

Connie looked skeptical, "Who would look after Mac and Caycee if we flew?"

"What about Mike Nelson, Honey? He and his family have always gotten along with Mac and Caycee when they've come to visit or when we've gone to visit them," Belle supplied.

"We could ask him, I guess," Connie said. "I at least know he can talk to Mac. Caycee, Mac, and Vera do like to play together."

Art got up from the table, "I'll give him a call so we can see if plans like this will work out." On the phone with Deputy Mike Nelson, Art explained they needed a dog sitter for Mac and Caycee in August so they could make a quick trip to Tingle Creek, Arizona to scatter Connie's parents' ashes.

Mike agreed. He said, "The advance notice gives me enough time to set up a kennel for them, next to Vera."

Art said, "You should see these two. They share everything, food, water, Connie and her bed."

Mike chuckled as he imagined Connie in bed with two German Shepherds sleeping with her. "The safest kid ever," Mike said.

"Just about," Art replied, "I'll make some travel plans and get back to you with the exact dates."

"Sounds good," Mike said, ending the call.

When he sat back at the table, Art said, "Mike would be happy to dog sit for Mac and Caycee. He needs time to build them a kennel, so if we go in August, that will work for him. What do you think, Connie? You game?"

Tears stood in her eyes as she contemplated Art's offer, "I guess." She paused, "This isn't going to be easy, is it?"

"No Honey, it's not, and if you don't want to scatter their ashes in Tingle Creek, we can do something else, but we can't keep them in a cardboard box in the closet forever," Belle said.

AUGUST 8-10, 1995
TINGLE CREEK, ARIZONA

MESQUITE RANCH WAS THE DUDE RANCH ART, BELLE, AND CONNIE stayed at a few miles outside the town of Tingle Creek, Arizona. The ranch operated as a B&B. The owners were Jack and Kate Sullivan. Their seventeen-year-old son Tom helped around the ranch after school.

Tom found he enjoyed Connie's company in the barn as he did his chores. She even helped him clean stalls. He just liked her even if she was a kid.

As they worked, they talked about books, movies, music, whatever came to mind, and dogs. They found that they enjoyed the same books, movies, and music. They talked about why they liked a certain book or movie and what put them off other movies and books. Connie talked about German Shepherds, and Tom talked about Aussie Shepherds.

Before he had to be in school, Tom took Connie horseback riding on the property in the mornings after an early breakfast. Art or Belle always chaperoned the morning trail rides into the surrounding desert and mountain foothills but gave the kids room to have fun. They toured the desert hills and talked, or sometimes rode the horses, not saying anything.

When Tom came home from school, he parked his pickup next to the barn in the lean-to. After he closed his truck door, he thought he heard crying from the barn. He went to investigate, and found Connie, crying in the hayloft. Not letting her know he was there; he left and found his mother.

"Mom, something's wrong, I just found Connie. She's holding a box and crying in the hayloft. Should I tell Mrs. Miller?" Tom asked. He dropped his backpack of schoolbooks onto a kitchen chair.

"I need to tell you why they came here from Wyoming," Kate said. Pointing at the kitchen table, she said, "Sit."

AUGUST 11, 1995
TINGLE CREEK, ARIZONA

MRS. GRANT, TOM'S BEST FRIEND PAUL'S MOTHER, WAS A NURSE, AND SHE had to work an emergency night shift at the hospital. Paul slept over and accompanied Tom as he took Connie and the Millers on the post-breakfast trail ride on their second to last day on the ranch.

In the barn afterward; as Tom and Paul removed the tack and brushed the horses, Tom told Paul, "I'm gonna marry her one day."

"Get out!" Paul responded. "She's a kid! You're a kid! You can't know that!"

"Yes, I can," Tom said. "I don't know how, but I do."

That night before he went to bed, he told his parents, "I'm going to marry Connie one day."

"Don't you think she gets a say in your plans?" asked Kate as she ruffled her son's hair. "You know why Connie's here?"

Jack added, "Don't put all your eggs in one basket. Especially one that is in a whole other state. Remember she wouldn't even be here if her parents hadn't died."

"I can't imagine that, ever, let alone at her age. In some ways, she's just a little kid. In others, I think she's older than me," Tom said. "Connie showed me an old photo today. She said it was where her parents got engaged. I thought she meant the Millers. Now I know it isn't." Tom paused. "Mom, I know where that is, I can take them to that exact spot if you don't want to," Tom volunteered.

AUGUST 12, 1995
TINGLE CREEK, ARIZONA

THE NEXT MORNING, AFTER BREAKFAST, TOM LED CONNIE AND THE Millers on the last trail ride of their visit. He took them to the place Connie wanted to scatter the ashes of her parents. Connie was quiet as she rode with the box containing her parents' ashes in her saddlebag, the photo of where she wanted to scatter the ashes in her hand.

When they reached the spot in the old engagement photograph, Tom, Art, and Belle waited on horseback in the shade of tall cottonwoods when Connie dismounted.

Tom reached over and handed her the saddlebag off her horse. The unshed tears he saw in her eyes when she took it from him made his heart hurt for her. He watched as she carefully removed her parents' ashes. Tom saw her shoulders rise and fall as she took deep breaths as she walked away. "She's not crying, is she?" Tom asked as he sat on his horse next to Art and Belle as they watched Connie walk into the trees.

Once off the beaten path in the bushes and trees, Connie opened the box containing her parents' ashes. Rather than dump them in a pile, she scattered them under various plants and trees, as tears ran down her face. "I'm putting you here so no one will walk on you. You can help the trees and plants grow," she told the ashes that were her parents. When she had spread her parents' ashes entirely, she sat down against a cottonwood and wept. She gave herself the luxury of a few minutes of absolute grief, then wiped her face off on her sleeves, and walked to the horses.

When they returned to the Mesquite Bed and Breakfast, Art, Belle, and Connie packed up and got ready to leave for the airport. Tom helped load the suitcases into the rental car. After, as the adults said their goodbyes, Tom slipped Connie a piece of paper with his email address on it. He told her, "If you ever want me to go check on them, send me a note, and I will. I can't imagine having to do what you did today. That took guts. You're lucky to be with Mr. and Mrs. Miller."

Connie mutely nodded her head as she took the slip from Tom and put it in her pocket. She turned her face to him and mouthed, "Thank you," as tears ran down her cheeks again.

Noting Connie's distress, Belle poked Art in the side and said, "Let's get a move on it, Dear. We don't want to miss our flight."

Art finished his conversation by telling Jack and Kate Sullivan, "If you are ever up in Wyoming, stop on by."

Tom stood with his parents as they watched the rental car head down the drive and out of sight.

In the afternoon, Tom stopped by the ice cream shop in town to hang out with his friends. The girls suddenly seemed younger than Connie, even though they were his age. He couldn't figure out why he wasn't having fun hanging out with his friends. He felt lonely. He left after a while to go home and check his email. The rest of the day had passed so slowly and seemed somehow empty to Tom. I miss her. That's what's wrong, Tom thought.

The next day, Tom found a picture of Mac and Caycee with Connie in his email.

PART TWO

JUNE 13, 1998
GLENROCK, WYOMING

Connie graduated high school at fifteen-years-old, with a 4.0 GPA. Today was her graduation party. She wasn't sure what the big deal was, but throwing the party was very important to Belle, so Connie went along with it.

Art directed the box truck that had the rented party tent and picnic tables as it backed up onto the lawn in front of the house. He supervised the tent setup and table placement inside the tent. When assembled, the tent had its sides rolled up to let air and light through, and the picnic tables were in rows inside. Perpendicular to the rows of picnic tables were the tables for drinks, food, plates, and utensils at one end of the tent. Garbage cans sat at the corners.

Connie played with Caycee and Mac during the afternoon to wear them out so they would ignore the disruptions of the party. They were older and moved slower, but still full of energy when they were with Connie.

Belle enjoyed watching the three of them run and play together.

The invitations Belle had sent out to everyone she knew said:
Help us celebrate Connie's early graduation from high school. The open house graduation party starts at 7:00 p.m. in the tent in our front yard. Dress comfortably.
We look forward to seeing you — drinks and cake for all. No R.S.V.P. needed.

Belle and Art went through the tent at 6:45 p.m., to ensure they had everything ready for when their company arrived. Cans of iced tea, lemonade or pop were in ice-filled coolers on the drinks table. Several sheet cakes lightly covered with plastic wrap sat cut and ready to serve. A large coffee urn sat on a nearby table that also held paper plates, plastic silverware, and Styrofoam coffee cups for those not drinking cold drinks. Napkins were held in place by a paperweight.

Connie happily visited with everyone who dropped by. She was delighted when she unexpectedly spotted her friend from Arizona. Tom Sullivan was in the crowd of friends and neighbors who came to wish her well on her journey into college life and adulthood.

Tom spotted Connie in the crowd. He threaded his way through the well-wishers to Connie and wrapped her in a congratulatory bear hug. All the emails hadn't taken into account how much she had gone from a small, skinny, kid to a gorgeous teen. He loved having her in his arms.

"Tom! What're you doing here? I've missed you," Connie said as she leaned into his hug.

"I've missed you, too," Tom said. Keeping her in his arms, Tom continued, "You sure grew up a lot since I saw you last. Are Art and Belle feeding you miracle grow for teens?" He asked as he smiled at her.

"A growth spurt that Belle says is from finally being happy," Connie replied as she grinned at Tom.

"Break it up, you two," Art said as he joined them. Art held his hand out to shake Tom's hand. "What brings you this way? I know Belle sent an invitation, but we never expected you to show up."

Tom released Connie and shook Art's hand then pulled him in for a quick hug. When Tom released Art, he said, "I was passing by. I'm on the way to my summer internship with the forest service in the Black Hills. I had to stop and congratulate Connie."

With Tom at the party, the rest of the guests faded into the background. Connie sat with Tom at a picnic table. They sat, heads together, and talked for hours about this and that. "Have you decided what you want to study in college?" Tom asked.

"Not yet. For a while, I thought I wanted to be a veterinarian, but that involves needles. And I would have to stick them in animals. I can't make myself do that," Connie replied and shuddered. She then asked, "How is school going for you?"

"Great! I finished my sophomore year in Fire Science with a 3.9 GPA overall," Tom said.

"That's cool! Good for you," Connie said.

"Say, when can I meet your dogs. You write about them and send pictures in email, but I want to meet them. If it's okay," Tom said.

"Sure, come on," Connie said. She led the way out of the tent around the back of the house to the fenced-in yard for Mac and Caycee. At the kennel fence, she had Tom sit on the ground. "Mac, Caycee, come. I want you to meet someone," Connie called the dogs. They ambled over to the fence from their spot on the back porch.

To Tom, she instructed, "Hold your hand out, palm down, in a loose fist up to the fence for them to smell you." To Caycee and Mac, she said, "Make friends."

"I thought you said one of them only knew German," Tom said, as he held his hand out for the dogs to sniff.

"That would be Mac, the one missing a back leg. When Art and Belle became my foster parents, I had to teach him English." She smiled shyly. "Don't tell them, but it was easier than trying to teach them German. Besides, Caycee only knew English," Connie said and shrugged.

The dogs sniffed at Tom through the fence. Connie watched. She was happy with the results of the sniffing through the wire enclosure. She asked Tom, "You want to go in? We can sit on the bench under the tree if you want."

"Do I? Heck yeah," Tom said, he stood and followed Connie through the gate. In the dog yard, Connie had Tom sit on the bench Art had built for her when Mac had joined them. She sat down next to Tom and watched as Mac and Caycee approached.

Tom was thoroughly sniffed over by both dogs. A few minutes passed before Mac, and then Caycee gave Tom a lick on the knuckles of his hand. Connie was ecstatic but hid it.

Dad always said, "*Trust your dog. If your dog likes someone, they are good people.*" She thought, *Dad, thanks for the tip. I guess if he likes me as much as I like him, I might marry him someday.*

Sitting with Art in the tent long after dark, Belle said, "We might as well start cleaning up. I don't expect anyone to show after 10:00 p.m." They rose and began cleaning up party remnants. Art dropped a few paper plates into a trash can when he saw Tom Sullivan's truck still parked out front. "Belle?" Art called, "Have you seen Connie or Tom lately?"

"Now that you mention it, she has been scarce the last couple hours, why?" Belle asked.

"Because that boy's truck is still out front," Art said. "Any idea where they might go?"

"If it was anyone but Connie, I'd worry and say look in the hayloft. Since it is Connie we're talking about, I'm not worried. Check the dog yard," Belle said.

Art quickly made his way around the back of the house, and sure enough, there they were. They were sitting next to each other, with the dogs at their feet. Mac was resting his head on Connie's knee. Caycee with her head on Mac's hip.

Unseen by the couple, Art stood and watched for a few minutes. When Art was sure that Tom behaved like a gentleman and Connie's virtue was intact, he made himself known. Art said, "Hey, kids. Time to head into the house."

"Is everyone else gone?" Connie asked. "Can I turn the dogs loose?"

"Go ahead," Art said. "And make sure they do their business. It's time for bed."

Connie released the dogs. They ran around to the front of the house and sniffed all the new smells the partygoers had left behind.

As Tom went to follow Connie, Art held up his hand in a "stop" motion. "A word, Tom," Art said.

"It's late, so if you want to stay the night, you can. It will be on the couch and you will not, and I can't stress this enough. You will not go down the hall to Connie's room. We understand each other?" Art asked.

Tom swallowed audibly. He answered, "Yes, Sir. I would never do that, and I understand completely."

Satisfied, Art said, "Okay, Tom, let's get you set up in the living room." Art yawned widely. "It's past time for this old coot to be asleep." Art led the way into the house. "Belle? You in here?" Art called out inside.

"Yes, in the living room. I got Tom sheets, a pillow, and blanket and put them on the couch," Belle replied, having anticipated the outcome.

Tom came in and said, "Mrs. Miller, thank you for letting me stay on the couch. I appreciate it."

Connie came through the house with the dogs at her heels. "Goodnight, everyone. See you in the morning." She yawned and kept going to her room with Mac and Caycee.

Art pointed at the dogs who followed Connie to her bedroom. "Those two sleep in her bed with her and protect her. Keep that in mind," Art instructed.

"Understood. Message received," Tom said. He sat on the couch and pulled off his boots. Art and Belle went to their room.

Tom turned off the light on the end table next to the couch, stretched out, and fell asleep.

JUNE 14, 1998
GLENROCK, WYOMING

At breakfast, Art asked Tom, "Will you be joining us for church this morning?"

"I'd like to. I really would. But I have to be in Rapid City to get signed in for my internship for school. I have to be checked-in by 3:00 p.m. or I lose my place. It counts for school credit, and I get paid to fight fires," Tom said. "I need to be on the road right after breakfast. And thank you both for your hospitality," he said. He looked at Art and then Belle. "I appreciate you letting me stay on the couch last night. I was planning to sleep in my truck."

"We couldn't let you do that when we had a perfectly good couch to sleep on," Belle said.

"I'm just glad you stopped by for my graduation party," Connie said. "I wasn't expecting to see you." She beamed at him before taking another bit of her mesquite flour waffles. Belle had made them for a celebratory breakfast.

Belle asked, "Connie, have you made any decisions about college yet?"

"I think I want to go my first two years at Casper College before I go over to the University of Wyoming. Those kids will be so much older than I am. I don't want to be that far from home yet. Is that okay?" Connie asked. "I want to study computer science. So that I can become an information technology specialist."

JUNE 20, 2002
LARAMIE, WYOMING

WHEN SHE LOOKED AT THE CLOCK IN HER ONE-BEDROOM APARTMENT, Connie expected Art and Belle to arrive at any time from Glenrock.

Upon their arrival, Connie enjoyed hugs from both of her adopted parents. At their request, she modeled her graduation gown before they left for the graduation ceremony at the University of Wyoming.

"I'd skip the ceremony, but I know it means a lot for you to see me get my diploma," Connie said. "I could be packing and on my way home tonight." She smiled at Belle and Art as she slowly turned in a circle in her graduation gown.

At the graduation venue, Connie guided Art and Belle to their reserved seats before she joined her classmates for the walk across the stage. Connie whispered, "Mom, Dad, I hope you can see me get my diploma, too. I miss you both so much." She sat and patiently waited for her turn to cross the arena.

During the ceremony, Belle and Art were all smiles, especially when they watched Connie walk across the stage in her graduation gown to collect her diploma from the University of Wyoming.

JUNE 21, 2002
GLENROCK, WYOMING

BELLE MADE SURE ALL PREPARATIONS WERE READY FOR WHEN CONNIE arrived with Art at the ranch from Laramie, Wyoming. She and Art had been in Laramie for Connie's graduation ceremony the night before. Then they had rushed home so she could plan the surprise graduation party and Art could retrieve the horse trailer.

Belle had restrained herself when it came to the guest list since she didn't want to overwhelm Connie when she got home tonight. Just a few close friends, including Jack and Kate Sullivan from Arizona, along with their son Tom. She knew Connie and Tom were sweet on each other. Time would tell if it turned into more than a close friendship over the computer with occasional visits in person.

LARAMIE, WYOMING

Art helped Connie load her belongings from the off-campus one-bedroom apartment where she had lived while going to college. The boxes were packed first into the horse trailer followed by her furniture. The things she had accumulated during her stay at the University of Wyoming were too many to put in the back of her father's old 1994 pickup truck that she still drove every day.

GLENROCK, WYOMING

It was late afternoon when Belle heard Connie's old pickup drive into the yard followed by Art pulling the rackety horse trailer. The noise was hard to miss when they pulled into the yard. Caycee barked to announce the arrivals then ran out the doggie door to greet them.

Stopped, Connie got out of her truck. She bent down to pet the old German Shepherd. Taking in the gray muzzle, she said, "You're getting old, girl. I missed you. I still miss Mac. I bet you do too." Connie hugged the happy wriggling dog, then allowed face licks. "I love you too," Connie said. She stood stiffly and stretched from the long drive home from Laramie.

Out of his truck, Art also was greeted with enthusiasm by Caycee. "You okay with me putting the trailer with your stuff in it in the barn overnight? I've had enough moving stuff today," Art said, then mumbled, "not as young and nimble as I used to be."

"Sure, go ahead," Connie answered.

In the house, Connie couldn't miss that Belle planned a party for her. When she saw the small number of places set, she said, "I know what you did. You planned another party. I forgive you, Mama Belle. I need to shower and change. I have time, don't I?"

Belle hugged Connie. "You even have time for a nap, as long as you are awake and dressed by 6:00 p.m.," Belle said.

When the guests arrived, they were all people who were important to Connie. Some she hadn't seen in a long time. Judge Harry and his wife, Dorothy, the lawyer Roger and his wife, Dena. Mike Nelson, now a lieutenant and his wife, Donna, had even come. The biggest and best surprise for Connie was Mr. and Mrs. Sullivan, and their son Tom. The man who made her heart sing. Tom being there, made the day extra special. And boy, had he filled out. He wasn't the six-foot, two-inch tall string bean she had first met. He was tall, filled out and muscled, and tanned. The sun had bleached his already blond hair almost white. Connie reminded herself not to swoon.

Graduation supper and dessert were over. Connie and Tom cleared the dishes from the table while their parents visited over coffee after all the other party guests had left. When they had completed rinsing plates and cups, had loaded and started the dishwasher, they returned to the living room.

Tom almost vibrated with anticipation. He had worked very hard all evening not to keep tapping the small velvet-covered box in his pocket. Tom held Connie's hand as they went into the living room and rejoined their parents. Before Connie could drop onto the couch next to Caycee, Tom pulled her to a stop. He pulled the ring box from this pocket. He dropped to one knee, opened the lid, then held it out to Connie.

"I've waited a very long time to ask you this," Tom said. "Connie, will you do me the honor of marrying me?"

"Yes! Absolutely yes!" Connie replied; her face lit with joy. Her left hand shook as she held it out for Tom to slip the ring on her finger. She stared, awestruck for a moment. "It's beautiful," she breathed out. Then she pulled Tom to his feet and kissed him.

PART THREE

APRIL 6, 2014
DALLAS, TEXAS

ALLEN WAS EARLY. TOO EARLY. HE HAD TOLD MANDY HE WOULD PICK her up for their date at 6:30 p.m. To waste time, he drove around the lower-middle-class neighborhood.

He saw the houses in the older neighborhood were small. They could fit in the ballroom of his grandparents' mansion. Well, what remained of it.

The houses here were in good repair, and the tiny yards were clean and kept up. Manicured grass lined the street. The people who lived here took care of their homes. He noticed the big trees in some of the yards that shaded the homes. Allen saw that the trees overhung some of the houses and could cause problems if they ever caught fire and fell onto the roof.

His smartphone began blasting his current favorite country song. It was the alarm he had set to let him know it was time to present himself at Mandy's house to pick her up.

When he had met Mandy at Dairy Queen and asked her out, she surprised him when she said yes. It had been easy to get her address and cell number after that.

The address was to a tidy red brick house with a two-car garage. There was a new four-door pickup in the driveway. Allen decided to park the old, green Ford station wagon he had stolen in Oklahoma City down the street a couple of houses and walk back to the house.

Before he left the car, he made sure he had his essentials in the pockets of his cargo jeans. A home-made sap he always kept handy, his wallet, smokes, lighter, and cell-phone. It was just dusk when Allen arrived at

Mandy's front door. He tugged his t-shirt into place and finger-combed his unruly wavy blonde hair then rang the doorbell. The door opened as he shoved his wire-framed glasses up his nose.

A tall, distinguished-looking man with broad shoulders, light brown hair, with a little gray at the temples, and a fit frame opened the door. He was in worn jeans and a chambray shirt. This man was not who Allen had expected to answer the door.

Allen saw that he barely came up to the man's shoulder. He didn't like that the man caused him to feel short.

Mandy made her appearance, barefoot and in a t-shirt and jeans. She ducked under the arm of the man holding the door open and said, "There you are, Allen. I was beginning to think you weren't coming." Mandy was excited to see Allen. He looked like a blond-haired, brown-eyed, teenaged, short Rob Lowe in wire-framed glasses. He had shown up for their date almost on time. Mandy turned and went back into the house. "I just need to grab my purse and some shoes," she shouted over her shoulder.

The man holding the door said, "Why don't you come in; this could take a few minutes."

Allen nodded his head and, as the man stepped aside, he entered.

After the man shut the door, he asked, "Who might you be? I don't think we've met. I'm Mandy's father, Mr. Bradley."

"My name's Allen," he said.

"Allen what, if I may ask?" said Mr. Bradley.

"Allen Stout."

"Where are you planning to take Mandy and when do you plan to have her back?" Mr. Bradley asked.

"I was thinking of Dairy Queen and then a movie," Allen replied. He disliked being asked his plans for Mandy that evening.

"How are you planning on getting there?" asked Mandy's father.

Allen paused before he asked, "Isn't there a bus line near here?"

Dan Bradley wondered what this boy in his foyer was really after. "You know Mandy is only fifteen years old, don't you?"

"Um, no. I never asked Mandy how old she was. I thought she was my age," Allen said.

"Where did you two first meet?" Dan Bradley asked. He led the way through the living room.

"The college library. We both wanted the same book," Allen replied. He shifted his weight from foot to foot before he followed.

"Just because Mandy is book smart and taking A.P. classes at the college, doesn't make her people smart. She can be quite naïve," Dan Bradley told Allen. "Let me see your driver's license." Mr. Bradley held out his hand for the license. Allen stared at the man.

"You do have one, don't you?" demanded Dan Bradley.

Allen nodded, and in an automatic response to the commanding tone, he dug his license out of his wallet and handed it over. He thought he shouldn't have done that, afterward, but it was too late.

Dan Bradley studied the Oklahoma license stating Benedick Allen Stout IV lived in Oklahoma City, Oklahoma, and was twenty-five years old. He asked, "Why is a twenty-five-year-old wanting to date my fifteen-year-old daughter? Let's go into the kitchen. We need to have a little talk while she gets ready."

"But she said she was getting her purse," Allen said.

"You'll learn," Dan Bradley said.

Allen followed Dan Bradley into the kitchen. As he walked, Dan slipped his smartphone from his front pants pocket, took a photo of the license, then dropped the phone back in his pocket. He handed Allen back his license in the galley style kitchen. Dan pulled his cellphone from his pocket and plugged it into the charger on the kitchen counter, then continued to the table in the breakfast nook.

Allen pocketed his license and pulled the sap from another pocket as he followed the tall man. When they reached the kitchen table, Dan pulled out a chair for Allen.

That was when Allen struck Dan from behind. He hit Dan several times on the back of the head and followed him as he crumpled to the floor.

Allen had repeatedly struck until he was sure that Dan Bradley was unconscious and would stay that way.

"No one tells me what to do anymore," Allen snarled at the unconscious man. Allen drug Dan up into the chair at the kitchen table and propped him up. When he heard the clack of Mandy's shoes as she came down the tiled hall, he returned to the foyer. When Mandy reemerged from the hallway, she asked, "Ready to go?"

"Sure," replied Allen. "Can we take that sweet ride of a pickup I saw in the driveway?"

"Dad, that okay with you?" Mandy called as she grabbed the keys that hung by the garage door. When she got no response, she shrugged and led the way to the garage, then pushed the button to raise the garage door.

As they walked through the garage, Allen held his hand out for the keys. "Give. I have a license. I'm driving."

Since he was cute and had an actual license, not a learner's permit like she did, Mandy smiled at him and gave him the keys.

Allen pushed the button on the remote to unlock the truck. He and Mandy were in the pickup, with the motor running, when Allen said, "Wait, I forgot to get my license back from your dad. I don't know why, but he wanted to see it."

"Oh, that's just dad, he's been overprotective since mom died," Mandy replied, as she adjusted the air conditioner to high. She then started spinning the knob to adjust the radio station as Allen went back into the house through the open garage door.

Inside, Allen hit the wall-mounted button that closed the garage door. Alone in the garage, he looked for anything that would start a fire. He found a five-gallon gas can next to the lawnmower less than half full. He spotted a roll of duct tape on a workbench and took that.

Once in the house, Allen did a quick search of the coat closet in the foyer. In there he found a hunting rifle standing on its stock on the floor and a box of shells on the shelf above. He took both and placed them by the front door.

Next, he splashed gas on the curtains and mismatched furniture in the living room and poured gasoline into the carpet leading to the dining room. He dribbled the last of the gas in the can on the floor of the kitchen. He used the duct tape to affix the unconscious Dan Bradley to his chair.

In the kitchen, he threw a bottle of whiskey from a tray of liquor bottles on the counter against the wall. He surveyed the kitchen as he looked for anything more he might want to take.

He saw the bulge of a wallet in Dan Bradley's back pocket. Allen pulled it free and checked the contents. There was $627.00 in cash and three credit cards. He pocketed the cash and credit cards then tossed the wallet on the kitchen table.

Dan Bradley moaned and moved tentatively against his duct tape restraints while Allen was still in the kitchen. He returned to the foyer, loaded the rifle, went back to the kitchen doorway and shot Dan Bradley in the back.

"Shit!" Allen shouted; his ears rang from the rifle shot. Adrenaline-fueled excitement coursed through him. Mandy was waiting for him. He needed to get moving, he ran into the living room, lit a cigarette, and threw it against a gas-soaked chair. The chair promptly ignited, and he fled the house, with the rifle and box of shells. He shut the front door to the house when he left.

The adrenaline rush was even better, stronger than when he had killed the grandparents who raised him in Oklahoma! Just outside the front door, he skidded to a stop to take a few slow, deep breaths. He ran in place a few seconds to burn off the rush. He knew he needed to be calm for Mandy.

He peeked at her and saw she was playing with her smartphone. When he got to the pickup, he opened the driver's side back door. He slid the rifle into the truck behind the front seat along with the box of shells.

Mandy had the a/c going full blast and the radio blaring country music, so he was sure she never heard anything when he shot her father.

In the driver's seat, Allen turned down the volume on the radio and asked Mandy, "Where do you want to eat?" He backed into the street and pulled up and parked in front of his old ride. He no longer needed it. When he got out, he said, "I need to get a few things out of my car. Then we'll go eat."

"Okay," Mandy replied, as she wondered how much stuff did he need to go on a date? She went back to playing the game on her phone.

Allen retrieved everything he owned from the car. His duffle bag, trusty wire coat hanger, and a jacket made up the first trip. He placed the items on top of the rifle in the backseat of the pickup. Returning to the station wagon a second time, he removed a small toolbox and an almost full box of road flares. It also went onto the back floorboard of the pickup truck.

After a last quick look in the car to make sure he removed all his stuff, he tossed a lit road flare onto the floor under the steering wheel. He returned to his new truck, and he looked back at the Bradley house. There was no sign of the fire from the back, but he could see thin wisps of smoke from the front of the house near the living room.

When Allen re-entered the truck, Mandy said, "Let's go to Denny's."

"Okay," Allen replied, then asked, "Do you have any family other than your dad?"

"Nope, just us. Why?" Mandy asked.

"Just curious," Allen replied.

Once they were heading to Denny's, Mandy asked, "What took so long in the house?"

Allen stalled as he rubbed his forehead with his left hand, right hand still on the steering wheel. He replied, "It took a while to get him to say it was okay to take you to the country music festival called Country Thunder in Arizona. Have you ever heard of it?

"Yes! I always wanted to go!" Mandy exclaimed. Puzzled, she asked, "He's letting me go to Arizona on a first date?"

"I promised to have you back in a few days, in time for school to start back up after spring break. I promised to be a complete gentleman and return you with your virtue intact. He said you were to treat it like summer camp, no electronics, you know? He wants postcards and letters during your trip. That way you can talk about them when you get home."

"Isn't he the coolest dad?" Mandy beamed, satisfied, then her expression dimmed, "But I didn't bring any clothes or my stuff."

"We'll get what you need there or on the way. Your dad gave me a credit card to pay for your stuff."

"Cool! I don't know how you talked him into it, but this is SO COOL!" Mandy almost shouted with glee.

Allen pulled into Denny's restaurant parking lot and said, "We're here. Let's eat. I'm starved." Allen drove slowly through the lot. "They must be full since there's nowhere to park. I don't want to wait that long to eat. We'll find somewhere else, okay?" Allen explained to Mandy.

They waited to get back on the street, to allow a police car to fly by with lights and sirens going. Moments later two fire trucks sailed by with lights and sirens going, followed by an ambulance. When no more emergency vehicles were in sight, they left the restaurant parking lot and got on to Interstate 30, westbound.

Just over an hour later, Allen stopped at the well-populated truck stop in Weatherford for food and fuel. He didn't think anyone would be looking for Mandy yet. After eating, while Mandy was in the ladies' room, Allen went out and found a pickup truck in the parking lot that looked just like what he was driving. It had New Mexico license plates. Using a screwdriver from his toolbox, he swapped the plates. He felt more comfortable now. His truck wasn't using Dan Bradley's plates. Job done, he went back in to the truck stop.

Mandy met him at the checkout line with a Mountain Dew in a four-cup cardboard drink holder, a bag of pretzels and some turkey jerky. Allen added two large black coffees into the drink holder beside her pop.

"Stay here while I gas up, so you can pay for the gas," Allen directed and handed Mandy two fifty-dollar bills. "I'll text you the pump number. Then wait and see if there is any change after you pay for the food, okay?" Mandy nodded her assent.

Truck gassed, they continued west on the interstate. Before long, the monotony of the nighttime drive made Mandy sleepy, and she fell asleep in the passenger seat.

It was difficult for Allen to stay awake by the time they drove through Big Spring, TX. He decided to stop for the night. He didn't want to get pulled over for erratic driving. Allen found a chain motel near a truck stop with an almost full parking lot. The motel sign still flashed Vacancy, so he pulled in.

Mandy was still sound asleep in the passenger seat. In the motel lobby, he had to wake the night clerk to get a room for cash. He used the name Allan Smith.

He parked in front of his ground-floor room at the back of the motel. Allen quietly exited the truck and opened the back door. He looked through what Dan Bradley kept in the back and found a blanket to cover the duffle bag, toolbox, and rifle on the rear floorboard of the truck. That done, he woke Mandy and guided her into their room. She was like a zombie, and once on a bed, went right back to sleep. He removed her shoes and pulled the comforter over her.

APRIL 7, 2014
BIG SPRING, TEXAS

THE NEXT MORNING, THEY ATE AT A McDONALD'S. AFTER ALLEN finished his breakfast, he went to the truck. He found and studied a map of New Mexico. He knew northern New Mexico was ready to burn. The drought had been all over the news, even in Oklahoma. It was sort of on the way to Arizona. There had to be someplace to start a fire. He liked starting fires. He loved starting fires. It was a rush to watch them grow, to become alive, independent, unleased, and uncontrolled.

The map didn't show any easy, quick, off interstate routes into northern New Mexico. There were too many turns, back roads, and state highways to get to Interstate 40 in Albuquerque. He decided to stay on the interstates.

If there were any interesting tourist spots along the way that Mandy wanted to see they would stop. Otherwise, hammer down to cool northern New Mexico and Interstate 40.

Growing up in Oklahoma had taught him that he hated the heat and humidity of the midwestern states in summer, and all the bugs that came out in spring. He hated tornado season even more. Those sons a bitches came out of nowhere. And with no warning, they just leveled everything.

According to his grandparents, he had been a little over a year old when tornadoes demolished the house he and his parents had been living in. They had spent the entire night sheltered under the basement stairs. There had been tornados and straight-line winds that night.

He didn't remember anything, but tornados still freaked him out. Up in the mountains, they didn't have tornado problems — at least none he had ever seen about on the news.

Allen walked back to the table where Mandy was eating when he glanced out the window. He saw a Texas state trooper casually cruise the parking lot and slow down by his pickup truck, then stop in front of it. Another one came and stopped behind the pickup truck, boxing it in.

He watched as the highway patrol officer in the back stopped for a moment, lifted the microphone to his lips, and spoke. Next, he saw the trooper in front of the pickup lift his mike and talk into it. He scanned the parking lot. The truck he had traded plates with was gone.

Sweat jumped out of all his pores as he watched, transfixed, to see what would happen next. Allen let out the breath he had involuntarily been holding when both cop cars slowly moved on. He turned and raced for the bathroom. He just made it before losing the breakfast he had just eaten. After, he rinsed his mouth out with water at the sink, then headed back to the table.

Mandy was finished eating. She was slow, and she ate everything she ordered. When he saw her pull her phone from her pocket, he quickly sat down to distract her. "Who ya calling?" he asked.

"Nobody. I was gonna text Daddy and tell him what a good time I'm having and thank him for letting me come along."

"Okay, but then we need to get on the road if we're going to make the music festival for the day our tickets are good for."

Mandy slid out of her side of the booth. "I'll be just a minute."

"Sure, meet me at the truck," Allen replied. At the fuel desk, he bought a pay as you go phone he saw for sale by the cashier. He paid for it and activated it at the register with one of Dan Bradley's credit cards. Allen set up the phone with an unlimited data plan, along with unlimited talk and text, and automatic billing to the credit card.

On the interstate, heading west, the answer for future lodging was on a billboard. A KOA campground. He glanced over at Mandy, who was playing a game on her phone. "Hey, Mandy, you ever been camping?"

"Yeah, sure, with my dad. We'd go to Hickory Creek campground and go fishing and camp for his weekend whenever he got two days off in a row. I thought you forgot I was here," Mandy said.

Allen said, "Sorry, I haven't forgotten you; it's just when I drive, I give it my whole attention to make sure I don't get in an accident or something."

"Oh, that makes sense," Mandy replied.

"So, we'll get some camping gear. We'd need it for the music festival anyway," Allen explained. Mandy resumed playing the game on her phone. After a few more miles she quit her game and reclined her seat a bit and went to sleep against the window.

LAS CRUCES, NEW MEXICO

ALLEN WAS ALMOST TO THE INTERSTATE 25, NORTHBOUND RAMP WHEN Mandy woke up and announced, "I'm hungry and need to pee."

In the distance, Allen saw a Wal-Mart sign. "There's a Wal-Mart up ahead, that work?"

"Yeah, it does for me," Mandy said. She squirmed a little in her seat.

Allen stayed on Interstate 10 westbound and headed for Walmart. He said, "We can also pick up something to eat and some supplies for the music festival while we're here." He took the exit for Wal-Mart.

Allen cruised the almost full Wal-Mart parking lot. He found a truck that looked virtually identical to what he was driving and parked nearby. It had Colorado plates, so that was perfect for switching out with the current plate on his truck.

As soon as he had the truck in park, Mandy hopped out. "I'll wait for you inside near the carts," she said, as she ran to the store entrance.

"Perfect," Allen muttered. He took his screwdriver and quickly changed out the license plates, then went inside in search of Mandy.

Inside, Allen met Mandy at the carts, shoved one towards her and directed, "Go find a backpack and get whatever you think you might need.

But not more than will fit in whatever backpack you pick, okay? Oh, and pick yourself up a few books if you like to read." He smiled at her and continued, "I'll get us some food, water, and pop, then meet you over in camping supplies."

Mandy nodded and went off to do her shopping.

First, Allen picked up petroleum jelly and cotton balls in the pharmacy area. He added two grill lighters to his cart, along with charcoal briquets, and the food and gear necessary for camping.

In her cart, Mandy had a tent, sleeping mat, and sleeping bag along with a flashlight, headlamp for reading, appropriate clothes and a couple of books.

Allen had paid for all their purchases with Dan Bradley's credit card. Their camping supplies included a couple of tents and comfy sleeping bags. They left the store with a mini-fridge Mandy had found, that plugged into a cigarette lighter socket in the truck. They also had sleeping paraphernalia, food, several 2-gallon jugs of water, and drinks. Allen placed the food that needed to be kept cold in the refrigerated cooler.

When he left Wal-Mart, Allen headed for Interstate 25. In Socorro, they stopped for food and gas so they wouldn't have to stop while they went through Albuquerque.

Mandy tapped on her phone again. She startled Allen when she asked, "Hey, up ahead, just past Albuquerque is a campground near an old volcano. Can we stop there? I've never seen an extinct volcano. I've never seen any volcano."

Allen asked, "Do you know how to get there?"

Mandy studied the screen on her phone. "Google maps says the closest campground is at Fenton Lake," she read the directions on her phone to Allen. "It says it's about two or three hours away," Mandy continued.

Allen shrugged as he drove, "Sure, we can stop there for the night and sightsee tomorrow."

FENTON LAKE CAMPGROUND, NEW MEXICO

AT THE CAMPGROUND, ALLEN SCOUTED AROUND FOR RESTROOMS, AND nearby campers. He was satisfied with their isolated spot. The campsites near theirs were empty.

Allen told Mandy to set up camp before he walked off to explore. Now back, he saw she wore her new fleece jacket and headlamp while she leaned against a tree and read a book. When he scanned the campsite, Allen saw the fire pit ready to light, kindling and varying sized sticks of wood were stacked nearby. Mandy had the tents set up, his near hers.

Allen went to the back of the truck. On the lowered tailgate, he prepared a cotton ball to start the fire. He coated it with petroleum jelly, then grabbed the grill lighter. Allen tucked the cotton balls into the center of the grasses and wood kindling and lit the fire. It took off immediately and began to burn through the kindling.

The breeze picked up, and the flames danced higher as they bit into the dry wood. He fed in some larger pieces of wood. The gorgeous fire grew with the added fuel. A peaceful euphoria enveloped Allen. When he looked into any fire, he felt it call to him and calm him. Flames hypnotically sucked him in. He loved staring into a fire.

Allen felt so at one with the flames. It was so peaceful to be one with the fire. But this was such a small fire.

Mandy ruined the moment when she asked, "Can I start cooking some hot dogs yet? I'm starved."

Allen turned and saw she looked at him as if she had asked this question more than once.

Allen shook himself out of the hypnotic state the fire had induced, and said, "Sure, I want two, not burnt, just cooked."

Mandy went to the truck and pawed through the bags of food. She pulled out paper plates, a bag of hot dog buns, and a large bag of potato chips. From the refrigerated cooler plugged into the cigarette lighter, she pulled cans of pop and hot dogs. She went through the groceries again. "Ah, ha! Got you." She pulled the ketchup and mustard from the bag.

After supper was done Mandy quickly and efficiently put out the campfire before Allen could stop her. "What did you do that for?" Allen asked, shocked.

Mandy tipped her head as she looked at Allen. She said, "This wind would be dangerous if we didn't make sure the fire was completely out. So, I put it out."

He watched as she added even more dirt and water, and more dirt. She stirred with a large stick after each item was added and checked the heat with her hand. The fire was dead. She hadn't been satisfied until the fire was cold.

"You're right, thanks for taking care of that," Allen barely got out past the lump in his throat. There was no way Allen could revive it without serious work.

APRIL 8, 2014
FENTON LAKE CAMPGROUND, NEW MEXICO

IT WAS AFTER MIDNIGHT. ALLEN STOOD NEXT TO MANDY'S TENT AND listened to make sure she was asleep. He heard her deep, steady breathing. Satisfied she wouldn't wake; he noted the breeze was gently from the west to the east. He went to the eastern most campsite.

In the fire pit, Allen placed petroleum coated cotton balls, pinecones, and kindling. On top, he stacked heavier wood sticks he had found. He constructed a trail of pinecones and pine needles from the fire pit into the drought-stressed Ponderosa pine woods to the east.

He placed dried grasses, then kindling on top of the pinecone trail to the forest. He surveyed everything before he pulled a cigarette from the pack in his jeans pocket and lit it. Allen placed the lit cigarette in between the cotton balls. He watched to ensure the cotton balls started burning, and those started the pine cones. He returned to the campsite he shared with Mandy and crawled into his tent to sleep.

It was still dark when a man's voice blared from a loudspeaker. "Everyone out! Pack up and leave! Forest fire!" He repeated his message as his loudspeaker announcement woke Allen and Mandy. He repeated over his vehicle-mounted P.A. system, "Pack up and evacuate. Now!" The sound of prolonged blasts on the vehicle horn punctuated the announcement. "Forest fire! This is a mandatory evacuation!" the campground manager announced over the loudspeaker. "Evacuate west on 550 towards Bloomfield."

His fire was burning better than Allen had hoped, to be getting evacuated from the campground already.

Allen helped Mandy collapse their tents and load their possessions into the truck. Other campers were packing up under the campground manager's supervision when they left the campground, which made Allen happy.

Panicked, people fled the fire and created a traffic jam due to poor decisions, and that caused road blocking accidents. Allen and Mandy didn't get far from the inferno. Traffic allowed them to get a few miles from the campground in just under two hours.

Their meals were snack food in the truck as they spent the day creeping along the highway. By afternoon, frustration got the better of Allen. He slammed his hand against the steering wheel and snapped, "I could walk out of here faster than we're driving!" His outburst caused Mandy to jump in her seat. Surprised, she turned and looked at him.

Their camp that night wasn't in a campground. Just a wide spot along state highway 550 where there was room to park, set up their tents, and make a fire. They spent the night as traffic continued its crawling pace past them.

APRIL 9, 2014
ROADSIDE on HIGHWAY 550, NEW MEXICO

ALLEN WAS HALF-AWAKE IN HIS TENT. HE REALIZED HE HEARD MANDY talking to a man. On exiting his tent, he saw a Park Ranger in a Forest Service truck. "Morning officer," he said.

"Fire is no joke, especially this one," the Ranger told Mandy as he looked at Allen.

"I know, my dad is a firefighter," Mandy replied.

The Ranger told Allen, "Young man, you need to take this fire seriously and get moving. Get out of here."

"We will. We stopped here because the traffic stopped last night. We'll get going," Allen replied.

"I'll be back in thirty minutes to make sure you cleared out. You better be gone. This fire is dangerous," the Ranger said, then got in his truck and drove off.

Mandy collapsed the tents to put into the truck when Allen announced, "Breakfast first. No, coffee first." He built a cooking fire. Allen took the cooking utensils, coffee, and food needed for breakfast from the truck.

Mandy packed tents and other gear into the truck. She was packed and ready to leave. "Allen, this isn't safe. The winds are still strong and could pick up sparks from this fire and cause a new one!" Mandy protested. "People could be hurt if your campfire got away from you!"

"I need coffee, then food. Then we can worry about packing up and leaving," Allen replied.

"But the fire. The Park Ranger said, . . ." Mandy barely got out before she was cut off by Allen.

He roared, "Coffee! Food! Then whatever!" His face was very red. His hand shook as he filled the coffee pot with water from a jug and slammed the jug onto the truck tailgate. He put the coffee pot into the edge of the fire. Pointing at the eggs and bacon, he ordered Mandy, "Breakfast isn't going to make itself. Hop to it!"

Mandy stared at him in shock for a moment, then made a breakfast of scrambled eggs, no-frills, no bacon. Protests she directed at Allen while she cooked, fell on deaf ears. "Don't you have any sense?" Mandy asked. "This is a big fire and dangerous!" Mandy dumped the eggs onto a plate for him. She would eat later; somewhere she felt safe.

As soon as Mandy gave Allen his eggs, she put out the cook fire. Dirt covered the fire before Allen could protest. Mandy refilled his empty coffee cup and dumped the rest of the coffee into the dead fire. She held her hand over the fire to verify it was out when Allen protested, "Hey! What did you do that for?"

Allen ate slowly, chewing each bite thoroughly. He watched the wide black column of smoke from the wildfire he had started the night before billowing into the morning sky, backlit by the sun. It was beautiful and made his heart swell. I did that, he thought.

"What is wrong with you? The fire needs to be completely cold! We need to go!" Mandy was adamant.

Mandy's question set him back. Why would she ask what was wrong with him? He looked to the sky and the huge column of billowing black smoke climbing to the heavens. Allen didn't think anything was wrong with him.

Mandy also watched the sky, for new, smaller columns of smoke, and to gauge the wind direction.

They packed and were ready to leave when the Park Ranger followed by a deputy flew by, lights flashing and sirens howling. They sped up the road in the direction evacuating traffic was taking, driving on the wrong side of the road. The traffic going by their campsite slowed and then stopped. State highway 550 was a parking lot, again. Curious to see why traffic stopped, Mandy approached a motor home she saw had a CB antenna. She knocked on the side of the vehicle. When the driver opened his window, she asked, "How come everybody stopped on the road?"

"I heard on the CB radio there's a big accident. It seems like a boat towed by a motorhome, a couple of cars, a truck and another motorhome all collided somehow. One of them caught fire. The vehicle fire has the road blocked in both directions while they put it out," said the gray-haired man who operated the motor home.

"Any idea how long until the road opens again?" Mandy asked.

"Haven't heard anything yet, we're listening. If I hear anything, I'll let you know." He shrugged at Mandy.

"Thanks, mister!" Mandy said and went back to the roadside campsite she shared with Allen. Mandy watched the sky. The column of black smoke grew wider and denser and blacker.

When she made a late lunch, Mandy invited the motorhome folks, Doc and Linda, to join her and Allen. That made Allen grumpy.

After lunch, Mandy repacked the truck for evacuation. Still, traffic didn't move. Mandy spent the afternoon visiting with Doc and Linda in their motorhome. It had air conditioning.

With Mandy out of the way, Allen sat and watched the black smoke billowing into the sky. By evening Mandy was antsy. She went to the motor home and asked, "Any update on why traffic isn't moving?"

"The fire from the accident damaged a bridge. From what we heard, a path is being bulldozed through a creek bed that should be open by early morning. At least that's the latest I heard on the CB," said Doc. "At least the wind is blowing the fire away from us."

"So far," Mandy said. "My Dad taught me never to trust fire. It's unpredictable and dangerous."

They spent another night camped along the highway. Doc and Linda pulled their motorhome onto the wide shoulder of the road so they could sleep, too. They didn't want to block traffic if it started moving before they woke up.

APRIL 10, 2014
ALONG HIGHWAY 550, NEW MEXICO

DURING THE NIGHT, ALLEN HEARD NUMEROUS VEHICLES PASS THE campsite going towards the fire. When he peeked out of his tent, he saw fire suppression crews had arrived in their crew buses, with their brush trucks and water trucks. The truck noises stopped just up the road from where Allen camped with Mandy, Doc, and Linda.

BASE CAMP
FENTON LAKE FIRE, NEW MEXICO

IT WAS WELL AFTER MIDNIGHT WHEN TOM SULLIVAN AND THE SOUTHERN Arizona wildland firefighters arrived at the fire suppression base camp set up by the Forest Service. They quietly set up their tents away from already sleeping firefighters so as not to disturb them. Tom led his arson dog, Ace, to the edge of the fire camp to take care of his business, before they got into their tent for a few hours of sleep.

The wake-up bell clanged. Ace licked Tom's face to wake him. "Good boy, Ace," Tom said. "If we don't get moving, we miss breakfast. It's hard to fight fire on an empty stomach."

After breakfast and the briefing from the incident commander, the wildland firefighter team from Arizona was sent to rebuild a neglected fire break several miles away from the central fire. That way, if the wind changed direction, the blaze wouldn't have any fuel to head into town.

Tom took a few precious minutes and used the satellite phone assigned to his crew to check in with his wife, Connie. She was his heart. He had to hear her voice to start the day. The phone rang twice before Connie picked up. "Hello?" she mumbled, not quite awake.

"Hey, babe. We got here safe and are about to go out to cut brush away from the fire. I'll call you tonight," Tom said.

"I miss you. Be safe. I love you too," Connie said through her sleep thickened voice.

"Gotta go now, love. Bye," Tom said.

"I love you," Connie said. She hugged the phone to her chest after the call ended.

Forest Service crew supervisor Joe Murphy led the Arizona wildland firefighter crew. On a map with the fire marked in, he detailed to the firefighters the attack plan.

"Firefighters, the goal is barren dirt for the width of the fire break. A starved fire is a dead fire," said Joe Murphy. "Now let's get to work!"

Shouldering their gear, the firefighters piled into the crew bus that would take them as close as possible to the area they were to clear. From there, they hiked to their assigned work area. Ace had a pack with his water, a first aid kit, and the satellite phone. When a rabbit flushed by their passing ran across the trail, Ace stayed with Tom at a loose heel position. Tom praised Ace for staying at his side.

ALONG HIGHWAY 550, NEW MEXICO

THE CHATTER AND BUZZ OF CHAIN SAWS STARTING AWAKENED ALLEN. He crawled out of his tent and followed the sound through the woods to the brush clearing crew. He clenched his jaw when he saw the firefighters preparing to kill his fire. The crew had cleared an open space to stop the fire from spreading, and they were expanding it.

As he watched, he saw two different men approach a guy with a dog. Allen figured he must be the one who gave the orders. There had to be a way to stop them, Allen thought.

He pondered his options. A fire wouldn't work; the wind was blowing the wrong way. Bullets would. If he took out the boss man with the dog, would that make the rest panic and run? Allen decided it was worth a try. He returned to the campsite. He noticed traffic was starting to move.

He roused Mandy and told her, "Get ready to leave, take down the tents and pack up the truck. It's time to leave. We'll get breakfast later."

Mandy mumbled something he didn't understand while he took the rifle and loaded it. She crawled out of her tent while he grabbed a roll of toilet paper from the truck. Waving the roll at her, he said, "I have to visit the bushes, if you need to go after I do, I can watch for wildlife."

Stretching, Mandy replied, "Nope, I'm good. You go ahead. I'll get packing."

THE FIRE LINE, NEW MEXICO

PAUL GRANT HAD HIS CHAIN SAW ROARING AS HE CUT INTO SMALL TREES. Tom Sullivan's fellow firefighter, rookie Corey Clements, pulled his cell phone out of his pocket to take a short video of the terrain where they were working.

Corey panned the area where they were to cut down small trees and scrape out the grass and brush to rebuild the neglected fire break. He saw Tom had picked a spot further into the fire break, still within sight of Corey. With his spot picked out, Tom dropped his pack, placed his chain saw on the ground then turned and removed Ace's load.

THE WOODS, NEW MEXICO

ALLEN RAN THROUGH THE WOODS TO WHERE HE COULD GET A SHOT AT the firefighting crew. He watched through the scope and was surprised when the dog lifted its nose into the air, scenting.

The dog's actions warned him that the dog would scent him if the breeze didn't shift. He chambered the first round, lined up his shot on the dog's head. The dog turned just as he fired but still dropped.

He quickly chambered another round. He went for another headshot. His target was the guy who was next to the dog, the boss. He missed; the man had turned towards the fallen dog. He chambered another round and fired. It hit, and the man dropped.

Allen stood and ran to the truck.

THE FIRE LINE, NEW MEXICO

BY ACCIDENT, COREY HAD RECORDED IT ALL. ACE, AS HE LIFTED HIS NOSE to scent the breeze. Tom when he removed the pack from the dog. Ace when he flinched, yelped and dropped to the ground. Tom when he jerked his head, crumpled and landed beside the where the dog had fallen. Ace as he ran off into the trees.

It was all on the video on Corey's phone. "Man Down! Help!" Corey bellowed as he shoved his phone into his pocket. He grabbed his EMT bag and ran for Tom. Corey's shout caused Paul Grant to look in Corey's direction.

Paul saw Corey run to a figure on the ground. Paul raced to his side. Tom was injured. Paul was stunned to see the gaping, bloody head wound. Paul checked for life signs. No pulse. No breath. There were none. Tom was dead. Paul looked around.

Ace, who was there a second ago, was gone. "What happened?" Paul asked Corey.

HIGHWAY 550, NEW MEXICO

When Allen got almost back to camp, he stopped running. He tried to look calm when he walked out of the woods.

Mandy asked, "Did I hear shots?"

"Yeah, snake. I hate snakes!" Allen manufactured a shiver. "You want to use this before we leave?" he asked as he held out the roll of toilet paper to Mandy.

"Nope."

Allen put the rifle and toilet paper back in the truck. He stood on the running board of the pickup and scanned the campsite to make sure nothing was left behind. As he slid behind the wheel, he asked, "Ready to go?"

Mandy was in the truck, "Yeah."

Courtesy of Doc and Linda in the motor home, Allen was able to easily merge into the moving traffic fleeing the fire evacuation zone.

THE FIRE LINE, NEW MEXICO

"What did you see?" Paul asked Corey.

"I don't know. I was shooting a video, for before and after we cleared the brush. I saw it while I was filming. One-minute Ace and Tom are fine, the next, Ace down, Tom down then Ace was gone," Corey said.

Looking around, Corey spotted a blood trail that led off into the forest.

"Make sure you save that video!" Paul ordered.

On his radio, Supervisor Joe Murphy announced, "Incident command, we are being shot at by a sniper. One down, deceased."

Incident command replied, "Evacuate the area immediately."

Murphy ran up to Corey and Paul, "Tell the crew to take cover and prepare to evacuate. I radioed this in."

Corey bellowed at the firefighters closest to him on either side, "Take cover, sniper! Prepare to evacuate! Pass it on!"

"I'm not leaving him," Paul said. He pulled a tarp from Tom's pack. Corey kneeled next to him and helped wrap Tom's body so they could carry Tom from the forest to the crew bus.

When Corey reached for the pack Ace had left behind, Joe Murphy said, "Leave it. That will let the investigators know where the shooting took place."

Tom's body was quickly bundled to be carried out to the crew bus. The ride back to the firefighters' base camp was quiet.

HIGHWAY 550, NEW MEXICO

ALLEN WAS PUMPED WITH ADRENALINE BUT COULDN'T LET ON TO MANDY. He drove, crawling along with traffic when he wanted to race through the small town of Cuba. He glanced at the diner they passed. It looked closed. Damn, he was hungry. He stayed with the bumper to bumper traffic as it crept up the highway.

BASE CAMP
FENTON LAKE FIRE, NEW MEXICO

ONCE BACK AT THE BASE CAMP FOR THE FIREFIGHTERS WORKING THE Fenton Lake fire, the state law enforcement officers took over caring for Tom's body until the FBI and medical examiner arrived since Tom had died in the National Forest.

TINGLE CREEK, ARIZONA

AT THE MALEY COUNTY PUBLIC SAFETY COMMUNICATIONS CENTER, dispatcher Claudia Thibodeau took the call from New Mexico. As soon as she disconnected from that call, she dialed the number for Sheriff Martin Barrett's desk. When he answered, she said, "Sir, I just got a call from...I should tell you this in person. You need to come in here."

"On my way," the Sheriff said. When he arrived in the communications room, he said, "Spit it out." He saw the strained look on the usually unflappable dispatcher's face.

"Sir, Firefighter Tom Sullivan from Tingle Creek was shot and killed in New Mexico. He was working on a wildfire with Forest Service. They want us to go tell his wife, Connie Sullivan."

"Crap!" Martin let out a sigh as he dropped in to a chair at an unused dispatch console. "What deputies do you have on today?"

"I have Denise Porter and Jesse Lopez," replied Claudia.

"Have Denise call in. She and Connie are friends. Don't let any of this go over the radio. Call it a special assignment when they get there. She can take Jesse with her if she wants," instructed the sheriff.

"Also, check the overtime list, see who signed up for this week. We'll need to call in a dispatcher for you so you can go home sometime today. I suspect Denise'll be tied up the rest of her shift, so check the deputy list and call someone in to cover for her."

"Yes, sir. I'll take care of it," the dispatcher replied.

GRANT RESIDENCE
TINGLE CREEK, ARIZONA

SHARON HAD FINISHED THE SNACK SHE NEEDED BEFORE SHE LEFT FOR work at the local E.R. Her cell phone rang as she loaded her dishes into the dishwasher. She checked the caller ID. It was Paul. "Hey Sweetie, I was just getting ready to go to work," Sharon said. "Why are you calling now? I thought you wouldn't call until late tonight."

Paul made a strangled noise over the phone.

Sharon asked, "Paul, Honey? What's wrong?"

Paul stammered, "Yeah... .um, . . . Tom was killed."

"Oh, no, Love, I don't know what to say....," Sharon responded. Tears burned the back of her eyes.

"It wasn't a fire. Someone shot him. We had just gotten to our assigned area to clear brush," Paul sniffed loudly and made a strangled sound Sharon couldn't identify.

"What?! No…" Sharon exclaimed.

"You have to get to Connie; this will destroy her. There are deputies on the way to tell her, but she will need you."

Sniffing, Sharon said, "Got it, on my way. Take care, my love." Sharon gave herself a minute to digest the news and cry for her best friend.

Talking out loud to herself, she said, "Time's up. Get it together, Sharon. Call the hospital, let them know you won't be in by 3:00 p.m., you'll be late." She did that.

"Okay, you need your purse, keys, and your emergency medical bag." She collected her things, went out to her SUV, and put everything on the passenger seat.

Once in the Ford Explorer, she rested her head against the steering wheel. "You can do this. You can do this. You do it when you need to for your patients. You can do this for your best friend," Sharon continued her self-pep-talk out loud. She straightened, wiped her eyes, started the Explorer, then backed out of the carport.

MESQUITE B&B
TINGLE CREEK, ARIZONA

Connie Sullivan had finished a light before work meal when she heard a vehicle pull into the B&B's gravel drive. Through the window above the kitchen sink, she saw Denise Porter had driven her Maley County Sheriff's vehicle into the yard, followed by Deputy Jesse Lopez in his truck. When Denise got out of her SUV, Connie went out to meet the deputies.

Connie's dogs met the deputies before Connie made it outside.

"Denise, Jesse, what are you guys doing here?"

"We need to talk to you for a minute," Denise said.

"Okay...?" Connie replied.

Denise led the way into Connie's private part of the B&B. "It's hot out here in a vest," she tapped the bulletproof vest under her uniform shirt.

"Okay, but my shift starts at fifteen hundred (3:00 p.m.), we need to make this fast," Connie followed Denise into the house, followed by Jesse and the dogs. Once they were all inside, she turned to Denise, "What's up?"

"Sit," Denise said, and she pointed at the couch.

Connie perched on the edge of the sofa, "You're scaring me."

"I don't mean to. Are Jack and Kate around? I need to talk to them as well," Denise said.

"No, they're camping in their RV. They left Tom and me to run the B&B this week. They should be home in the next couple of days. You can't talk to Tom. He's at a fire in New Mexico," Connie replied.

Jesse leaned against the door. Denise sat next to Connie on the couch.

"Connie, Tom was killed in New Mexico this morning." Denise watched Connie's face turn gray as Connie slowly shook her head "no."

"No, He can't…I talked to him this morning, he's fine," Connie said, tonelessly while she got even paler. "They weren't going to be in the way of the fire…"

"Connie," Denise said gently, "Tom was shot in the fire break, and Ace is missing."

"No," Connie mumbled, then fainted.

Denise caught Connie's limp body and guided it to the floor, laying Connie on her side. The dogs milled around Connie on the floor. Magic nudged Connie with her nose and licked her face. Misty lay down against Connie's back and rested her chin on Connie's shoulder. Denise pulled a throw blanket from the couch and covered Connie.

Denise knew Connie was safe with the dogs, so she used her cell phone to call Dr. Sharon Grant, "Hi, Sharon, it's Denise. I'm at the B&B with Connie. I just told her Tom is dead. She fainted on me. I don't want to leave her alone, and I know you two are tight. Any chance you could come over?"

"Already on my way," Sharon said and disconnected the call.

"Jesse, you might as well get back on patrol. I'll be clear when I can," Denise told her co-worker. "Nothing for you to do here anyway, I'll write the case report."

Jesse left. When Sharon arrived, she told Denise, "Go ahead and take off. I'll stay with Connie."

"I'll hang around while I write my report," Denise said. "Just in case…"

BASE CAMP
FENTON LAKE FIRE, NEW MEXICO

PAUL GRANT NEEDED A QUIET MOMENT TO HIMSELF. AFTER THE RETURN to base camp with Tom's body, he had provided a verbal report of what happened. Corey had sent a copy of the video to the incident commander for review and to pass on to law enforcement. Paul saw the video showed Ace as he dropped to the ground, then Tom shot and falling.

"Keep that video, son," the incident commander had ordered Corey. "Don't mess with it, don't post it on Facebook. Keep it safe. It's evidence."

"Yes, Sir," Corey said. The incident commander had stomped around in circles a few times then picked up his satellite phone and began making calls.

Paul walked out to the edge of base camp and ducked behind a screen of trees. His best friend since he was a kid, was gone. Dead. Paul dropped to his haunches against a large tree, put his head in his hands, and for a moment, he allowed himself to weep for his friend.

After he pulled himself together, Paul called his old college roommate and friend, Rand Hansen. Rand was now an FBI agent based in Dallas. Paul, Rand, and Tom had shared a house all through college. Paul waited, breath held, for Rand to answer.

When the phone stopped ringing, Paul heard, "FBI, Hansen," when Rand answered his phone.

"Rand, it's Paul Grant." Without giving Rand a chance to say anything, he continued, "Tom Sullivan and I were working a fire in New Mexico." Paul paused, then blurted out, "Rand, Tom Sullivan died at the fire."

Rand drew in a sudden deep breath, "Paul, I'm sorry to hear that, that's a tough way to die, in a fire."

"No! Not in a fire, *at* a fire! It was a headshot. A sniper killed him!" Rand heard Paul almost panting over the phone, as Paul explained what happened to Tom Sullivan.

Taking a breath himself, Rand questioned, "You're sure? Cuz that doesn't make sense!"

"It may not, but it did!" Paul exclaimed.

"And this was in the National Forest, not state land?" Rand asked.

"Yup," Paul responded. "The FBI will investigate, right? Can you get assigned? Keep me up on what is going on?" Paul paused for breath.

Rand answered, "I'll do what I can. I can't promise anything."

"That's all I ask," Paul replied.

"And please let me know when and where the funeral will be," Rand said. Then Paul heard someone talking to Rand, who mumbled a reply Paul couldn't understand.

Rand said to Paul, "Listen, gotta go."

"Yeah," Paul said, and disconnected. He returned to the incident command tent for a briefing that was already in progress when he arrived. He stood at the back.

The incident commander continued, "… A team of investigators is en route. Until investigators give an 'all clear,' no one goes into the area of the forest where Tom died."

The Arizona team was given the rest of the day off to document the morning for the investigators. They were to report for reassignment tomorrow. Once the briefing concluded, Paul, worried about Ace put out water for him at Tom's tent in the hopes the dog would come back to base camp.

FBI OFFICE
DALLAS, TEXAS

RAND KNOCKED ON THE DOOR FRAME OF HIS BOSS' OFFICE, THEN WALKED in.

"I was just going to have you come in, got a new case for you," his boss said.

"Is it the killing of a firefighter on Forest Service land in New Mexico? I wanted to be assigned that," Rand said.

"No, a stranger abduction of a teenager and the attempted murder by shooting and arson of Dallas firefighter Daniel Bradley. He's currently unconscious in a local hospital. According to Dallas Police Department, Bradley's Captain, a Captain Shawn Murray, is reporting the fifteen-year-old daughter, Amanda, missing. So is his truck."

Rand waited for more information as to why it was an FBI case.

His boss continued, "Captain Murray told Dallas P.D. her father had told him that Mandy had a date last night. Someone new. The captain's adamant the girl would never leave her dad and never hurt him. He insists Mandy is tight with her dad and isn't the runaway type. It's been just the two of them since mom died when she was a toddler."

"I'll get right on it," Rand replied. His boss handed him the case file and contact information for the officer handling the case for the Dallas Police Department.

At his desk, Rand read the file on the victim, Daniel Bradley. Accelerant was throughout the house. Bradley was duct-taped to a chair, beaten, and shot. The interior of the house was set on fire while he was unconscious. Trajectory indicated the shot was from slightly above and some distance behind the victim while he was in the chair.

Rand remembered reading about something similar in Oklahoma a few weeks back. He thought it might have involved an elderly couple, and the grandson was the suspect.

He researched online to verify his recollection. He was right. Now he knew how, when, and where. If there were forensics that matched his new case, it would help narrow down who the suspect was.

FARMINGTON, NEW MEXICO

ALLEN HAD STAYED WITH THE FLEEING TRAFFIC UNTIL THEY GOT TO Farmington. Hungry, he stopped at a Golden Corral restaurant to eat. After he parked, Allen roused Mandy, and they went in.

The smoke plume was easily visible to the southeast when they left the restaurant. The air tankers were tiny but easy to see against the smoke in the air. Allen cringed when he saw the airplanes and helicopters attacking his fire.

Mandy pulled her phone from her purse after she got in the truck. She buckled up, asked, "So where are we going today? Will we get to the music festival today?"

Her dad still hadn't answered any of her texts. But a text wasn't a postcard. The battery in her phone was getting low. She sent a quick text to her father, *"Safely out of the fire in New Mexico. Please answer,"* then shut her phone off and returned it to her purse.

"We should; it depends on how crowded the highways are. Because of the fire, we may have to take a detour," Allen replied. "If we can get there today, we should make the opening day for Country Thunder."

"Cool. So, you think they'll be someplace I can plug in my phone? The battery's almost dead, and I haven't talked to my dad in a couple of days."

"He knows where you are and what the plans were. I'm sure he doesn't expect a call from you from a music festival campground," Allen explained to Mandy. "Don't worry so much. You feel like staying in a hotel for a few days instead of camping?"

"Yeah, heat at night and a/c during the day would be great. Plus, a shower and a bed sound wonderful," Mandy said. "Separate rooms?"

"We'll find out when we get there," Allen replied.

Allen checked the map app on his phone and mapped out how to get Florence, Arizona, and where the nearest hotel was to Country Thunder. He was ready to sleep indoors and shower and sleep in a real bed, as well.

He used his smartphone and Dan Bradley's credit card to reserve a suite with two bedrooms, for the next two weeks. "It's so nice of your dad to give us this card for our trip," Allen said when he saw Mandy looking at the credit card he was using.

TINGLE CREEK, ARIZONA

WHEN CONNIE CAME AROUND, SHARON HELPED HER TO BED. THE DOGS stayed with Connie and hopped in to bed with her after she lay down. Sharon asked, "You want me to stay for a while?"

Listlessly Connie answered, "No, you can't do anything but watch me cry. You have better things to do."

"I'll check in on you later, by phone. So, you better answer, you hear me?" Sharon asked.

"I do and I will," Connie said. "Oh! God! He's gone!" She wept into her pillow. Sharon left Connie and went to work at the local hospital emergency room.

Shortly before supper time, Tom's parents, Jack and Kate Sullivan returned to the B&B a day early from their anniversary camping trip through northern Arizona. They got a subdued greeting from the dogs when they got out of their RV.

Kate noticed right away; something was off with the dogs. "What's wrong girls?" Kate asked the dogs as if they could tell her.

Magic gave her a half-mast tail wave and quickly returned into the house. Misty bumped her nose against Kate and then Jack's leg in greeting, and also returned to the house.

"Something's wrong with those two," Jack said. "Let's get the perishables into the house. We can finish unpacking the RV later after we know what's what."

They took the food from the RV into the house. The dogs were scarce. "That's odd. Misty and Magic always help put away groceries," Kate commented.

Jack said, "Since she isn't out here helping unload, Connie must be at work. Except, her Yukon XL is here. I wonder if it broke down?" He put the leftover meat in the freezer. "I'll look at it after supper."

From her bed, Connie heard Jack and Kate arrive home. She stayed in bed, hugging Tom's pillow. Tears were silently running down her face. She decided to let them finish supper before she told Tom was gone. It would be best to let them enjoy the last minutes they had left in a world with Tom healthy and alive.

After they had emptied the food from the RV, Jack pulled it into the machine shed behind the B&B and parked it next to Tom's tractor.

Groceries put away; Kate wandered through the empty B&B. There were no scheduled guests this week. That's why she and Jack had taken this past week for vacation while leaving Tom and Connie in charge of running their B&B. She checked the guest rooms anyway for unscheduled guests; they were clean and empty.

The door to Connie and Tom's part of the house was ajar, for the dogs, but that was normal. Where are those dogs, and where is Connie? Something isn't right, Kate thought.

Jack came into the kitchen. "Everything's put away. I looked; Tom's truck is gone. Did you find her?"

"No. I didn't find those dogs of hers either," Kate replied.

"Well, I need to eat, keep my blood sugar up, then we can sort out what's going on," Jack said. "I'll go out and start the charcoal in the grill."

Kate prepared to start dinner for Jack and herself. She set the steaks to marinate for grilling, prepared the salad, and got out plates and silverware. She noticed she was entirely alone. No canine supervision. When Jack came back into the kitchen, she asked him, "Any idea where the dogs are?"

"No, want me to look for them?"

"I think so, this isn't normal, even if Connie isn't home. They always supervise me when I make meals," Kate replied.

Jack searched the B&B, beginning in the guest areas. When he got to Connie and Tom's room, he pushed the door completely open. He was surprised to see Connie in bed, curled up around a pillow, Misty with Magic lying against her back.

"Connie! What's wrong, are you sick?" Jack asked as he went to her. Connie shook her head. When Jack got to her, he saw her tear-streaked wan face; he demanded, "What's wrong? Tell me!"

"You don't want to know," her voice broke, Connie wept into the pillow she clutched.

Jack left the bedroom and hollered down the hall, "Kate get in here, Connie's room, quick! Something's wrong!" Jack returned to Connie until Kate ran into the room.

"What?" Kate asked out of breath. She directed Misty to the floor and sat next to Connie on the bed. Jack sat at Connie's feet as Kate stroked Connie's hair. "Come on, Connie. We can't help if you don't tell us."

Connie sobbed out, "Tom's dead. I was going to wait until after you ate to…," sobs wracked Connie's body.

Kate looked at Jack; her face went white. Staring back at Kate, Jack mumbled, "I'm sorry, Connie. I don't think I heard you right."

Connie sobbed out, "Tom is dead. He was killed this morning at a fire in New Mexico."

Kate suddenly bolted to Connie's attached bathroom. Jack followed and saw her hunched over the toilet. She was vomiting violently.

"Honey!" He went to her and held her hair back as she was sick.

Stomach empty, Kate sat on the floor next to the toilet as Jack flushed it for her then wiped her mouth with a damp washcloth. He noticed she was panting in shallow breaths. Her face was somewhat gray and sweaty, as well.

He bellowed, "Connie call Kate an ambulance! Now! I think she's having a heart attack!" He gently wiped Kate's face with the backside of the washcloth. Her face got grayer, and her eyes unfocused and dilated.

When Connie didn't move right away, Jack bellowed, "Now Connie, call 9-1-1."

Connie drug herself off the bed, picked up the bedside phone, put on her emotionless dispatcher persona and made the call, efficiently passing on information to the dispatcher. She was still on the phone with the dispatcher when Connie heard thumps from the bathroom.

"Tell them she is unconscious!" Jack yelled from the bathroom.

Connie passed the information on to the dispatcher. Connie heard Jack saying over and over, "Stay with me, Katie, stay with me, come on baby, we can get through this, but only if you stay with me."

Jack yelled, "Connie! She stopped breathing! I need help with CPR!"

Connie advised the dispatcher of Kate's deterioration, ordered the dogs to stay by the bed, and ran to the bathroom to assist Jack.

When the paramedics arrived, they took over CPR and treated Kate as they rushed her to the hospital. Jack rode in the ambulance with Kate. Connie followed in her SUV.

HOSPITAL
TINGLE CREEK, ARIZONA

ALL ATTEMPTS TO REVIVE KATE THAT EVENING FAILED. THIRTY MINUTES after arriving at the hospital, Kate was declared dead.

Jack was in shock. "This can't be happening, it isn't real," he muttered to himself over and over. He was stunned, numb, and only able to follow simple directions given to him by the hospital staff.

Over her radio, Deputy Denise Porter heard the ambulance dispatched to the B&B, and the follow-up rescue call dispatched to the hospital. Worried, she volunteered to take it.

When Deputy Porter arrived at the hospital, she saw Connie. "Are you okay?" the deputy asked.

"No, but it's Tom's mother, Kate. I told her and Jack…" Connie's eyes teared up as she took deep, slow breaths, in and out. "I told them Tom was dead. I killed Kate." Connie began to sob.

Deputy Porter sat next to Connie and pulled her into a hug. "I am so sorry, Connie. Today's got to be the shittiest day ever. So, you told Kate about Tom and…" Denise let the sentence hang to see what Connie said.

"She had a heart attack or something. She got sick, vomited and then stopped breathing," Connie said. "Jack's with Dr. Grant now to get checked out. I think he was going into shock."

After she talked to the doctor and paramedics, Deputy Porter wrote the case report on Kate's unexpected death. When she finished the report, she checked on her friend. She asked Connie, "Have you called your parents?"

Connie looked at her friend, hollow-eyed. She shook her head.

"Give me your phone," Denise ordered. Connie handed it over, Denise scrolled through the numbers. When she found "Home – WY," she dialed.

"Mr. Miller, Art, I don't know if you remember me from your last visit to Tingle Creek. I'm Connie's friend, Denise. I am also a deputy. I'm calling you in that capacity."

"I remember you, what happened?" Art replied. "Is Connie okay?"

Denise answered, "This afternoon I had to inform Connie her husband had died." Denise heard Art gasp. "When Connie informed Tom's parents, his mother, Kate, died. It would help Connie a great deal if you could come to Tingle Creek and stay for a while. Help Connie get back on her feet again."

It took a moment for Art to respond, "We'll be on the road in an hour, it will take two days to get there. We can't do the non-stop drive anymore."

"That's okay, Art, I'll let Connie know you're on the way," Denise replied.

FLORENCE, ARIZONA

Allen handled getting them checked in to a motel that evening. Mandy spent her time in the lobby browsing the rack displaying other places with things to do in Arizona. She pulled out flyers for the Arizona Sonora Desert Museum, the Pima County Fair, and The Thing!

It would give them places to see and things to do on their way back to Dallas. For as long as she could remember she'd seen billboards for The Thing! Now maybe she could find out what the fuss was about.

The two-bedroom suite they had enchanted Mandy. Her room had a jacuzzi tub in the private bathroom, and the motel had a pool! They settled in quickly.

Allen glanced at Mandy when she came from her room in her swimsuit, carrying a towel. She was a hot chick, but she didn't turn him on like fire. He liked having her around, so he wasn't alone.

Mandy plugged in her phone to charge before she left for the pool. Allen watched and figured, so what, daddy can't answer anyway from where he is. There aren't phones in hell.

While Mandy swam, Allen watched CNN so he could monitor his fire in New Mexico. The newscasters enraged Allen. He shouted at the TV, "What the fuck! Who cares about some lame-ass dead firefighter? The inferno is what's important, not the people putting it out!"

Vibrating with rage, he turned the TV off and paced the suite to calm himself. He stepped out onto the private patio while Mandy continued to swim.

He enjoyed the always moving air. It was so restless like him.

APRIL 11, 2014
CASTLE ROCK, COLORADO

AFTER MIDNIGHT AND THROUGH DENVER, ART PULLED INTO THE FIRST hotel he saw with a vacancy sign. He needed to rest. Belle couldn't drive after dark.

Belle roused him before sunrise for breakfast. "But I just laid my head down," Art groused.

"It's dawn; we need to get moving. Connie needs us," Belle replied and set a freshly brewed cup of coffee on the nightstand next to the bed. As Art dressed, she went to the lobby for eggs, bacon, hash browns, and another cup of coffee from the complimentary breakfast bar and brought it back to the room. After eating they continued to Tingle Creek.

FLORENCE, ARIZONA

MANDY AND ALLEN ATTENDED COUNTRY THUNDER EVERY DAY FROM the start until closing. They returned to their rented suite every night and the festival every morning. Mandy enjoyed every day of the music festival.

Allen was getting itchy to start another fire. He wished he could muster up the enthusiasm Mandy had for the music festival. He needed a fire; that would make him feel better. It had been too long.

TINGLE CREEK, ARIZONA

ART AND BELLE ARRIVED AT THE B&B IN TINGLE CREEK AFTER DARK. As soon as they got past the dogs, and through the kitchen, they saw a wan Connie seated on the couch clutching a pillow, as tears ran down her face. The dogs raced ahead and jumped on the couch next to Connie.

Belle and Art went to her and enfolded her in their arms. "I'm so sorry sweetie," Belle said as she and Art hugged Connie.

A pale Jack wandered into the room at the sounds of new people in the B&B. Belle left Art hugging Connie as she went to enfold Jack in a hug.

Jack allowed her to hug him but was too emotionally numb to lift his arms to hug her back. He rested his forehead on her shoulder for a moment.

"I am so sorry, Jack. I can't imagine what you're going through. I'll help any way I can," Belle said, as she rubbed his back with her hand.

Jack mutely nodded against her shoulder, made a strangled noise, then fled down the hall to his bedroom, closing the door.

APRIL 12, 2014
TINGLE CREEK, ARIZONA

In the morning, Art and Belle took it upon themselves to fix breakfast. Art noticed Belle was moving slower than usual. "Honey, what's wrong?" he asked.

"Just a headache, I think I'm getting a migraine, but let's get Connie and Jack fed. After that I'm going to lie down," Belle said. "Get the lazy bones to the table in five minutes."

Breakfast was a quiet affair, with no conversation at the table. Belle rubbed her head, then excused herself to go lie down without eating anything.

Art split her meal between the dogs after adding the eggs and toast that wasn't eaten by Jack and Connie. Art rinsed the dishes and loaded the dishwasher.

Connie went to check on Belle. She shouted, "Art, come quick! Mama Belle is sick!"

Art raced into the guest room he and Belle shared. When he entered, he saw Connie on the floor, cleaning up vomit from beside the bed with a towel. Art looked at Belle and noticed the difference in her face. It was so limp, somehow.

He sat on the side of the bed next to Belle and soon realized the seat of his pants felt wet. He stood, pulled back the covers, and saw she had wet the bed.

"Belle, Sweetheart, talk to me. Come on, open your eyes." He stroked the side of her face. "Connie, call 9-1-1. She's had a stroke or something. Belle, Honey, open your eyes for me please."

Connie called for an ambulance, as she threw the vomit filled towel into the trash.

When the paramedics arrived, Belle was unresponsive. After checking Belle over, the paramedics told Connie, Jack and Art she would be flown to Tucson for treatment. Whatever had happened was too complicated for the local ten-bed hospital.

"But she's healthy! There's no history of stroke in her family. Her normal blood pressure is low," Art said.

"We don't know this is a stroke. That's why the patient has to go to Tucson," paramedic Joyce said. "They have the MRI and CAT scan machines."

HOSPITAL
TUCSON, ARIZONA

In the hospital waiting room, Art went over Belle's medical history and insurance information with a nurse. Connie paced nearby. After an eternity, the doctor treating Belle came out.

"The tests show Belle has had a hemorrhagic stroke, possibly from an aneurysm. We'll develop a treatment plan as soon as we know more. I'm waiting for her records from her doctor in Wyoming. Only time will tell how much she'll recover if she does," said the emergency room doctor.

"Can I see her?" Art asked.

"As soon as we get her settled in a room, a nurse will come to take you to her."

"How long until I can take her home?" Art asked the doctor.

"Back to Tingle Creek? It'll be a while," the doctor said.

"No, Wyoming. We live in Glenrock, Wyoming," Art replied.

"She won't be going back there. She wouldn't survive the trip," the doctor bluntly said.

Art dropped into a chair. Connie sat beside him. Head in hands Art mumbled, "So what do I do?"

"For now, rent someplace local to stay. In a few months, your wife's situation could change," the doctor suggested.

"You can stay with me," Connie said. "Go home, get what you need, and stay with me. We can convert and update the bunkhouse. I'll look after Belle while you're gone. We can talk on the phone every night until you get back."

COUNTRY THUNDER MUSIC FESTIVAL
FLORENCE, ARIZONA

ALLEN FELT TWITCHY AND OUT OF SORTS. HE NEEDED A FIRE. HE WALKED around the music festival, and he found the dumpsters. He went back to his truck for a road flare.

Mandy was at the bandstand listening to the last band of the night when he started the dumpster fire. They met in the parking lot at the truck to go back to the motel. On their way back, fire trucks blew past them, lights and sirens going, heading for the festival site.

Mandy commented, "I sure have seen a lot of fire trucks this trip. Of course, I have never been this far from home, so I don't even know if it is normal."

"It's Arizona, the place is so dry, sneezing wrong can start a fire," Allen replied.

Mandy said, "Oh," and looked out the window as they drove back to the motel.

HATCH, NEW MEXICO

EXHAUSTED, EMOTIONALLY, AND PHYSICALLY, ART PULLED IN TO A NO-name motel after dark. He had pushed himself to get this far since leaving the hospital, so in the morning, he wouldn't have to drive east, into the sun.

From his motel room, he called his lawyer in Wyoming, Roger Smith, to inform him of Belle's condition and ask for help with selling the ranch in Glenrock. When he and Belle had adopted Connie, they had set up a revocable family trust that included the ranch.

APRIL 13, 2014
FLORENCE, ARIZONA

The next morning, Allen and Mandy packed up their truck and prepared to leave the motel for the last day of the festival. The need for a real fire, a big fire, rode Allen hard.

"Mandy, wait in the truck, I'm going to do a quick check of the rooms before we leave. We don't want to forget and leave something behind," Allen directed.

In the suite they had stayed in, Allen set fire to the room he had slept in during their stay. His aftershave had a high alcohol content and made a significant accelerant along with alcoholic drinks from the mini-bar.

Mandy was unaware Allen had torched their suite as they headed off to the final day of Country Thunder. Mandy enjoyed the music festival immensely and planned on telling her dad the two fo them should go together next year.

After spending the last day at Country Thunder, Allen planned to drive as far as Benson before he stopped for the night.

TUCSON, ARIZONA

The drive from Tingle Creek to the Tucson Medical Center had been easy. No construction or accidents on the Interstate. And no construction on Kolb Road, when she got off the interstate.

At the hospital, Connie drove around the parking lot for a few minutes before she found a spot to park at the very edge of the lot. Connie hoped Belle would demonstrate some improvement when she saw her. Connie entered the hospital carrying a small CD player and went to Belle's room.

There, she set up the CD player and plugged in the USB drive with Belle's favorite music. She had been unable to sleep, so she had spent the night downloading a few classical music albums, The Best of Mozart and Greig's Peer Gynt Suite, and a few other light classical albums she had come across online.

She set the USB drive of music to play softly, on repeat. Then she sat and read to Belle. After an hour, she prepared to go home. She told Belle,

"I'll be back tomorrow. Get better. I love you, and I need you, and so does Art." She kissed Belle on the forehead.

FLORENCE, ARIZONA

Allen had an idea for the main stage at the festival. It would be spectacular when he executed it.

The headlining act had just finished when the very faint smell of smoke carried by the gentle breeze began to drift across the crowd.

The band's roadies were breaking down equipment when a roadie near the drum set yelled, "Fire! The stage is on fire! Call 9-1-1!"

The breeze strengthened, fanned the fire, and took the intensifying smell of smoke into the gradually dispersing crowd.

Allen couldn't hang around long after setting the stage on fire and hustled Mandy out to the parking lot. He said, "Come on, I want to get going before traffic snarls all up, and we sit in the parking lot forever."

The stampede of festival-goers fleeing to the parking lot began when the stage curtains erupted in flames.

"I want to get as far as I can tonight," Allen said. "I need to pay attention to traffic now." He wove the truck through the people running to their cars in the parking lot.

"I can drive some if you want. I have my learners permit, and you're an adult so that it would make it legal," Mandy said, as she tried to be helpful.

"I'm not comfortable with that, I didn't ask your dad if you were allowed to drive on the highway," he said.

APRIL 14, 2014
INTERSTATE 10 TUCSON, ARIZONA

They drove past a billboard announcing the Pima County Fair. April 17- 27, 2014 at the Pima County Fairgrounds on South Houghton Road as they approached Tucson.

It was after midnight, Allen was tired and cranky. It had been a long and satisfying day. "What the hell?" Allen muttered as he saw the sea of red brake lights ahead of him. Advancing sirens and flashing red and blue lights from behind him began to work their way up the left lane.

"Crap! Traffic is supposed to be easy this time of night!" Allen grumbled as he pulled as far to the right as he could without hitting the car next to him. The traffic backup had Allen looking for a way off the interstate. He finally made it off at the Speedway exit.

Mandy spotted a sign for the Arizona Sonora Desert Museum. "Can we go there tomorrow? Since we're taking two days to drive home, do we have time to stop there?"

"Sure, in the morning, right now, hotel and sleep," Allen said.

A few hours later, the sun was up, and so was Mandy. She was ready for her desert museum adventure. She packed and then had to wait for Allen. He woke up grumpy later that morning. He had wanted to enjoy his fire last night at the festival in Florence but had known that it wasn't wise to hang around.

They spent the whole day at the Arizona Sonora Desert Museum. Allen found he enjoyed the trip as much as Mandy. Once they got past the geological stuff and into the areas that had live animals, it was fun.

Mandy found the strange animals who lived in the desert enchanting. She could do without the snakes, scorpions, and spiders. Some of the other reptiles, like the horned lizard and desert tortoises, were interesting, but she loved the mammals and birds. The coyote pups, the pumas and bobcat kittens were cute!!

She almost danced after taking pictures of them with her phone. "This is so cool! Wait until I show this stuff to Dad!" Mandy exclaimed; happy. The aviary was cool. A hummingbird sat on her hand! At closing, there was still so much more to see. "Can we come back tomorrow for a little while?" Mandy pleaded.

"Sure," Allen replied, "What's one more day." They checked in to the Days Inn. There was a restaurant nearby for meals.

TUCSON, ARIZONA

AFTER LUNCH, CONNIE DROVE TO TUCSON TO SPEND A FEW HOURS WITH Belle again. She still had not regained consciousness. In talking with the nurse, Connie decided when she got home; she would read a book onto a USB drive so that Belle could hear her voice during the day. At night Belle could listen to music. If she asked, she was sure the nurses would change out the USB drives.

APRIL 15, 2014
HOSPITAL
DALLAS, TEXAS

IN THE EARLY MORNING HOURS, DAN BRADLEY WOKE FROM HIS COMA frantic, mumbling, then yelling, "Mandy! where's Mandy?"

The nurse who was still in his room after taking his blood pressure had to restrain him when he tried to pull out his I.V. as he tried to get out of bed. "Mandy!" he called.

The nurse pressed the call button for help and tried to calm Dan. "Sir, you need to calm down. You're in the hospital. You're badly injured. Lie still!"

"As soon as I see Mandy!" Dan replied as he fought to escape from his bed.

"Lie still or I will sedate you!" the nurse threatened as the on-call night doctor strode into the room.

"I need to see Mandy. I need to know my little girl is all right. Where is she?" Dan asked.

"I don't know who Mandy is," Dr. Swanson said. "Let me ask the other nurses if she has been in to see you."

When the doctor returned, he said, "Your only visitors have been firemen according to the floor nurse."

"Let me talk to the cops now! He has her. I know he does."

While he returned from the coffee machine, Paramedic Stan Hubbard heard the commotion from Dan Bradley's room. As soon as he walked into the room, he told Dan, "Settle down. Captain Murray has already reported Mandy missing. The police took a runaway report on her."

"She's not a runaway; he took her!" Dan insisted.

"I'll call the cops and tell them she's an abduction victim, not a runaway," Stan said.

"I know who took Mandy. He's the one who did this to me. I have his photo. I need my cell phone. His picture is on my phone," Dan carried on.

"Dude, calm down," Stan said. "You're hurt. You got hit on the head, shot and burned. He burned down your house, with you in it, and you're still alive. Mandy wasn't there."

"Mandy! What about Mandy? I need my cell phone," Dan demanded as his agitation increased. The doctor nodded to the nurse, and Dan was sedated. His strength ebbed as the sedative the nurse injected into his I.V. took effect.

Paramedic Stan Hubbard left Dan's room and contacted the officer who had taken the initial report on Mandy. He passed on what Dan had said about Mandy.

The officer initiated an attempt to locate (ATL) and had it sent out to Texas and neighboring states. Mandy's updated information was entered in the National Crime Information Center (NCIC), to include the new information provided by her father.

FBI OFFICE
DALLAS, TEXAS

AFTER HIS MORNING ARRIVAL IN THE OFFICE, FBI AGENT RAND HANSEN reviewed Dan Bradley's financials. He found the most recent credit card use in Florence, Arizona.

When he contacted the local police department, Rand learned the hotel where the card was used to rent a suite was also the scene of an arson fire.

Rand asked if they had a photo of the user of the credit card. The deputy he spoke to told him, "We're in the process of getting that right now. If the picture is any good, we'll send you a copy."

"Thanks, deputy, I appreciate it," Rand replied, then terminated the call.

TUCSON, ARIZONA

MANDY WOKE AS THE SUN CAME UP. SHE DRESSED, GOT PACKED TO LEAVE, then knocked on the connecting door to Allen's room.

Instead of opening the door, he said through it, "Go away. I have a migraine. I need to stay in a dark, quiet room. Too much sun yesterday at the Desert Museum."

"When are we going home?" Mandy asked.

"As soon as I feel better. Tell the receptionist we'll be here one more day. Please? You'll have to entertain yourself today, quietly."

Standing at the connecting doors, Mandy was surprised when he slid one of her dad's credit cards under the door. "Here, use this for meals today, I can't deal with anything," Allen said. "We'll go to the Desert Museum tomorrow, okay?"

Mandy walked to a nearby restaurant to eat. She paid her bill with her dad's credit card. At the register, she asked to have the bill increased by twenty dollars, so she had some cash in her pocket. The cashier was happy to comply.

Mandy's use of the credit card caused Agent Hansen to get a notice of its use in Tucson on his computer at the FBI office in Dallas.

GLENROCK, WYOMING

It was dark when Art got home. Without Belle or Connie with him, the place was lonely. After Caycee had passed away, they hadn't gotten another dog. Connie wasn't there to train it.

He was exhausted by his worry about Belle and the long drive. He hated having to talk to realtors, his lawyer, estate sale people, plus figuring out what to take and what to leave for auction without Belle's input. He needed to arrange for a cattle and horse auction as well. Any livestock not sold would stay on the ranch.

After a brief nap, Art called Connie so she would know he was home, in Wyoming. "It's going to take me a few days to take care of loose ends. How is Belle?" Art asked.

"No change, still unresponsive," Connie said. "The doctor says not to worry yet. It is still early days in her recovery. I made a recording of her favorite music to play in her room for her. I see her every day. Today I started reading her the book, 'Kinship With All Life,' by J. Allen Boone. It's one of her favorites."

Art sighed. "I miss her," he sniffed and wiped his nose, took a deep breath and said, "Enough with the mushy stuff. I'll call you when I leave here."

"Okay, Papa Art. I'll see Mama Belle tomorrow. I love you, too," Connie said, hanging up the phone.

APRIL 16, 2014
HOSPITAL
TUCSON, ARIZONA

THERE WAS STILL NO CHANGE IN BELLE'S CONDITION. CONNIE READ TO Belle for an hour while she held her hand. Before she left, Connie started up the music she had copied for Belle to listen to.

There were no guests at the B&B. Connie went on the website and closed it for the summer without consulting Jack. Since Kate died, he hadn't been able to decide what to wear, let alone run his business. She couldn't run the B&B either. They both needed time to deal with the deaths of their spouses without guests around.

APRIL 17, 2014
TINGLE CREEK, ARIZONA

SINCE IT WAS JUST THE TWO OF THEM, CONNIE SAW NO NEED TO RUSH Jack out of bed for breakfast. She wasn't sleeping much since Tom's death. Jack was sleeping a lot since Tom, and then Kate had died.

After breakfast, she took the dogs out for a long run in the back pasture. Afterward, the dogs flopped on the cool tile floor in the kitchen to supervise Connie when she called the hospital to check on Belle.

There was no change. Connie told the dogs, "I'm going to Tucson to see Belle after lunch. You be good for Jack while I'm there."

When Jack didn't show up for lunch, Connie went to his room, followed by the dogs and knocked on his bedroom door. She called through the door, "Jack? You going to want lunch?" When she got no answer, she opened the door. The dogs waited with her in the doorway.

Connie saw Jack was in bed, on his back and looked like he was sleeping, with one arm thrown over his eyes. But she didn't hear him snoring. He was a champion snorer.

"Jack?" Connie called from just inside the doorway. "Jack!" she said louder.

Still getting no response from him, she went to shake him. He was cool to the touch. Connie immediately checked for a pulse and found none. "Jack! Nooo! Not you too!" In tears, Connie left the room to go to the kitchen to call 9-1-1. She'd need a deputy to come out to take a report of his death. Then she'd have to wait for the funeral home to come to get his body.

She wasn't going to see Belle today, after all. She had to take care of Jack. She called Art and told him what was happening.

TUCSON, ARIZONA

AFTER A LATE BRUNCH, ALLEN AND MANDY LEFT THEIR HOTEL.

"So, I should be home sometime tomorrow, right?" Mandy asked. Allen had just merged onto the interstate when Mandy heard sirens approaching. Looking around, she saw fire trucks on the surface street heading in the direction of the hotel they just left. She thought it was odd how there was always one or more fire trucks on the way to a place they had just left.

"Depends on traffic, but with the late start today, more like the day after tomorrow," Allen replied.

Mandy took her phone from her purse. She texted her father when she thought she would be home. When she saw the red "undelivered" message below the text, it confused her.

They had been traveling for only twenty minutes when traffic on the interstate slowed way down. Allen slammed his hand on the steering wheel, "Now what? This is supposed to be a highway, not a damn parking lot!"

Traffic crawled until it got to Houghton Road. There all traffic was directed off the interstate and sent on a round-about detour before it returned to the interstate.

Allen was in the wrong lane on Houghton and traffic forced him to the parking area for the Pima County Fair.

PIMA COUNTY FAIR
TUCSON, ARIZONA

"Don't," Mandy said when Allen was going to pay for parking. "Tell him you just want to turn around."

"You don't tell me what to do! Deal with it!" Allen snapped. He paid, parked the truck, and stalked towards the entrance to the fairgrounds.

Surprised at his surly response, Mandy jumped from the truck and ran to keep up with him. She caught up at the fair entrance. He paid for a day pass for both to enter the fair. "I'll text you when I'm ready to leave," Allen told Mandy over his shoulder and stomped away from her.

She wanted to protest, but this was a new Allen. Different from the one she had left Dallas with. The longer they were traveling, the more Allen had changed. At loose ends, Mandy figured she might as well visit the ladies' room then she would hang around near the exit to watch for Allen.

After waiting a couple of hours, she was hot, tired, and hungry, so she went to a food truck and got a medium iced tea, a hot dog and a bag of chips. She sat in the shade against a nearby building to eat while she watched the exit. When she finished, she moved closer to the exit.

By late afternoon she wondered if Allen had dumped her at the fair and left without her. Upset by the thought, she retreated to the ladies' room.

Safely in the privacy of the empty ladies' room, at the sinks, she began to weep.

A few moments later, she heard a toilet flush. She wasn't alone. She looked and saw a uniformed Maley County deputy walk out of a distant stall. The deputy washed her hands a few sinks away from Mandy before she approached and asked, "Are you alright? Is there anything I can do to help you?"

"I don't know," Mandy got out between sobs. "Allen, the guy I'm with, said he had my dad's permission to take me to Country Thunder for our date..." She tried to slow down but couldn't. The rest came out in one long summary of her trip. "...But he only told me that after we left the house. When I left with him, I didn't know that, or I wouldn't have gone. I thought we were going to Denny's and a movie. Then I would go home —not this big long trip. And now when I try to call my dad, he won't answer the phone! I don't know what's going on. I want my dad. I want to go home!" Mandy began bawling.

Deputy Lujan put an arm around Mandy, "It's okay. You're with me, and I'll get you home. Let's get out of here and go over to the county fair office. We can get you sorted out over there." Mandy nodded her assent.

In the county fair office, Deputy Lujan had Mandy sit at a desk with her. Deputy Lujan put her note pad on the desk as she prepared to take notes. "Okay, what's your name, honey?"

"Mandy."

"Your full name and I also need your date of birth," Deputy Lujan clarified.

Mandy provided her details to the deputy who then used her cellphone to call her dispatcher and have Mandy run through the computer databases.

Mandy saw a box of tissues on a shelf and got up and helped herself to a few to mop her teary face. She threw her used tissues in the trash and grabbed a few extras.

When she was back in her chair, she saw the deputy suddenly straighten up, hold her notepad with the elbow of the hand holding the cell and start writing in her note pad. "I'll call you back," Deputy Lujan said into the phone, then disconnected.

"Where do you live, Mandy?"

"Dallas."

"How did you get here?"

"In my dad's truck? I had a date with Allen."

"Details, tell me everything, and I mean everything, even if you don't think it is important."

"Like I said, I thought we were going to Denny's and a movie and then back home. I was in the truck, . . ."

Deputy Lujan interrupted, "Describe the truck for me."

Mandy did. "It's my dad's gray 2013 GMC pickup. It's a four-door pickup."

"Do you know the license plate number?"

"I don't, no," Mandy replied.

"Okay, sorry, continue. . ."

"Anyway, we stopped at another car up the street, . . ." Mandy gave the deputy a complete rundown of the places she had been, what she had seen and heard, and her increasing distress at not being able to contact her father.

"I hope you don't mind, but you may have to tell all this to another deputy. Working here at the fair is my off-duty job, and it isn't even in my county."

Mandy started to tear up at that news. "Does that mean I can't stay with you until we reach my dad?"

"Maybe, I need to call my supervisor."

"I just want to go home to my Dad," Mandy said.

Allen was ready to leave and searched for Mandy around the food trucks shortly after she had gone to the fair office with Deputy Lujan. He was ready to go. Now.

He looked around the exit and didn't see Mandy anywhere. He walked a little way back into the fair and still not seeing her, walked past a cluster of dumpsters behind the food trucks. He threw in a lit cigarette.

He walked back to the exit and out into the parking lot to the pickup. He sent her a text, "parking lot, truck! now!" and waited.

He looked back towards the dumpsters. He was satisfied to see the thin trail of smoke that rose into the sky.

Patience at an end, Allen got in the truck when his text went unanswered, and she didn't show up at a run. He started the truck and waited.

There was still no sign of Mandy.

He drove slowly by the exit from the fairgrounds then left without her. It took time for him to get into traffic headed south on the detour from I-10.

With her Sheriff Barrett's permission, Deputy Lujan let Mandy stay with her in the county fair office until a relief deputy could arrive.

It took five minutes for Deputy Jesse Lopez to show up. "You got here fast," Deputy Lujan said.

"I was on my way home from Superior Court in Tucson," Jesse said. "Thanks for the off-duty hours. My bank account will love it."

Staffing levels maintained at the fair, Deputy Lujan and Mandy went to the deputy's truck in the parking lot. Radio traffic over the law enforcement radio increased while Deputy Lujan maneuvered out of the parking lot with Mandy.

They were leaving the fair when the sound of approaching sirens caught Mandy's attention. "Oh, yeah, it seems I keep hearing sirens and seeing fire trucks everywhere. What's that about?" Mandy asked Deputy Lujan.

"Right now, it's about the dumpsters behind food truck row being on fire," Deputy Lujan said. "Know anything about that?"

"No! My dad's a fireman! I would never do that!" Mandy was adamant. "I just thought it was strange how often it was happening while I was with Allen. He said it was because of a drought."

Deputy Lujan advised her dispatcher over her radio. An ATL needed to go out on Allen. "… with focus at and areas surrounding the fair for the next couple hours. He's to be considered armed, dangerous, unstable, and likes to set fires."

This was news to Mandy.

"Notify Dallas P.D. and FBI that Mandy is safe and I am taking her to the office for a statement," Deputy Lujan told her dispatcher.

FBI OFFICE
DALLAS, TEXAS

IN THE LATE AFTERNOON, RAND WAS NOTIFIED BY THE DALLAS POLICE Department that the car torched near the Bradley house was a stolen vehicle from Oklahoma City near a house fire believed to be arson.

In Oklahoma, the current theory was the fire had been set to hide the deaths of an elderly couple who were raising their grandson, now in his mid-twenties. The local police had been out several times in the past for domestic violence calls where the grandson was the suspect, but the grandparents had consistently refused to press charges.

INTERSTATE 10, EAST OF VAIL

ALLEN HAD JUST GOTTEN BACK ONTO EASTBOUND INTERSTATE 10 WHEN he saw the overhead sign. It warned of road work, blocking one lane at mile marker 317. Based on the mile marker given, it was miles away.

Guard rail replacement closer had traffic moving slightly faster than a tortoise as early evening traffic combined into one lane.

"Why damn it? Why! Move!" Allen shouted. He blasted the horn then slammed his palm against the steering wheel as he crept along in traffic.

When he saw a chance to get off at Marsh Station Road, he took it. He followed the signs to the small town of Tingle Creek, population 1342.

The information sign along the road listed a campground east of town, as well as a restaurant, gas pumps, and motel in town.

Allen went to the campground to claim a spot.

After he got his tent set up, he went back into town to eat. As he drove into town, Allen passed a house with the porch light on and a package on the porch. The house was close to the road. The angle of the setting sunlight was just right when combined with the porch light, to let Allen see the package on the porch.

He decided to keep an eye on the place. If no one were home, he'd break in and live there for a while. The night spent at Fenton Lake Campground had taught him he preferred to sleep indoors at night, away from all the bugs and not having to worry about wildlife when he heard a noise outside his tent.

TINGLE CREEK, ARIZONA

When Deputy Lujan arrived at the Sheriff's Department's substation, she began her paperwork. Mandy sat with her as she began typing her report into the computer. Then she recorded Mandy as she had her formal videotaped interview.

Mandy detailed all the places she and Allen had been and where she had seen fires or fire trucks.

After completing her report, Deputy Lujan forwarded a digitized copy of the videotaped interview to Dallas P.D. and the Dallas FBI office. Then, she took Mandy to the local diner for a very late supper for both of them.

HOSPITAL
DALLAS, TEXAS

Dan muted the ten o'clock news on his TV when the police officer entered his hospital room. He pushed the button to raise the head of the bed. "Mandy has been found, she's okay," the officer told Dan.

"Oh, thank God!" Dan felt like he could breathe easily for the first time since he had woken up in the hospital. "Where?"

"Tingle Creek, Arizona. She's with a female deputy who is taking her to a safe house until we can get her back here," the officer said. "We'll arrange for you to talk to her once she's settled. Probably tomorrow."

"Where's Tingle Creek?" Dan asked.

"Near Tucson somewhere," the officer responded.

"You said she's okay, but was she hurt at all?" Dan asked.

"As far as I know, she's unhurt, a little shaken and wants to get back home. She didn't run away and had no idea this wasn't just a date for the evening. We're still getting more details, so as hard as it is, you'll have to be patient a while longer."

Dan pressed the call button for the nurse. When he arrived, the officer left. "I need to get out of here. I have to get my daughter," Dan said.

"Take it easy, Mr. Bradley," the nurse said. "You just woke up. It will be a few days yet; your injuries need more time to heal before you can go anywhere. And it will take some time for your stamina to rebuild. Now get some rest, I'll be in to check on you again, later."

MESQUITE BED and BREAKFAST
TINGLE CREEK, ARIZONA

CONNIE HAD WATCHED THE TEN O'CLOCK NEWS FOR THE WEATHER report and just shut off the TV when she heard the lobby bell for the B&B ring. The closed sign was out there.

When Connie arrived in the lobby, she saw Deputy Lujan with a teenage girl.

Deputy Lujan said, "I know you're closed, and this has been a crappy couple of weeks for you, but it's an emergency. I need a place to stash Mandy until tomorrow. She's fifteen and a kidnapping victim I just got away from her abductor. You're my last hope for her before I have to take her to juvie in Tucson for the night. Can you help?"

Connie took a deep breath and let it out slowly before saying, "Of course, come in. Mandy, have you eaten supper?"

"Yes, LeAnne fed me at the diner in town, after I gave my statement," she said. "I won't be any trouble I promise. I'll help with chores, whatever you want me to do."

"That's not necessary. Besides, how could I not take you in?" Connie asked. "Twenty years ago, I was you."

"Really?" asked Mandy.

"Yes," Connie said. "We can worry about chores tomorrow after you've had a good night's sleep."

Connie led Mandy to the unused guest room, trailed by Deputy Lujan. Art and Belle's belongings were still in the other guest room.

Mandy took in the queen size bed, love seat, dresser and en suite bathroom, "It's beautiful. But I don't have any pajamas or anything. When I left, I left everything."

"I can give you a t-shirt and sweat pants to use as pajamas," Connie said.

"Can you stay with me, LeAnne? Please?" Mandy asked Deputy Lujan.

Deputy Lujan looked over at Connie, who said, "The loveseat is a hide-a-bed."

LeAnne said, "Sure. If it will make you feel better."

"It will. Thank you so much!" Mandy said.

Connie provided Mandy and LeAnne with similar outfits for substitute pajamas.

"Thank you," LeAnne said, taking the items from Connie.

"When should I be up in the morning?" asked Mandy.

"Whenever you wake up. I don't sleep much, so don't feel you have to get up if you hear me moving around. You need your rest. I'm sure you will have a big day tomorrow," Connie replied.

Mandy and LeAnne settled in for the night. "I am so glad you're staying with me," Mandy told LeAnne.

"Not a big deal. I've always wanted to spend a night here. Now I can. Now go to sleep," LeAnne said.

APRIL 18, 2014
TINGLE CREEK, ARIZONA

CONNIE LAID OUT A COLD BREAKFAST FOR HER GUESTS SO THEY COULD help themselves when they awoke. She wanted to get to Tucson early to talk to Belle's doctor this morning. Even though she saw Belle almost every day, she couldn't see any progress, and she hated telling that to Art.

THE ROAD TO TINGLE CREEK

Deputy Lujan was awake and getting coffee in the kitchen while Connie set up breakfast.

"LeAnne, I have to go to Tucson today, to talk to Belle's doctors. You guys help yourselves whenever you're ready to eat breakfast," Connie said. She showed the deputy the options: cold cereal, fresh fruit, yogurt, juice, coffee, or milk.

"Don't worry about us; we can take care of ourselves. I hope the docs have some good news for you soon," LeAnne said.

"Me, too," Connie said. "The dogs will be in their room or their yard and not bother you. Lock up when you leave, please," Connie said as she left.

Deputy Lujan was dressed in her uniform when Mandy finally woke late in the morning. She hadn't felt this refreshed since leaving Dallas with Allen. She liked how safe she felt here.

Mandy opened the curtains and saw their room had a private, west-facing patio with pillowed lawn chairs and a chaise lounge, a small gas grill, and a small yard that it was all enclosed with a four-foot-high block wall with a wrought iron gate that led to a walking path into the desert. It was perfect. A large mesquite tree shaded the whole patio area.

After breakfast at the B&B, Deputy Lujan brought Mandy with her to the Sheriff's substation in Tingle Creek for a second recorded interview that would be conducted by Sheriff Martin Barrett. When Mandy had completed the interview, Deputy Lujan sent a copy of the second recorded interview to the Dallas Police Department.

Dispatch buzzed her desk to advise her she had a phone message. Agent Randall Hansen from the Dallas FBI office had called about Amanda Bradley and her abductor.

Deputy Lujan called and gave Agent Hansen the details she had gotten from Mandy.

"Do we know if he's still in the area?" Agent Hansen asked.

"It's a good bet. There have been fires in Florence and the Tucson area where we know he's been. There has been a hay truck fire, but I don't know if that's him, but my gut feeling is, yes, he's still around," the deputy answered.

"I better get out there," Agent Hansen said.

Mandy was finished, emotionally, after her interview with the sheriff. She sat slumped in her chair while Deputy Lujan completed her paperwork.

Mandy looked forward to a nap when Deputy Lujan returned her to the B&B. She'd need it to recover.

CAMPGROUND
TINGLE CREEK, ARIZONA

IT WAS WARM WHEN ALLEN WOKE. OVERNIGHT THE TEMPERATURES hadn't cooled off like he had hoped they would. It was warming up fast today. The heat made him fidgety. Allen desperately wanted out of the campground. He had to be too careful around all these other people. He ate breakfast at his campsite and had to fight the urge to let his morning fire go big. Instead, he reluctantly put it out.

FBI OFFICE
DALLAS, TEXAS

RAND HANSEN CALLED PAUL GRANT IN TINGLE CREEK. "HEY, ANY recommendations for accommodations there or do I need to stay in Tucson? I have a kidnap victim in Tingle Creek that I need to go talk to."

"When I left the fire station this morning, the motel was closed for the summer for renovations. So, the only other place in Tingle Creek is the B&B. Tom's parents' B&B," Paul said.

"Crap," Rand said.

"Have you made any progress on who killed Tom?" Paul asked.

"No, not my case, but things are moving along," Rand replied, then asked, "Directions to this B&B?"

"You're flying into Tucson, right?" Paul asked.

Rand said, "Yeah."

Paul provided instructions from the airport, ending with, "If you get into town, you went too far."

CAMPGROUND
TINGLE CREEK, ARIZONA

Later, he wanted to cool off, so he drove into town to eat lunch at the diner. He saw the package still on the porch when he passed the house with the porch light still on. Curious, he pulled into the dirt driveway and parked in front of the garage. He walked around the house and saw no evidence of occupants. The only clear tracks in the dirt other than his own belonged to birds, rodents and other critters. He broke into the house through the back door. Inside, he flipped a light switch, happy the power was on. He found the thermostat for the air conditioner and set it down to seventy-six degrees. It began to blow cold air. He decided he was moving in that evening if the package was still sitting on the porch. He left the house and continued into town. He parked in front of the diner. It was an old railroad dining car that someone had converted into a restaurant. It was cool inside when he entered.

While he ate his burger and fries, he heard the old cowboys at the next table. When he first sat down, they were complaining to each other about the abnormal early heat. Then they began to compare tales they had told to the guests when the B&B used to be a guest ranch.

"My favorite is when I used to tell the kids about a cave with gold in it," the cowboy in a battered John Deere baseball cap said, laughing a little. "Their eyes would get so big. They wanted to search the caves for gold."

Another cowboy who wore glasses and a big white Stetson laughed, then said, "I liked telling the investment bankers when they were here, that there was gold to be found in the hill across the street. That the abandoned mine just needed someone with deep enough pockets to work it."

The old guys chuckled about the easterners and their dime-novel beliefs about the modern West. "Most of those easterners think it's still like those old John Wayne westerns out here. The early ones," said one old cowboy, then he laughed.

Allen listened to the loud conversations as he ate. Done eating, he paid his bill and returned to his truck. The breeze was warm.

On opening the door to the locked pickup, the heat billowed out of the vehicle and slapped him in the face as if he had opened an oven. Gingerly he sat inside and put his hands on the steering wheel.

"Damn! That's hot!" he shouted and quickly removed his hands from the steering wheel. Looking at the car next to him, he saw it had a towel draped over the seats and another over the steering wheel. He started the truck and let it run, giving the A/C a chance to cool down the vehicle.

While he waited, he spied a hay truck with two loaded trailers parked on a side street next to the diner. He left his running vehicle and went to the semi-truck. No one was with it, so he climbed up the trailer, lit a cigarette, and tucked it into a hay bale. He tucked another lit cigarette, into another hay bale on the second trailer, then got in his truck and left. He enjoyed the sounds of sirens when they started. He was the conductor of this siren symphony. He smiled.

APRIL 19, 2014
TINGLE CREEK, ARIZONA

IN THE PRE-DAWN LIGHT, ACE FINALLY MADE IT HOME TO THE B&B. He was scared, tired, injured, hungry, footsore, and underweight. He whined at the closed yard gate. When no one opened the gate for him, he did it himself. He entered the house through the doggie door into the dog room. He hobbled to the water pail and drank.

Magic heard a noise and launched from Connie's bed, growling. Misty followed right behind her. The sharp motions of the bed when the dogs leaped off and the growling woke Connie.

Magic's growl increased in volume as she raced to confront the intruder. Next, Connie heard a yelp. The growl turned to yips of excitement. Misty also barked happily.

Connie got up to investigate. The doggie door repeatedly flapped as the dogs exited and reentered the house.

In the dog room, Connie saw Ace was home and the cause of the commotion.

Ace had come home.

Magic and Misty licked at him, danced around him, whimpered and barked in excited greeting.

Overjoyed, Connie said softly, "Ace, am I glad to see you."

When she saw him cringe at her approach, she immediately stopped and sat on the floor and allowed him to come to her. "You poor baby. I missed you so much. Come on, let me have a look at you," Connie murmured to the skittish dog. Magic went to Connie, gave her a lick, and returned to Ace; Misty remained at his side.

Hesitantly, he belly-crawled the last few feet to Connie. He sniffed at her outstretched hand, gave her a lick on the knuckles, and moved up and settled his body along her leg, his head resting on her thigh. He let out a long sigh as he relaxed against her.

Connie gently stroked his head, then what she could reach on his body, as she said, "I am so glad you're home. My brave boy, getting yourself home."

She found his ribs were too prominent; he had a tender spot with swelling along his spine near his shoulder blades, he stank and was in very rough shape. From the way he lay against her, she could see the bottom of one foot. The pad was bloody and raw. "It's okay now, Ace; you're home. I'll take care of you," Connie murmured to the scared and malnourished dog as she continued to stroke his fur.

After some cuddling, Ace heaved himself to his feet and limped to the water pail for more water. He drank and drank and drank. He promptly vomited the water back up onto the floor.

Connie moved slowly so as not to frighten Ace. She got to her feet, took some old towels from a drawer, and put them over the water on the floor. "Easy, boy. You've got to go slow," Connie said as she lifted the pail of water onto a table out of his reach.

Connie got Ace a small bottle of Pedialyte from the mini-fridge. She poured a small amount into a puppy bowl and let him drink it in small increments until he finished the bottle. Once she was sure he would survive while she was on the phone, she called the vet. Connie described what she could see of his condition to the vet.

"Put on the coffee, I'll be there in a little bit," said the sleepy veterinarian.

Magic and Misty ran out of the doggie door to announce Doctor Larsen's arrival in her mobile vet clinic. Ace stayed glued to Connie as she went to invite the veterinarian into the B&B.

When the vet entered, Ace moved around Connie to keep her between him and Doctor Larsen. At the kitchen table, Connie poured coffee for the vet and herself. They drank slowly to give Ace time to remember and accept Doctor Larsen.

Doctor Larsen watched Ace as she drank her coffee, keeping one hand down at her side for him to smell.

S. GUETTER

"What do you know?" asked Dr. Larsen.

"Ace was with Tom in New Mexico when Tom got shot. I was told Ace ran off after falling. That was one week and three days ago," Connie sniffed and wiped her eyes. "I never thought I'd see Ace again. He just let himself in maybe fifteen minutes before I called you. I haven't been out to look, but I think he committed the ultimate no-no and opened the gate himself. Once in the yard, he came into the house through the doggie door."

"Okay, when he's ready we'll take him out to the clinic and check him over."

Ace was ready to accept the vet after her second cup of coffee was done. He licked her hand she held down at her side while she sipped her coffee.

Connie led him as they went to the mobile clinic. She stayed with him as the vet worked on him. When the vet finally finished treating Ace, Connie asked, "Staying for breakfast?"

"Sure, and thank you," Dr. Larsen said. "I'll be just a minute. I want to update his records before I come in."

Ace followed Connie and cowered when she closed the gate he had left open. She ignored Ace's distress and led the way into the B&B. Connie started making breakfast.

CAMPGROUND
TINGLE CREEK, ARIZONA

AFTER BREAKFAST, ALLEN PACKED HIS GEAR INTO HIS TRUCK AND DROVE to the house he planned to squat in. It was comfortable inside from the a/c as he dumped his things on the living room floor. He went through the cabinets as he inventoried the kitchen, taking note of what he would need to buy at the grocery store.

MESQUITE BED and BREAKFAST
TINGLE CREEK, ARIZONA

MANDY SLEPT MOST OF THE DAY. SHE SLEPT THROUGH BREAKFAST, AWOKE briefly for lunch and then went back to bed. Connie was okay with that. She had Ace to look after. She called Art to let him know she wasn't going to visit Belle. "I'll go tomorrow; I need to see how bad off Ace is and get him settled. I hope that's okay, Poppa Art," Connie said.

"I know how much your animals mean to you. It's okay. When you see Belle tomorrow, you'll have some good news to share with her," Art said. "Now go look after your boy." Art hung up.

TINGLE CREEK, ARIZONA

At lunchtime, Allen was back at the local diner using the free wi-fi. He sat at a back table as he nursed an iced tea, while he checked what was going on in the world on his cell phone. He enjoyed the dimly lit, quiet ambiance of the restaurant. It let him think. He checked on his fire in New Mexico. It was still uncontained. Yes!

After a while, Allen left the diner and drove around. He wanted to find the mine and the B&B he heard the old cowboys mention yesterday.

It was easy to find, west of town. Allen spotted the old mine on the hill across the street and east of the B&B. It was an excellent, high point to check out the surrounding area.

He parked his truck in a nearby wash, grabbed binoculars out of his duffle bag, and hiked up the hill to the mine entrance. Inside the mine, the shelter from the sun felt good.

Allen enjoyed the cool shade as he surveyed the surrounding area. He noticed the dry grasslands around the B&B. He looked over the B&B more closely and saw a gold-colored, full-sized SUV parked to the back and lots of fenced areas around it. After a while, he saw three dogs in the back fenced area, surrounded by a privacy fence. They didn't spend much time outside before they went back into the B&B.

After supper at the diner, Allen wandered around Tingle Creek, to get a feel for the place. He avoided walking past the town Public Safety Building. Allen took in the brush-choked wash and the paved walking path that ran parallel to the wash and behind the businesses on the main drag. He thought the wash could be promising for a future fire. He kept walking.

He came to an abandoned house with a few broken windows, some of them partially boarded up, with a weedy yard, and falling down wooden fence. To burn that down would be much more satisfying than another dumpster fire.

Allen broke into the empty old house. He was happy to see old furniture. He picked at an old couch and pulled some batting out of a torn cushion. He lit a cigarette and placed it into the batting. It caught quickly. He looked outside to make sure no one was around to see him leave.

He wanted to stay and watch but knew that was a bad idea, especially if anyone took pictures of the crowd. He would listen to the siren serenade when it started. He walked slowly back to his truck and drove over to the bar.

He sipped the beer he had ordered and heard the sirens as they started to howl. He relaxed and enjoyed his beer. His fire lived.

APRIL 20, 2014
TINGLE CREEK, ARIZONA

AFTER MIDNIGHT ALLEN RETURNED TO HIS SQUAT. THE A/C IN THE house was perfect, the shower refreshing, the bed comfortable. Allen slept soundly.

He got up late in the morning. He wandered into the kitchen in his shorts and looked for coffee for the fancy one cup coffee maker on the counter. Then he remembered he had forgotten to go shopping. He returned to the bedroom and dressed for his drive into Benson to grocery shop.

MESQUITE BED and BREAKFAST
TINGLE CREEK, ARIZONA

MANDY GOT UP EARLY FOR BREAKFAST WITH CONNIE AND WAS AMAZED at the dogs. "Where did they come from? They're so beautiful," Mandy told Connie. "I always wanted a dog. Can I pet them?"

"Let them come to you. Give the German Shepherd some room. He just got here. He's hurt and is still settling in," Connie said.

After breakfast, Mandy did the dishes before Connie could. Then she followed Connie around the rest of the day. Mandy helped Connie pack up the belongings Art and Belle had left behind in the other guest room.

Connie had no idea when Art would be back. Connie and Mandy hauled the sealed boxes and stored them in the vacant old bunkhouse behind the B&B.

TRUCKSTOP
BENSON, ARIZONA

AFTER HE HAD FINISHED HIS GROCERY SHOPPING, ALLEN STOPPED TO FILL the gas tank in his truck. He saw another hay truck while he gassed up the pickup. It was a spur of the moment thing. Allen lit and tossed a cigarette on top of the bales as he slowly drove by.

TINGLE CREEK, ARIZONA

ALLEN GOT BACK FROM BENSON IN THE AFTERNOON. AFTER HE PUT HIS groceries away, he didn't know what to do to entertain himself. He flopped on the couch and turned on the TV.

The screen flashed "Breaking News" followed by an announcement that Interstate 10 was closed in both directions at Mescal due to a hay truck burning in the median and dense smoke from the fire had reduced visibility to zero. His fire had flourished. He smiled.

MESQUITE BED and BREAKFAST
TINGLE CREEK, ARIZONA

AS CONNIE PUT SUPPER ON THE TABLE FOR MANDY AND HERSELF, SHE got a text from Paul. Two FBI agents would be over shortly to talk with Mandy. One of them was afraid of dogs. Connie put the dogs in their room, "Quiet," she ordered.

Connie and Mandy had just finished supper when FBI agents Rand Hansen and Stacey Baune followed Paul Grant into the parking area of the B&B in their rental car.

In the B&B kitchen, Connie told Mandy, "Since some guests might be afraid of dogs, I make sure no one knows we have dogs until I know how they feel about dogs. Understand?"

"I do. I won't tell," Mandy said.

"Since I'm not sure who this is, please go to your room. We can't be too careful. I want to keep you safe, okay?" Connie instructed.

"I'm going," Mandy said and went to her room. She locked the door once she got inside.

Connie met Paul and the FBI agents in the lobby, and he made the introductions. "Connie Sullivan, these are FBI agents Randall Hansen and Stacey Baune. Rand, Stacey, this is Connie," Paul said.

"Nice to meet you. I am so sorry for your recent loss. Tom was a good friend," Rand said, holding out a hand to shake Connie's. Her appearance saddened him. Tom's death had taken quite a toll on her. She was hollow-eyed and looked underweight.

Stacey stepped forward, "Nice to meet you, and thank you for letting us stay here. It's beautiful," she said.

"What?" Connie asked as she shook the agent's hand. She gave Paul a quizzical look. "I don't know what Paul told you, but I'm closed for the summer. I thought you were here to talk to Mandy."

"I didn't think you'd mind, they're FBI and here for Mandy," Paul said. "Besides, the motel in town is closed for renovations. If they don't stay here, they have to go to Tucson or Benson."

Connie heaved a sigh, then checked the FBI agents in. She observed Rand was as tall as Tom had been, but not as muscled. He had brown hair and dark eyes. Stacey had blonde hair long enough to put in a bun and had a fresh farm girl look. She had a sturdy build and looked like she could handle herself in a fight.

Connie gave them a brief tour of the B&B guest areas. In the hallway that led to the guest rooms, she said, "As I only have two rooms, you can either share a room or I can have Stacey bunk with Mandy."

Stacey said, "I'll bunk with Mandy as long as she doesn't mind."

"Okay, Rand, you'll be here," Connie said as she gave him a key and pointed at a door with a coyote plaque on it. Rand opened it, put his bag through the door, and closed it.

Across the hall, Connie knocked on a door with a roadrunner plaque on it. Mandy opened it a crack.

Connie asked, "Mandy, would you mind if FBI agent Stacey Baune stayed with you? She'll sleep on the love seat hide-a-bed the way Deputy Lujan did."

"I'm fine with that! I don't like being alone," Mandy said. Stacey brought her bag into the room and left it next to the love seat.

"The kitchen is down the hall," Connie said as she led the FBI agents on a quick tour. "This is the guest fridge. You can buy food for meals other than breakfast if you want. It should go on the shelf matching your room picture. If it isn't on your shelf, it isn't yours. You can cook in here, as long as you clean up after yourself. All of us share this area. Buffet breakfast is from 7:00 a.m. until 8:00 a.m. If you want to eat before or after that, you can fix something yourself."

Still walking, she led the group to a door marked "Private." She pointed out the doorbell mounted on the door frame. "This is where I live. Ring the bell if you need me and can't find me."

Back in the hallway between the guest rooms, Connie asked, "Any questions?"

Rand stepped into his room, turned on the light and surveyed it this time, and exclaimed, "That's a *dog* bed!" He pointed to the corner.

"Yes, it is. Every room has one, and outside is a dog run. It's for guests who may have dogs. That doesn't mean you have to use them. You can sleep in the people bed, it is allowed." Agitation caused Rand to miss the sarcasm that dripped from Connie's voice.

Paul and Stacey saw Connie was annoyed with Rand. In an attempt to keep the peace with Connie, Paul said, "Rand, maybe this was a bad idea. I am so sorry, Connie, but I think maybe this wasn't my best idea. I thought it looked like a good fit. I guess not. Stacey can stay here, and I can have Rand sleep on my couch."

"No, no it's fine," Rand said. "I'm sorry. I overreacted; not enough sleep in the last few days. The room is fine."

Stacey added, "He'll be fine, he's just a little jumpy when it comes to dogs. He's even jumpy when the canine team does their weekly bomb sweep at the office. He can hold it together around dogs. Just give him a chance."

Sleeping arrangements sorted, Rand and Stacey sat in the great room with Mandy. They sat in chairs that faced Mandy so they could ask her some questions.

"Can Connie stay too?" Mandy asked.

"That's up to her, if she wants," Rand answered. "I want to show you some pictures. You tell me if you recognize anyone, okay?"

Connie shook her head. She said, "I've still got chores to do. You'll be fine Mandy, Stacey is with you," and left the room.

Stacey changed seats to sit next to Mandy on the couch, as Rand laid out the photos he wanted her to look at on the coffee table.

"If you see anyone you recognize, let me know. If not, that's okay too," Rand said.

Mandy pointed to one out of the twelve men and said, "That's Allen."

"You're sure, no doubts?" Stacey asked.

"No doubts. That is Allen." Mandy was firm.

"You see any car he might have driven other than your dad's truck?" Rand asked.

Mandy described the old station wagon he had gotten his stuff out of near her home in Dallas. She pointed at the photos again and said, "He isn't shaving anymore. He looked like this when he picked me up. Now he's more scuzzy and rough looking."

"Thank you, Mandy, that helps a lot," Stacey said.

"Anything else you can tell us about Allen?" asked Rand.

"No. When can I go home?" Mandy asked.

"We need to talk about your father first," Rand said.

"What about my dad? Why won't he answer my calls or texts?" Mandy asked as tears filled her eyes. "Is he mad at me or something?"

Stacey hugged Mandy. "No, Honey, he isn't mad at you. He was hurt. He's in the hospital," Stacey explained.

Mandy began to weep, "What happened? I thought he was mad at me when I couldn't talk to him."

"He'll be okay; it's just going to take a while for him to heal. He lost his phone. He'll call us from the hospital in . . ." Rand checked his watch, "about another ten minutes."

Stacey stroked Mandy's back to soothe her. When Rand's cell rang, it was Dan Bradley.

After she got to talk to her dad, Mandy calmed down and so did Dan.

Plans were made with Stacey to get Mandy home later in the week. Dan wouldn't be released from the hospital for a few days so she might as well stay there. Plus, Dan needed to find a place for them to live since their house was burned down.

Allen was edgy. He needed a big fire, a real inferno, not the little ones he had set. Even the house fire had fizzled. He hadn't realized the house had adobe walls. The need gnawed at him and wore him down. He got in his truck and drove around in the dark.

He found the grasslands at the east edge of town was the best he could do at the moment. He scouted the area and found a derelict house that had a great line of sight into the grasslands. Perfect for taking out a firetruck or two. He parked behind the house and took his rifle up onto the roof of the dilapidated house and chose a place that would provide cover while he shot at firetrucks. He left the rifle up there.

Back on the ground, Allen lit the fire using a few road flares, then climbed to his perch on the abandoned house. The position was perfect for simple shots at the firefighters' equipment as they fought the grass fire.

Allen waited, prone on the roof of the abandoned house, his rifle at the ready and a handful of extra shells at his elbow. It took a while for the fire to build enough to be seen and reported.

When he heard the approaching sirens, he felt high as his adrenaline flowed. He slapped his hands on the roof with excitement. Soon red lights strobed the night as the approaching sirens announced the fire trucks that raced to the scene.

The brush truck, a four-wheel-drive flatbed with a pump, hose reel and water tank, arrived with the large water tanker truck right behind it, followed by the fire engines. Allen watched the firefighters set up. When the water began to discharge from the fire hoses, Allen picked his targets.

As the firefighters arrived and fought the grass fire, Allen followed their activity through the rifle scope. "Where to start," Allen mumbled to himself. "This is gonna be fun!"

He fired at the water tank on the brush truck and missed it. He tried again — another miss. His first hit went into the pump on the front bumper of the brush truck. He missed two more shots and reloaded. His second hit nicked the hose from the tanker truck to the fire engine.

An even larger tanker truck lumbered onto the scene. Allen's hands shook from excitement, and he missed the next few shots. The next hit went into the little water truck near the base of the tank.

The shots created mayhem amongst the firefighters as they tried to compensate for the equipment failures. One firefighter even looked around, suspicious.

Allen giggled as he watched them scurry around. He pulled the trigger again and hit an unlucky firefighter right in the shoulder. The man spun to the ground. Panicked firefighters ran to the injured man to pull him to shelter behind the engine and render aid. Allen enjoyed the confusion he caused by shooting at them. His last shot went through the windshield of the newest tanker that had arrived.

Then the cops began to arrive — that was Allen's cue to leave. Once off the roof of the old house, Allen had to do quite a few jumping jacks to burn off the adrenaline. He hid the rifle behind the back seat of the pickup before he sedately drove into town to the bar.

The taciturn barman was efficient at keeping the nuts bowl full, and the bar wiped down. Allen sat quietly at the end of the bar and sipped his beer. He jumped when a drunk guy with a greasy gray ponytail down his back slammed his hand flat on the bar.

The drunk yelled, "I said I would get the money for you and I will!" into his phone. He slammed his hand flat against the bar again, as he tried to emphasize his comment to the person on the other end of his call.

"Keep it down or leave," the tall, rail-thin barkeep advised the inebriated man. The drunk waved his acknowledgment at the bartender and continued his conversation at a lower volume. Allen could tell from his slightly slurred speech he was intoxicated.

Allen went back to scrolling through his phone, looking for news of his latest fire while trying to blend in with the other patrons of the bar.

APRIL 21, 2014
TINGLE CREEK, ARIZONA

When the bar closed at 1:00 a.m., Allen drove out to see how things were going with the brush fire east of town. It was another disappointment. The winds had dropped off. The grass fire was almost contained — Allen needed a sure thing fire.

He broke into the house he had used as his shooting perch earlier in the evening. He took his time, and he ensured this house was combustible. He had the privacy he needed.

The next-door neighbors had a wooden fence.

He prepared the house to burn. He laid a trail of dried weeds and twigs from dried up trees on the abandoned property back to the derelict domicile.

When everything was ready to his satisfaction, he set his delayed fuse of a lit cigarette leading to petroleum jellied cotton balls in the twigs and brush. He would be safe at "home" when it went up in flames. He would have to let the sound of the sirens be enough tonight.

He fell asleep after the concert of sirens had ended.

GRANT RESIDENCE
TINGLE CREEK, ARIZONA

PAUL GRANT WAS SITTING WITH HIS WIFE, DR. SHARON GRANT AT THEIR kitchen table. They were enjoying their first coffee of the day as they waited for the sun to rise over the mountains to the east. It was barely 6:00 a.m. when his cell rang. Checking the number, he saw it was Rand and answered it.

"It's our lucky day. I know who shot Tom. Now I just need to find him. The same asshole shot his grandparents in Oklahoma, then a firefighter in Dallas before Tom," Rand said. "And get this, the grandfather was a firefighter in Oklahoma City."

"So, this scumbag is targeting firefighters? Any idea why? And where he is now?"

"None and I don't know, other than probably nearby," Rand replied.

Rand heard Paul's pager go off. "All off duty firefighters report to the station. This is an all-call. All off duty firefighters report to the station," the dispatcher said.

"Gotta go!" Paul hung up on Rand, kissed Sharon goodbye and raced out the door to his pickup.

MESQUITE BED and BREAKFAST
TINGLE CREEK, ARIZONA

IN THE EARLY MORNING, CONNIE WAS OUT IN THE GARDEN BEHIND THE barn and out of sight of the B&B with her dogs. Ace stayed close to her not willing to be far from her side. Magic and Misty ran around the fenced ten acres, scaring the jackrabbits.

The sun was almost ready to peek over the mountains. Connie had just stretched out her first 100 feet of a garden hose when she smelled wood smoke mixed with something less appealing and more chemical like in smell. Facing into the breeze, she saw a thick column of billowing, dense, black smoke backlit by the sun as it poured into the morning sky from the direction of town. She was thankful the fire was so far away as she laid out the next hose. Every time she finished a line, she checked the smoke from the fire. With the stiff breeze, she hoped the fire was contained quickly. This kind of weather was the kind that could burn out a town if not stopped.

Finished in the garden, she took the dogs inside and fed them in their room. She made sure the doggie door slide closed the canine exit into the yard — no need to have them seen and scare Rand.

After Mandy woke and dressed, she found Connie setting up breakfast in the kitchen. Mandy asked, "You want any help?"

"Sure," Connie replied.

A loud, deep, resonant boom made both Connie and Mandy jump. Ace bolted from the dog room to Connie. He whimpered and leaned hard against Connie's legs, almost knocking her over. She bent to comfort him. Magic and Misty followed Ace to Connie.

"What was that?! And where were they hiding?" Mandy asked as she pointed at the dogs. "I looked for them earlier."

"They stay with me in my room or in their room that has access to a private yard through a doggie door. Remember, Rand's nervous around dogs, so we hide them and don't say anything, okay? Can you keep the secret?" Connie asked.

"Oh, yes, no problem," Mandy said. She smiled at the idea of hiding things from the FBI. Her eyes sparkled as she nodded her acknowledgment.

"In answer to your other question, there's a fire in town," Connie pointed, and Mandy turned to look out the picture window of the great room.

Black smoke billowed in a thick, dark column into the sky. After a few minutes, grey smoke mixed with the black.

Connie calmed Ace and led him and the other dogs back to their room and ordered them to stay. Ace, Misty, and Magic all touched noses.

When Connie returned to the kitchen, Mandy had three place settings out, with napkins.

"Thanks for doing that, Mandy," Connie said.

Rand and Stacey had a tasty breakfast prepared by Connie with Mandy's help. The dogs stayed quiet throughout the meal, and Rand remained unaware of the dogs in the B&B. After she had finished eating her breakfast, Mandy left with Rand and Stacey for Tucson.

They were going to the FBI office for a formal recording of Mandy identifying Allen as her abductor. That would allow more research into Allen's background. Now they had a suspect in the firefighter shootings.

At mid-morning, a FedEx Ground delivery truck arrived at the B&B. Her once a month delivery of dog food and treats. The driver asked Connie, "Did you hear the explosion all the way out here?" He unloaded her boxes from his truck onto his hand truck.

"Yes, it made me jump," Connie said.

"House fire in town. The propane tank exploded," the driver informed Connie.

"Ouch. Anyone hurt?" Connie asked.

"Not that I heard. Do you want these on the back porch like always?" the FedEx driver asked. He had stacked four large boxes onto his hand truck.

"Yes. Please. I can carry the bags into the house and break the boxes down from there," Connie said.

Delivery complete, the driver roared off to his next delivery address.

Connie opened the large boxes and took the bags containing treats into the dog room. She came back and one at a time dragged the 30-pound bags of dog food into the dog room and leaned them against a wall. Later she'd pour one into the airtight container she used for dog food.

She flattened the used boxes for subsequent use. She carried them out to the metal shed and added them to the stack near where the RV was parked. She let the dogs accompany her and let them stay out to play in their yard.

When the dogs came into the B&B, she locked Ace in his kennel with a dirty t-shirt of hers to keep him company while she was in Tucson. She called Sharon to have her stop to check on Ace while she was gone. "I have to go see Belle, I've missed so many days already," Connie said.

TUCSON, ARIZONA

WHEN SHE GOT TO THE HOSPITAL, BELLE'S CONDITION HADN'T CHANGED. It was so hard to see someone she knew to be such a vital person look so old and infirm. She read to Belle for an hour as she held her hand before she returned to Tingle Creek.

Rand and Stacey spent the day in Tucson to collect background on their suspect, Benedict Allen Stout IV. They also pondered how to find their suspect. Was there a safe way to draw him to them?

Mandy talked with a victim advocate and a therapist to learn how to cope after her ordeal while Rand and Stacey worked the computers and phones.

As a treat, the three of them went out for pizza before they returned to Tingle Creek.

MESQUITE BED and BREAKFAST
TINGLE CREEK, ARIZONA

LATE IN THE AFTERNOON, PAUL STOPPED BY TO VISIT RAND BEFORE HE went in to work. They sat in Rand's room. Paul said, "Compared to previous years, we're having way more fires than we should, even with the drought. And this is the first time we've been shot at when we respond to a fire. It happened last night."

"Can you show me where?" Rand asked.

"I'm working a half shift today, from 6:00 p.m. to 6:00 a.m. Then I have two days off," Paul said.

"Know anyone with a metal detector? Maybe we can find the bullets," Rand said.

"I'll ask around at the station," Paul said as he rose to leave.

"Tomorrow we take Mandy into Tucson for a grand jury deposition about her kidnapping. So, day after tomorrow, in the morning?" Rand asked.

"Yeah," Paul said and left.

APRIL 22, 2014
TINGLE CREEK, ARIZONA

CONNIE FED HER GUESTS AN EARLY BREAKFAST. THEN THEY LEFT AS SOON as they finished. They didn't plan to be back until suppertime. The dogs could run today.

Connie finished her first glass of iced tea for the morning, the dogs at her feet in the kitchen. "You want to go out?" she asked them. The dogs ran to the porch door and waited for her to open it, rather than use the doggie door from their room into the yard.

As she walked to the shed, she heard, then saw the low flying helicopter as it left Tingle Creek Hospital on a flight path to Tucson. Connie briefly prayed for the occupant of the medivac helicopter to quickly recover from their injury or ailment.

Accompanied by the dogs, Connie went to the large metal building that housed the tractor, a boat on its trailer and Jack and Kate's RV. There, she taped together old boxes the dog food had arrived in, so she could begin to pack Jack and Kate's stuff. She wasn't ready to pack Tom's things yet.

Connie was taping the bottom of her fourth box when Magic gave her Akita yodel and Misty her happy yips that let her know someone was at the B&B. Someone they recognized and liked. They raced for the gate.

Ace leaned against her legs, shaking. She calmed Ace. With the insecure dog glued to her side, she walked through the yard to the gate.

The first vehicle she saw when she got closer to the house was the fire truck as it loomed over the height of the privacy fence. She suspected Paul Grant was on the fire truck. When she got closer to the gate she saw next to it was a blue Ford Explorer. She knew it belonged to her friend Dr. Sharon Grant.

Waiting at the yard gate was Paul Grant, in his firefighter uniform and his wife Sharon, her best friend, almost her only friend since her husband died. Now she was a widow; most of the people she had thought were her friends were just too busy to stop by and visit. When someone did stop by, she made every effort to not wallow in grief at her loss.

Connie waved to them as she walked to the gate. She saw Sharon cradled a shoe-box against her chest, out of dog reach. Connie opened the gate to let Paul and Sharon into the yard before closing the gate again.

"Is Rand here?" Paul asked.

S. GUETTER

"No, he and Stacey left for Tucson while it was still dark. They took Mandy with them," Connie said.

"Good. Remember I told you Rand is terrified of dogs? I think anything canine larger than a mouse would have him airborne. I never knew that about him before. I knew he got a little nervous around dogs, but I didn't know that dogs made him panicky."

"Yeah, it's a good thing he hasn't noticed my pack yet," Connie almost grinned as she glanced at her three dogs.

Misty was first to notice the shoe-box. She tried very hard to get a sniff of what was inside. She stood on her back legs, front legs gently placed on Sharon's thighs for balance and reached out with her nose to inhale deeply.

Connie immediately corrected her, "Misty! Feet down!"

Misty promptly removed her front feet from Sharon's legs but stayed balanced on her back feet a moment more, getting in one more deep sniff before she dropped to all four feet.

Paul petted Magic and Misty. He stayed out of the delicate negotiations over the contents of the shoe-box. Ace wouldn't come to him. He opted to stay glued to Connie's side.

It made Paul sad to see the once confident and happy dog so apprehensive and unsure of himself.

Sharon held the box close and up, out of reach of Magic who approached and remained on all four feet while she reached out with her nose and sniffed at the carton.

"I know right now isn't the best time to foster motherless pups, but no one else will take them. I don't know why everyone is so afraid of dogs when they are puppies this young. Close to five weeks, I think," Sharon said. She opened the box to reveal two small black puppies that would fit in Connie's hand.

Connie reached into the box, stroked the head of one tiny pup and then the other. "What happened to Momma dog? And the owner?" Connie asked as she continued to stroke first one pup then the other.

"Rattlesnake," Paul said. "According to the paramedic, Joyce, she asked for you to care for them as she was loaded into the ambulance."

In the yard, Sharon led the group to the shade of the shed, where she handed the box to Connie. "They're Schipperkes, two sweet little girls," Sharon explained.

Connie took the box. "No one at animal control would take them?"

Paul said, "Deputy Sandoval said County Animal Control is on a hoarding case somewhere past Willcox. They'll be busy all day and overcapacity when they get done. When Sandoval found that out, he called me. Since the helicopter pad at the hospital is near the fire station, Deputy Sandoval asked me to meet Joyce and the ambulance there. That way, I could pick up the pups while the patient went to the hospital in Tucson."

"Why a hospital in Tucson?" Connie asked.

"The patient needs anti-venom treatment for the snake bites since she got bitten several times. She was trying to save her dog and the puppies. I called Sharon to meet me and take custody of the pups. I didn't want to risk taking them. If I got called out, they risked sitting the truck for hours," Paul replied. "If Sharon had them at least then I could be sure they would get to you safely."

While the women negotiated the care of the pups, Paul wandered into the large metal shed and leaned on the bucket of the bright red International 460 parked next to Jack and Kate's thirty-plus-foot RV.

Tom had kept all his equipment in tip-top shape and had used the bucket to level the dirt road to the B&B as soon as the driveway got the least bit bumpy. When Tom was alive, he had let Paul drive it once on the property. Paul had loved it. He wanted that tractor.

Paul put his attention back on the conversation between Sharon and Connie.

"I don't know," Connie said as she continued to stroke the pups with a finger. "With all the lawyer crap and doctor shit for Belle. With trying to get three estates settled. God help me," she swiped at a tear trying to drop from her eye. "Who knew it was so hard to deal with the legal stuff after someone dies? I don't know if I can give them the care and attention they need. At any other time, I'd say yes, no hesitation, but I don't know. The B&B is closed, and somehow, I currently have a full house."

The puppies began to squirm and whimper a bit. Not quite awake and demanding food, but working up to it. That did it for Connie. She blew out a breath and said, "Okay, I'll take them. You know I am such a pushover when it comes to puppies in need."

Paul reinforced to Connie, "You know of all the animal shelter's foster moms, you're the best with tiny puppies. And in a few weeks, they'll be ready for adoption. Everybody wins." He smiled. "I've got to get back to the firehouse."

Sharon followed her husband as they left the yard.

Connie's dogs continued to try to smell the contents of the box.

"Puppies," she told her dogs, "be nice." She lowered the box to nose level for her dogs.

The puppies started to yip and squeak. "They're hungry," Connie said. She hurried to the house with the pups, dogs following.

By the time she had gotten into the dog room with the pups, they had pottied in the box that held them. She got them an old t-shirt from her dog rag bag. It was full of old soft towels and t-shirts that she washed and reused for raising pups. She prepared a small kennel for the puppies to go into after she washed them. The squalling grew louder as they demanded food.

In the parking area of the B&B, Sharon gave her husband a long hug before they went their separate ways. Sharon worried, "She looked so tired and worn out. Those dark circles under her eyes keep getting darker, and I think she's lost more weight. I'm concerned about her. And I don't know what more I can do for her."

Paul held his wife in his arms as he returned the hug. He said, "She does look rough. She's been looking worse and worse since Tom died, and now with Belle in the hospital. It's a heavy load to carry. If it had been just Tom, I think she'd be adapting more by now. I don't know. I was hoping that having people at the B&B would help. Ace looked rough, too. I'm so glad she has him back."

"Is she even back to work dispatching?" Sharon asked.

"She's not working right now. The Sheriff put her on bereavement leave when Tom died," Paul said. "He extended it when Kate died and again when Jack died."

"But still, the stress, it's so much work," she shuddered. "It's like the pressure just won't let up. I don't know how much longer she can keep this up. At some point she has to rest, face everything that's happened and recover before she can hope to move on," Sharon said. "I'm her doctor, and I feel so useless to her right now."

"When she does collapse, you'll be there for her," Paul consoled his wife.

When she had the puppies clean and safe from big curious dogs, she prepared puppy formula. She poured the milk-substitute powder into two small bottles she plucked from a shelf over the small sink in the dog room.

She added water and shook them vigorously. She made enough formula to fill both bottles. She pulled an additional bottle from the shelf and made some extra formula to mix with and soften kibble into mush.

The pups were tiny in size, no bigger than her small hands, but the volume of noise they generated when hungry was ear-splitting. As soon as she got the bottles and mush ready, she set the food on the table next to her recliner. She grabbed the pups out of their kennel and sat, both puppies in her lap and put a bottle in each of their mouths. Ace immediately leaned against her legs. Magic and Misty lay nearby.

There was contented silence as they ate. When the puppies finished their bottles, Connie put a little mush on her fingertips and offered it to the pups. After some consideration of this unaccustomed food, they tentatively licked it off her fingertips. They enthusiastically ate the little bit more she offered them.

"You only get a little this time, we're gonna start you slowly, so no one gets an upset tummy," Connie explained to the pups as they nibbled the mush.

The big dogs supervised Connie as she fed the tiny pups. When the dogs came to sniff the new arrivals, Connie said, "Puppies. Be nice and easy. Leave it." The big dogs knew no picking up the pups with the "leave it" command and to be very gentle when ordered to "be nice and easy." The big dogs had experienced Connie foster puppies before and understood the rules.

Magic gave each of the puppies a welcoming lick then flopped next to Ace at Connie's feet. Misty stretched out on the tile floor with a groan, belly on the cool tile and back legs spread out behind her like a parody of a flat frog.

When they finished eating, Connie took the pups outside for a potty break before she put them in their new kennel for a nap.

APRIL 23, 2014
TINGLE CREEK, ARIZONA

CONNIE CALLED ART TO DISCUSS BELLE. "HER CONDITION HASN'T changed," Connie reported. "I don't know what to think. Also, I can't go for a few days. I hope that's alright?"

"Why not?" asked Art.

"Sharon dropped off two foster puppies too young to be away from their mother, but the mother is dead. I have to feed and potty them every ninety minutes. In a couple of weeks, I can visit Belle every day again," Connie said. "How long until you can come back?"

"I don't know exactly. But, as soon as I can, Honey," Art said.

"I miss you so much, Papa Art," Connie said.

"I miss you too, Sweetie. Now, I have to go," Art said. Connie held the phone to her chest for a few moments, even though the call was no longer connected.

ABANDONED MINE
TINGLE CREEK, ARIZONA

FROM HIS HIDDEN PERCH IN THE MINE ENTRANCE ON THE HILL EAST OF the B&B, Allen spent the afternoon watching the B&B again. He had decided to keep a low profile after the last fire he had set. Observing the B&B was as good a way as any to spend his days. He was sheltered and comfortable as he sat inside the mine entrance.

Through his binoculars, he saw a woman go out with the three big dogs, and now she had two small critters she put in the grass separate from the dogs. That was new from the routine Allen had seen previously. In less than fifteen minutes, she picked up the small critters and went inside. The dogs followed. Ninety minutes later, she was outside again. She followed the same routine as the last time. Curious, he wanted to see better what she was doing. He wondered what the small critters were that she kept separate from the dogs. Kittens? He needed a telescope.

FIRE STATION #1
TINGLE CREEK, ARIZONA

VETERINARIAN DR. LARSEN STOPPED BY THE FIRE STATION TO PROVIDE the Chief with her evaluation of the department's accelerant detection dog, Ace.

"Chief, physically, Ace is in rough shape, but he's coming along with Connie's meticulous care. Mentally, he's a mess. Everything scares the crap out of him except Connie. She's his anchor. We have to remember; no one knows what happened to him. I want him to stay with Connie as right now he needs a security blanket, and she's it. He'll need time. I suggest we wait for about six months and see where he's at then."

The veterinarian was firm with her decision, so the Chief grumbled his assent with the plan.

MESQUITE B and B
TINGLE CREEK, ARIZONA

RAND, STACEY, AND MANDY CAME HOME FROM TUCSON AFTER DARK. They had eaten supper in Tucson before leaving for Tingle Creek. Stacey and Mandy went into the room they were sharing.

Restless, Rand went looking for Connie. He wanted to see her. More accurately, he needed to see her. He roamed the B&B as he searched for Connie. He knew she was here somewhere, but he couldn't find her.

Rand hadn't seen her since yesterday or was it the day before? He'd been so busy he couldn't remember. Rand wondered where she was and why she stuck in his head the way she had.

He was sorry now that he hadn't made the time to visit the many times Tom had invited him. He'd always thought there was time, later, to meet Tom's wife. Strange it bothered him now, but not then. Maybe it was meeting Connie for the first time as Tom's widow, not Tom's wife.

APRIL 24, 2014
TINGLE CREEK, ARIZONA

PAUL PICKED RAND UP FROM THE B&B AFTER BREAKFAST TO GO TO THE brush fire scene at the edge of town. Paul pointed out the small flags on metal stakes that marked where all the trucks were when the bullets flew. Paul then pointed out to Rand the house that had burned in the early hours of the next morning, explaining how big it had been as now it was just a charred heap on a cement slab.

Rand took in the sightlines from where the house was and its size before burning. "That would be the perfect spot to shoot from," he said. "Were you able to get a metal detector?"

Paul opened the shell on his pickup and removed the device. "Got it right here."

"Okay, let's get started," Rand said. They took turns sweeping the metal detector over the ground and digging up the spots where the machine beeped.

ABANDONED MINE
TINGLE CREEK, ARIZONA

ALLEN WAS BACK IN THE MINE AFTER BREAKFAST. HE LIKED TO WATCH the B&B. He was still trying to figure out what the small critters were that the woman kept bringing outside.

They moved around the small area she had fenced off for them. They only stayed out for a little while before being taken back inside. But they were out almost every ninety minutes according to Allen's watch.

The next time the black critters were outside the woman had company. Two other people were with her. He recognized one of them was Mandy! The other woman he didn't know.

The conniving bitch! Mandy had to die by fire. It was the only way to keep fire his friend. She had to pay for her callous extinguishment of his fires when they had camped out.

He wondered how in the world did she get there? She knew who he was, so she had to die. The B&B would have to be his next fire. Then he would need to leave town.

Rage flooded him; he didn't like it when other people dictated to him what he would do and when he would do it.

He studied the construction of the B&B through his binoculars. He figured out what he thought would guarantee the B&B burned to the ground. He was going to need to burn the house he was squatting in to ash, as well. It would be a good diversion for the fire department while the B&B burned.

MESQUITE B and B
TINGLE CREEK, ARIZONA

MANDY AND STACEY MARVELED AT THE SCHIPPERKE PUPPIES. "THEY'RE so tiny," said Mandy. "I keep asking Dad for a dog, but he says I have to wait until I graduate from college. To get one now wouldn't be fair to the dog."

"I always wanted a dog, but my job just makes it unfair for me to get one," Stacey said. "You do know if Rand sees any of these dogs he is going to freak completely out, right?" Stacey asked Connie.

"Yes, I know. But there's no reason for Rand to know. You wouldn't know if I didn't allow you to see them," Connie said as she cleaned up after the pups.

She let them play with each other as she and her company sat in the shade of the large mesquite tree that sheltered the yard. Magic and Misty flopped down next to the women for petting; Ace had remained glued to Connie's side.

When the pups were tired, she took them in the house and put them in their crate to curl up and nap. Her scent on the t-shirts kept them calm, and she napped when they did. Exhaustion was her constant companion and had been since before the puppies had arrived. With puppies as young as these, she had to get what little sleep she could, and she slept when they did.

With the puppies asleep, and Connie preparing to take a nap, Stacey and Mandy left for Tucson. Mandy had to continue her testimony in front of the federal grand jury against Benedict Allen Stout IV. The charges against him were for kidnapping, arson, auto theft, and identity theft for using Dan Bradley's credit cards.

Mandy hadn't witnessed the shooting of her father and the subsequent house fire. She was unable to provide any information to the jury about that. She was able to tell the grand jury he had gone back into the house while she sat in the truck.

ABANDONED MINE
TINGLE CREEK, ARIZONA

WHEN HE COULD LEAVE THE MINE UNSEEN, ALLEN RETREATED TO HIS truck and headed to Tucson for supplies to incinerate the B&B.

TUCSON, ARIZONA

AT A SHOPPING MALL NEXT TO A BIG CAR DEALERSHIP, ALLEN FOUND A truck that looked identical to Mandy's dad's truck. The paint on the outside and the colors of the interior were an exact match. He swapped plates with it. He now had Arizona plates on the stolen truck he was driving. That done, he drove out and went looking for a Home Depot or another mall.

He needed someplace with a massive, full parking lot with lots of activity, but where no one was paying attention to other people in the parking lot.

He found a Target, in a large strip-mall with a full parking lot. A furniture store was holding a promotional event. They had all kinds of furniture out in the parking lot on display.

A roped-off area at the front of the strip-mall forced people to park further away from the store entrances and walk through the lot. There were plenty of people who moved around in the parking lot. It was perfect. He parked his truck around the side of the strip mall, in the shade from the building, away from the celebration in front of the furniture store.

He parked, pulled on a ball cap and sunglasses before taking his trusty straightened wire hanger with him as he went looking for an old pickup. He had to love Tucson for that. So many people kept their "vintage" trucks that didn't have ignition lock-outs on the steering wheel. It made them so easy to borrow.

He found an early 1960's era Ford F-100 pickup that had seen better days. He had it unlocked and hot-wired in seconds. He checked the gas gauge and saw his first stop had to be a gas station. It would only need a few gallons for him to complete his shopping.

He planned to return the truck as soon as he was done running his errands. He was going to get hot, as there was no air conditioning in the old truck. It ran, and that was what was necessary. He took a chance and turned on the radio. He hadn't expected it to work. The antenna was a wire coat hanger. He was delighted when clear country music poured out of the speaker. He hummed along with a song he recognized as he eased the truck out of the lot and into traffic.

He gassed up the stolen pick-up, his way of paying a rental fee to the owner for the use of the pick-up. After the gas station, he went to a mom and pop auto supply store for road flares, a chain drug store for large containers of petroleum jelly for coating clothesline, then a big box hardware store. There he purchased six full propane tanks for a gas grill, several hundred feet of cotton clothesline, a pallet of bags of fertilizer and four 5-gallon gas cans. Next stop another gas station to fill the gas cans with diesel before he returned to his truck. He parked next to his truck and transferred all his purchases into the truck bed of his pickup.

He was unhappy that he had to be the one to throw the pallet's worth of fertilizer bags from one truck bed to the other. It was hot, sweaty work, but necessary if he wanted to stay under the radar.

When he had it emptied, he parked the borrowed truck at the opposite end of the parking lot from where he had taken it. Satisfied with his shopping trip in Tucson he headed back to Tingle Creek to set up his best fire yet.

TINGLE CREEK, ARIZONA

THE PUPPIES WERE READY FOR A NAP AFTER ANOTHER OUTSIDE PLAYTIME. Connie set the puppy crate next to her bed. She got herself a glass of water and drank some as she listened to the dogs as they slopped water from their pail in the dog room.

She stretched out on top of the covers for her nap. It seemed she had just dozed off when the Schipperke pups started to whine and yap. Potty time again.

88-8 RANCH
TINGLE CREEK, ARIZONA

ON THE ROAD THAT LED BACK INTO TINGLE CREEK, ALLEN DROVE PAST the Double 8 bar 8 ranch sign that hung over a dirt track that teed off the paved road he was on. He'd driven passed it before. The pasture next to the dirt track was so golden and dry. So ready to ignite.

He scouted around and saw where he could park the truck out of sight over a ridge. On the hillside, there were lots of rocks he could shoot from, undetected. He poured diesel from one of the gas cans in a large puddle, then threw a lit road flare into the fuel to ignite the blaze. Then he scampered up into the rocks with his rifle to wait for the firefighters to show. Fire made him feel good; the buzz he got from taking potshots at firefighters was even better.

MESQUITE B and B
TINGLE CREEK, ARIZONA

PAUL BROUGHT RAND BACK TO THE B&B AFTER THEY HAD SPENT THE morning and early afternoon looking for spent bullets. They had found a couple soot-covered empty shell casings from spent rifle-rounds at the burned-out house. In the grassland burn area they found, an old rusted hinge, a part of a car spring, some cans, old pull tabs from cans before pop tops became the standard, and lots of nails with other metal scrap dumped by people in the past.

They also found what might be expended bullets near where the fire trucks had been. On the drive back, Paul asked, "How's Connie holding up?"

Rand replied, "She doesn't talk much, and she's always doing something. Sometimes she vanishes." He shrugged.

Paul asked, "Is she sleeping or eating?"

"I don't know about sleeping. When Connie eats with us, she doesn't eat much. It seems more like she shoves the food around until she can politely leave the table. I know Connie's running a bed and breakfast, but she also fixes us supper. I think she does that because of Mandy," Rand said.

"Sharon and I are worried about her," Paul said.

"I think someone needs to worry about her. I don't know her, but a break down seems inevitable," Rand said.

After their potty break, Connie tucked the pups into the large pocket of her puppy smock while she prepared their bottles in the kitchen. Before she got started, she heard a truck drive up to the private gate. Before she went out to see who it was, Connie hurried to put the big dogs in their room. Then she went out on the porch.

She hoped the puppies would stay quiet in their smock pocket. If she put them in their crate without food, they would complain - loudly, and that would upset Ace. He was already stressed by being separated from her.

Rand got out of the passenger side of Paul's truck and stretched out the kinks. "You call that a road?" Rand asked Paul. "Cuz it's not. It's someone's imagination of a road. The potholes could have swallowed my rental car, easy."

When he shut his truck door, Paul shrugged and said, "Yeah, those are roads. We have goat paths too. We know how to drive on them, not like you city slickers."

Paul saw Connie wearing her puppy-smock standing on the porch. He thought it was cool how she carried the puppies around with her. He hopped onto the shaded porch and gave her a gentle sideways hug so as not to squish the pups in her smock.

As he stood and stretched beside Paul's truck, Rand finally saw Connie on the shady porch. Since he had arrived, she had always been around, until she all but disappeared a few days ago. She was always in motion.

He saw her short light brown hair was clean, uncombed and wild, as usual. He noticed she barely came up to Paul's chin. Her clothes still looked a few sizes too large. And there was something wrong with her shirt. There was no breeze, but it seemed to be moving. Rand slowly approached the porch. He had just stepped onto the porch when a tiny furry black head peaked up from her smock pocket.

"Shit!" he yelled as he jumped away from Connie. Rand almost fell off the porch.

The puppy whined, looked around, then blinked. Rand's shout woke the second puppy. She popped up out of the pocket to survey the situation.

Connie was astounded at Rand's extreme reaction.

"They're puppies. They can't hurt you. They're just hungry; you guys got here at their mealtime," Connie said. "I need to make them their bottles." She stoked the puppies' heads. "It's okay kids, just a big jumpy man," she soothed the pups. She looked at Paul, perplexed.

Paul said. "I didn't know he would be afraid of them. They're the size of small rats."

"I can hear you," Rand announced from the yard as they talked about him. "They are dogs! And I didn't know they were there!" Rand defended himself.

Connie was perplexed, "Paul, I thought you told him about the puppies."

Paul responded, "I did! Before I brought them over to you."

"Paul told me you had them. I didn't know they were with you," Rand defended himself again, "and, and, they're still dogs!"

"They will be with me most of the time right now, in their pocket or their crate. Pretend they're kittens, small guinea pigs or large hamsters, or rats or mice, whatever! And come in the house," Connie was annoyed. "It's hot out here, and I need to feed them," Connie said as she turned and retreated inside.

As they went inside, Paul switched his pager to vibrate. Paul followed Connie to the kitchen, and Rand reluctantly trailed behind. He watched as Connie prepared the puppy bottles, and she and Paul held and fed them.

Bottles finished; the puppies were restless. Connie said, "Time to take these girls out to go potty. You want to come along and see what you're so afraid of?" she asked Rand.

"I want to," Paul said with a broad smile lighting his face. "I haven't seen them since we brought them over!"

"That was just the day before yesterday, and you just fed Jet," Connie replied.

Paul smiled as he shrugged. "I love puppies, so sue me," he replied.

Not given much choice, Rand trailed after Paul and Connie as they went through the B&B to the dog yard. Paul waited for Rand to pass him onto the porch so he could close the sliding glass door.

Connie looked at Rand, standing in the doorway. "In or out," she ordered. "Make a decision. I can't afford to air-condition the whole outdoors."

Rand took a deep breath, then stepped onto the veranda, followed by Paul. A huge mesquite tree shaded the porch and grassy area.

Connie put the pups on the ground. They wandered a few feet away from her and did their business. Connie quickly cleaned up after them. The pups played with each other, rolling and growling. They completely ignored the humans.

Rand stood uncertainly on the porch while Paul got down on his knees in the grass near where the pups played. Reaching out, Paul picked up one of the puppies. "Hi, little one." He nuzzled her. "Which one is this?" he asked Connie.

"Jet," she replied. "The one you just fed?"

Jet gave him a small lick on the face. "You are one sweet puppy; you know that?" Paul asked the puppy. He put Jet down and picked up the other one. "And who is this?" Paul queried.

"Dash, she makes friends a little more slowly," Connie replied.

Paul repeated his greeting and snuggled with Dash. She took a little longer to give him a lick on the chin. He smiled and chuckled then he put her down. He looked at Connie, and said, "They're doing great. I don't think anyone else could have kept them going and growing like you."

Rand watched Paul's whole dog greeting thing from the porch, his back against the closed sliding glass door.

Paul said, "Come on over here, Rand, they won't hurt you. I promise."

Rand stayed where he was.

"Move it!" Paul ordered Rand.

Rand shook his head. He said, "I always thought I wanted a dog as a kid. I was eight when I saw my friend mauled by a feral pack of huge dogs. They killed him. Those dogs shook him like a rag doll. They were trying to drag him away when the cops showed up. And the dogs went after them." Rand paused and shuddered involuntarily at the memory.

"These two are tiny, they can't hurt anyone," Paul said.

"The cops had to shoot them to get to Ralph's body. I'd gone up a tree for our kite. He'd stayed on the ground because of his broken arm. I saw the whole thing. The fire department had to pry me out of the tree. I've been scared of dogs ever since."

Considering what Rand told her, Connie asked, "You want to get over that fear?"

Rand nodded uncertainly, then said, "Of course." He didn't sound at all convincing.

"If so, Rand, sit on the ground under that tree over there." Connie pointed to the shade thrown by a large Mesquite tree. "If the pups come to visit you, let them. I can promise they will not hurt you. And these two will be my constant companions for the next two weeks. After that, they'll start to spend some time by themselves, but not much. If you get to know them now, then they won't be scary as they grow up. Fully grown, they may weight about eighteen to twenty pounds and be the size of a house cat."

Rand considered following Connie's instructions. Connie sat in the shade under a different Mesquite tree closer to the pups.

Paul stretched out in the grass in the shade near Connie.

Rand finally worked up the nerve to leave the porch and go where Connie had told him to sit. He watched the little black puppies play and tumble in the grass several feet away on the far side of Connie and Paul.

The B&B business phone rang from inside. She rose to answer and asked, "Paul, can you watch these two while I get the phone?"

"Sure," Paul responded.

After Connie went into the house, Rand asked, "Watch them for what? They're too little to do anything. Intellectually, even I know that."

Paul responded, "Says the guy who almost pissed his pants when he first saw them. Seriously, watch them so that a passing hawk or other large bird doesn't fly off with one and eat it."

"No, shit?" Rand asked.

"None. With all she's going through, if anything bad happened to these little girls, Connie would skin us both alive, no hesitation. After that she would stake us out on an anthill, cover us with honey and let us die a slow, painful death by fire ants while baking in the sun. That's if she's feeling charitable," Paul said as he produced an exaggerated tremor.

"Not someone to get on their bad side?" Rand asked.

"If you value your life, you won't. Remember, she's a dispatcher. The rules apply universally. Rule number one: Never piss off the dispatcher. Rule two: see Rule one," Paul said. "She hasn't been at her best since Tom died. I was hoping caring for these two would help somehow. Otherwise, knowing how you feel about dogs, I never would have brought them to her."

Played out, the puppies were tired and looked for a likely place to nap. Dash crawled up onto Paul's chest, flopped down and in short order fell asleep on him. Jet wandered around, found Rand, and crawled into his lap. He forced himself to stay put. Once in his lap, the pup was soon fast asleep. Rand stared down in wonder and some apprehension at the little fur-ball asleep in his lap.

Paul's pager vibrated. Paul covered it with his hand to muffle it when the dispatcher spoke so that the puppies would keep napping. He cradled Dash as he rose slowly, and placed Dash in Rand's lap next to Jet.

Rand whispered to Paul, "What do I do?"

"Stay put until Connie gets back," Paul said, he smiled at Rand with two puppies in his lap. "I've got to go — brush fire. Dispatcher just put out an all-call. Just stay here. You'll be fine," Paul murmured, then ran for the gate and out to his pickup.

Rand heard Paul's truck race out of the driveway and down the road. The pups slept on, undisturbed. He sat and marveled at the sleeping puppies in his lap. He enjoyed the small warm bodies cuddled on him. He smiled to himself at his amazing accomplishment. He was touching dogs. And he liked it.

When Connie returned from her phone call, Rand saw she appeared more tired and pale, more than she had been on the porch earlier. He was amazed she could get any paler. The phone call must have been something else.

"Is everything all right?" Rand asked.

"No, but thanks for asking," Connie answered. "Are you doing okay with them?" Connie asked, pointing at the puppies in his lap.

Rand nodded, a grin lit his face. "Can I pet them while they're asleep?"

"Sure, they'll probably sleep through it. The puppies have tired each other out, playing."

Rand stroked the pups; Connie saw the wonderment on his face as he did.

"They're so soft," Rand marveled.

Connie asked, "Ready to stop being a dog bed?"

"How do I pick them up?" Rand asked. He didn't want to wake the sleeping fur-balls.

"Scoop them up with your fingers spread, making sure you support their bodies and heads. The feet can dangle." Connie demonstrated the move to Rand. He handed the pups to her one at a time, then stood and brushed off his pants.

"Since they're taking a nap, I will too. You all right on your own?" Connie asked.

"Yeah," he replied. "I've got some work to do."

Rand's cell rang. He pulled it from his pocket and checked the caller ID, then answered, "Hey, Paul."

"Rand, if you're interested, you might want to come out here. This fire looks like arson. Don't know if it's your guy."

Rand pulled out a note pad he kept in his shirt pocket along with his pen.

As Paul gave Rand directions to the fire and the G.P.S. coordinates, he wrote down the instructions to the Double 8 bar 8 ranch pasture fire.

Rand told Paul, "On a different topic, you might want to have your wife touch base with Connie. She got a phone call just after you left that upset her, a lot."

Paul said, "I'll call Sharon right now." and disconnected the call with Rand.

Rand went in search of Connie. He found her in the great room as she carried the puppies in their crate. "I know this is asking a lot, but do you have a car I can borrow? Stacey has the rental, and Paul wants me at the fire he's working at," Rand said.

"Sure, take the gold Yukon XL in the shed. Flip down the visor, and the keys will land on the seat. Just fill it with gas before you come back, please," Connie said.

In Connie's GMC, Rand programmed in the G.P.S. coordinates and hoped he wouldn't get lost. He left.

When Connie heard Rand leave, she opened the doggie door slider so the big dogs could roam in and out of the house at will. She put the puppies' crate next to her bed. Weary, she kicked off her sneakers and stretched out on the bedspread. Just as she got comfortable, her cell phone rang. The particular ring tone was only for her friend Sharon, so Connie answered.

Sharon asked, "Can I come by and puppy sit for a while?"

"Sure, I need to get some sleep," Connie replied.

Sharon said, "Perfect; I can puppy sit, and you can sleep longer than a wink. I love looking after puppies. You can rest and not worry about anything."

Connie said, "You have a key, and the dogs will let you in, they know you."

At the B&B, Sharon went into Connie's room and carried the crate with the sleeping pups out into the great room. Connie's adult dogs chose to stay in the bedroom with her. Sharon left the dogs with Connie.

Puppy sitting while Connie slept, finally gave Sharon a chance to read. She was enjoying her book in the great room at the B&B when the business phone rang. Sharon pounced on it after the first ring. "Mesquite Bed and Breakfast, how may I help you?" she asked.

A male-sounding computer distorted voice said, "Sell or pay up! This is your last warning! Sell or die like your old man! Tell anyone. They die," said the voice. More threats and heavy breathing followed the demand. The entire call lasted less than ten seconds and terminated before Sharon had time to process everything she had heard.

Sharon checked the caller ID. It showed 'Arizona Wireless' and a phone number. Sharon wondered if this was what had Connie so rattled lately. It had to be more than just Belle in the hospital and Art in Wyoming to sell the ranch.

Sharon figured there had to be a way to get Connie to let someone help her. Heaven knew she would never ask for assistance. Sharon wrote the phone number down on a note pad. Then, she texted Paul to pass on to Rand that Connie was getting threatening phone calls. She included the number the call came from in her text. Then she took the startled awake puppies outside for a break with food to follow.

DOUBLE 8 BAR 8 FIRE

WHEN HE ARRIVED AT THE FIRE, RAND SAW CONTROLLED CHAOS. He parked on the shoulder of the road well away from the fire trucks. A water tender pulled up and provided water to a fire truck that blocked one lane of the dirt road. Another water tender disconnected from the fire engine it supplied and left for a refill from a nearby stock tank.

Rand surveyed the terrain from the Yukon XL. The blaze was in a pasture down in a draw, with the hills on either side that funneled the prevailing winds into the fire and pushed flames and burning embers into the dry grasslands beyond. Rand scoped out the surrounding hillside cover for a shooter. There were several significant rock outcroppings on the hill to his left and another likely spot in some creosote bushes partway down the ridge to his right.

A strong gust of wind threw embers into the long dry grass as the wind pushed the fire ahead of the firefighters. The flames branched out in the grasslands. The smoke thickened and darkened as the fire intensified. New blazes started in the grass further away from the primary fire.

Firefighters either handled fire hoses or used hand tools to combat the fire. The firefighters used shovels and Pulaskis as they worked along the sides of the fire, digging up small trees and brush to deprive the blaze of fuel. A couple carried large extinguishers on their backs like backpacks and put out small fires as they ignited away from the primary blaze.

Rand continued to scan the hillsides, one side then the other. Even sitting in the Yukon XL with the a/c on, the noise was horrendous from the motors of the water tenders, the pumps on the brush truck and the big fire engines. The different radios on the trucks were cranked up and blared from speakers on the vehicles.

The firefighters took turns as they rotated into the grass to use the shovels and Pulaskis to fight the fire out of range of their hoses. When they got overheated, the firefighters switched to the fire engine for shade and cold water, then returned to fighting the fire as soon as they cooled down.

Allen could hardly contain his excitement. The fire had taken off just like he hoped. He had hidden in the rocks and waited after he threw lit the road flare in the fuel he had poured in the tall, dry grass. The wind had picked up just like the local weather people on his phone app said it would. And wow! Did that fire take off! Nothing there, then small wisps of smoke, a gust of a breeze as the afternoon winds picked up and then, Bam! Grass and brush on fire like nobody's business.

Settled in the rocks on the hillside, he hadn't waited long for the fire trucks and looky-loos to show up. By then the fire was big and gnarly, with thick black smoke twisting skyward in the wind. Embers sailed ahead of the fire on the breeze and started new fires.

Allen waited until they almost had control. That was when it was his turn. Allen opened fire. On his second shot, he managed to knick the water hose. He had wanted to put a round right through the hose, but he'd take the nick. It still deprived the firefighters of some water.

Rand scanned the ridge to his right, then the hillside to his left. On the hillside, he saw a flash of movement. He continued to scan the hillside. He wondered what had attracted his attention. All of a sudden, Rand saw a towering fountain of water erupt from the firehose about halfway between the truck and the firemen who handled the hose. The sunlight made the water sparkle as it fountained from the fire hose into the air.

The water supply was shut down for a quick hose swap as firefighters scrambled to restore water flow. They needed the water line back in operation as soon as possible. The breeze was getting stronger. The fire grew bigger.

Allen fired several more rounds before his next hit took out the front bumper mounted pump. He wanted to take out the tires on the water tanker, but he wasn't in the right place for that to be an easy shot. He wasn't as good with the rifle as he wanted to be. He didn't stop the firefighters, just slowed them down, but anything to help his fire baby grow.

He dragged the rifle with him as he crept slowly through the large granite rocks. He moved slowly, paused for a couple of minutes then moved again until he was over the hill.

Concealed by the ridge between the fire and himself, Allen raced for his truck, stowed the rifle and drove off slowly down the road. The adrenaline rush made him want to race the truck back to town. He loved the adrenaline rush. He restrained himself, barely.

ABANDONED MINE
TINGLE CREEK, ARIZONA

IN PREPARATION FOR THE B&B FIRE, ALLEN STASHED HIS RIFLE, BOXES of ammunition for the gun and water and snacks in his blind, the mine entrance on the hill across the road from the B&B. It would make an excellent vantage point from which to watch the B&B burn down. He had to make sure Mandy died, by fire, shrapnel or gunshot didn't matter. Maybe he could pick off a few firefighters in the process, that would be a bonus.

DOUBLE 8 BAR 8 FIRE

AFTER THE EXCITEMENT OF THE HOSE LEAK AND REPLACEMENT, PAUL went to the support truck and got a couple of bottles of cold water. He drank some and poured the rest over his head and neck to cool his body down in the blistering heat. Refreshed, he joined Rand in the air-conditioned SUV. He asked, "Hey, Rand, did you see anything weird before the hose blew? I've never seen one leak like that without warning, or a pump suddenly freeze-up with no prior indication of trouble. Corey's working on the pump now."

Rand replied, "I'm not sure. Just before the hose leaked, I thought I saw movement up in the rocks over there." He pointed to the hill on his left. Paul scanned the rocks Rand indicated.

"I don't see anything," Paul said. He opened his second bottle of cold water and drank it empty. Rand continued to scan the hillsides. A deputy pulled up in her Tahoe, got out, and walked over to the men in the SUV. They got out of the Yukon XL.

Deputy Porter asked Paul, "Anything out of the ordinary with this fire?"

Paul said, "Yeah, everything. There's no reason for it to have started. Clear skies, nothing here to cause a spark. It has to be human-caused. Also, a fire hose ruptured spontaneously; we replaced it, then the front-mounted pump quit."

Rand said, "I thought I saw movement in the rocks on the hill to the left just after the hose ruptured. It was too noisy from the fire equipment to hear if shots were fired. I don't know what caused the movement I saw. I plan to check the area of the rupture for a bullet in the ground after the fire is out."

"Intriguing idea," said Deputy Porter. "Who are you?"

Rand handed the deputy his FBI credentials.

She looked at his creds thoroughly. "Why are you here?" Deputy Porter asked as she returned them.

"Paul invited me out to see this fire. I'm working a related case," Rand explained.

"Someone shot the pump!" Corey yelled. "I found a bullet hole!"

TINGLE CREEK, ARIZONA

AT THE HOUSE HE HAD BEEN STAYING, ALLEN GATHERED EVERYTHING HE wanted to take with him when he left and stacked it by the door. Everything he was leaving, including Mandy's stuff he piled in the living room. Then he showered, ate a snack, and slept.

MESQUITE B and B
TINGLE CREEK, ARIZONA

SHARON SPENT FOUR HOURS DOG SITTING FOR THE PUPS BEFORE SHE LEFT. It was the most sleep Connie had gotten in weeks. After Sharon had taken the pups for a potty break and fed them, she returned the pups and their crate to Connie's bedroom. She patted the adult dogs goodbye as she left them in the bedroom with Connie. "Look after your mom. She needs you. I have to get to work," she told the dogs. She closed the bedroom door. She locked the exterior door behind herself when she left.

HOSPITAL
TINGLE CREEK, ARIZONA

IT WAS DARK IN THE HOSPITAL PARKING LOT WHEN SHARON ARRIVED AT work. She checked her cell to see if Paul has answered her text. Nope.

DOUBLE 8 BAR 8 FIRE

FIVE HOURS AFTER THE FIREFIGHTERS HAD ARRIVED AT THE GRASS FIRE, they finally got it out. They had gotten lucky at dusk when the wind shifted and blew the flames into an area already burned by the fire. Whatever had gotten the grassfire started, the efforts to extinguish it destroyed any readily visible evidence. Arson investigators would make the final determination in the morning on the cause of the fire.

With the fire out, Rand and Paul put evidence flags in the ground to mark where each fire truck was and where the hose had ruptured. "This will help in the morning when we come back with a metal detector," Rand said. "If there's anything to find, we have a better chance in daylight."

"Great, I'm exhausted," Paul said.

"I also want to look around those rocks on the hill. See if I can find any tracks to tell me what I saw up there," Rand said.

Paul rode the fire truck back to the fire station. Rand followed the fire truck as it headed into Tingle Creek, but turned off at the B&B.

MESQUITE B and B
TINGLE CREEK, ARIZONA

RAND PARKED THE BORROWED YUKON XL WHERE HE HAD FOUND IT when he arrived at the B&B. He was hungry, tired, dirty, smokey, and sweaty. Connie had left him a cold supper, according to a note on the table. The plate he pulled from the fridge had a thick roast beef sandwich with lettuce and tomato. A second plate held two large slices of watermelon. Next to the note on the table was a bag of chips and a large glass of water with a full pitcher beside it.

Rand was surprised to be eating supper alone. Usually, he had Stacey and Mandy to accompany him at meals. It had been common for Connie to hang around to put dishes in the dishwasher after meals, despite her speech about cleaning up after themselves. He wondered why Connie was avoiding him tonight. He'd have to ask Stacey what she thought. His stomach rumbled, demanding food and water. Connie was still an enigma to him.

Connie heard Rand come home after the fire. She didn't think she could stand the smell of him after he had spent so much time at a fire. He'd smell like Tom did. Sweaty and smokey. In her recliner in the dog room, Connie cried silent tears as the big dogs crowded around her. They wanted to comfort her.

She wept, for Tom and his parents, for Belle in the hospital, for Art having to sell the family ranch, for her lonely, broken, empty heart. Even with a full B&B, she felt so alone. She knew, emotionally, she couldn't do it again. She'd lost her whole family once and had to find a new one. She didn't think she had the strength to do that again.

At least she still had Art and Belle, although Belle hadn't responded to treatment, yet. She stroked the dogs in thanks for their comfort. With Ace in her lap cried herself to sleep in the recliner. Magic and Misty lay at her feet.

Rand had put his dirty dishes in the dishwasher when Mandy and Stacey dragged in. "You guys just now are getting home?" he asked. He saw they looked exhausted.

"Yeah, an accident blocked the highway in both directions. We parked on the interstate, on the top of a long hill, for hours. We just couldn't get here from there," Stacey said as she dropped into a chair at the kitchen table. Mandy poked around in the fridge and pulled out a soda.

"Did you eat?" Rand asked.

"Before we left Tucson, thank goodness, or we would have starved," Stacey said, she rested her head on her crossed arms on the table. Mandy sat at the table and drank from a can of 7-Up.

"Okay, ladies, I need to shower. Anything we need to discuss?" Rand asked.

"I have to take Mandy to the airport tomorrow morning. Connie told me that Mandy and I need to be up at 4:00 a.m. to make our flight home," Stacey said.

"You plan to go with her?" Rand asked.

"You seem to have things under control here. Mandy's a minor, and a kidnap victim, so yeah," Stacey answered.

After he burned the B&B down, Allen knew he would have to find someplace new to live. California had a drought problem, worse than Arizona. He decided he'd burn the B&B down in the early morning tomorrow and be on the road by sunrise. When he got tired, he'd stop and sleep before continuing to sunny, dry California. His brush fire had relaxed him, enough, so he got some much-needed sleep before his final fires in Tingle Creek. He was happy.

APRIL 25, 2014
TINGLE CREEK, ARIZONA

ALLEN WOKE JUST AFTER MIDNIGHT. HE WAS VERY EXCITED ABOUT torching the B&B. He dressed all in dark clothing. Then he loaded all his belongings in the truck, along with a handgun and ammunition he had found in a nightstand in the master bedroom.

Using cooking oils, some kerosene he found for lamps, and liquor, he splashed accelerant throughout the house and soaked Mandy's belongings.

No need to make this look like anything but what it was, an intentionally set house fire.

In the living room, he lit a candle for his fuse. Satisfied, he blew out the pilot light on the propane gas stove, then turned on all the burners, opened the oven door and turned on the broiler. That should keep the cops and fire department busy while he burned the B&B to ashes. He imagined the B&B as it disintegrated in flames, and his blood hummed in his veins at the vision in his head. This house would burn completely and destroy any evidence he had stayed here.

Allen drove through town with the pickup's windows open. He had nearly passed the diner when he heard the house blow up. The resonant boom rattled windows up and down Main Street. Moments later the town siren began to wail.

That was discouraging to Allen, but he reminded himself that his nemesis' would be busy while he arranged the incineration of the B&B with Mandy inside. He just wished he knew exactly where in the B&B she was staying. He could make that part burn the hottest.

HOUSE FIRE
TINGLE CREEK, ARIZONA

ONCE THEY ARRIVED, THE FIREFIGHTERS FOUGHT VALIANTLY TO SAVE the homes next to the one Allen had demolished. The propane explosion of the house launched sparks and embers into the air. The wind carried the mini-torches throughout the neighborhood. The wind spread the burning embers into the dry trees and brush and started new fires.

When the fire chief arrived, he saw the multiple fires caused by the house exploding. He got on his radio and said, "Dispatch, put out an all-call for all off duty firefighters to respond, then ask Rincon Valley and Mescal fire departments if they can send us any units. We need everything. Personnel, engines, and water tenders, whatever they have available. Then have the sheriff's department evacuate the neighborhood. We have fire everywhere."

The dispatcher said, "Copy, will advise."

MESQUITE B and B
TINGLE CREEK, ARIZONA

ALLEN PARKED HIS TRUCK AS CLOSE TO THE B&B AS HE COULD, THEN unloaded his supplies that he would use to burn it to the ground. When the pickup was empty, he moved it to a nearby wash to hide it from anyone who might see it as the drove by. He ran back to the B&B and went to work.

Howling sirens shattered the night as the firetrucks that responded from neighboring departments roared down the road to help fight the fires Allen had started on the east side of Tingle Creek.

Allen smirked, "Going the wrong way, guys. The real fun will be here in a couple of hours. Wait and see." He giggled as he began to set up his destruction plan for the B&B. The outside spotlights at the back of the B&B came on. He checked his watch and mumbled, "Puppy potty break. Right on time."

At 4:00 a.m. Connie was awake and prepared to make breakfast in the kitchen. She heard the wind that had blown all night begin to shriek in the eaves. Wind gusts pummeled the house. It sounded like a Wyoming blizzard to Connie. She started the coffee maker.

The smell of fresh-brewed coffee brought Mandy into the kitchen. She saw the pups were in their crate near the wall, still asleep. She knew they would need attention after breakfast.

Ace followed behind Connie closely, while Magic and Misty sat in their designated corner of the kitchen. That kept them out from under her feet as she prepared breakfast. Normally, Ace would have had to sit there as well.

Connie knew the big dogs would need to go into their room before Rand woke. She figured she had time since he'd come in late from the fire last night. Connie didn't need him to freak out on her when she was on a tight schedule to get Mandy and Stacey fed, and off to the airport.

She opened the fridge and pulled out eggs, bacon, and a loaf of homemade multi-grain bread. She put those on the counter then scanned the freezer. She looked through her haul from last year's garden. She decided she would use the diced zucchini and chopped spinach.

Ace moved with Connie as she moved and leaned gently against Connie's legs when she stood still. "It's okay big guy, just wind," she told Ace as she made breakfast. Magic sat in a vigilant posture in her corner of the kitchen. She watched Connie closely. There might be treats. The dogs knew when it was bacon and eggs, if they behaved, Connie would make them each an egg. Misty was flopped next to the puppy crate and washed her front paws.

Allen swore when he saw that lights were on in the B&B. He dropped a propane tank, and it clanked against the house. No one should be getting up for another hour or more. He had watched them. He knew their schedule. The last puppy potty trip was at 2:00 a.m. They shouldn't be out again until about 5:30 a.m. to six o'clock. He stayed alert in case a door opened. When nothing happened, he continued to ready the B&B.

Connie had heard a thump and thought it was wind thrown furniture that hit the side of the building. Mandy asked, "Can I help with anything?"

"You can set the table if you want to," Connie answered.

The bewitching scent of fresh-brewed coffee drew Stacey to the kitchen. Rand had also smelled the coffee. He had dressed and exited his room. He followed Stacey to the kitchen.

"Is Connie expecting you for breakfast?" asked Stacey.

"She should be," Rand said. "I'm a guest here, too."

"Okay…," Stacey said skeptically, as she led the way down the hall.

A gust of wind slammed into the building. "Listen to the wind," Rand commented as he followed Stacey into the kitchen. He continued, "If this were winter, I'd say we were in for a nasty blizzard."

When Connie heard the rumble of Rand's voice, she ordered, "Rand, stop! Don't come in here."

"Why not?" he asked and entered the kitchen anyway.

"Shit," Connie muttered when Rand entered the kitchen.

Rand froze. He saw three massive dogs in the kitchen. Enormous adult dogs. "Where? Where did they come from?!" Rand stammered as he backed up into Stacey.

Mandy was transfixed as she watched the big FBI agent terrified by the well behaved and non-threatening dogs that she thought were adorable. She froze next to the table, silverware still in her hands.

"Easy big guy," Stacey said, she stepped in front of Rand. "They've been here the whole time, and you're are still in one piece."

"No, they haven't! Just the little ones," Rand declared. He peered over Stacey's shoulder at the big German Shepherd that leaned against Connie's legs, then at the German Shepherd - Akita mix as big as the German Shepherd and then at the fluffy Aussie Shepherd mix that lay nearby.

Connie turned from her bags of frozen vegetables and saw Rand was white as a ghost. Stacey stayed between him and the dogs as she led him to a chair at the table.

"Sit!" Stacey ordered, "before you fall. Head down between your knees, get some blood back in your brain."

Connie watched astonished.

Rand said, "I never dreamed there were dogs that big in here...I mean I... the little ones are scary enough..." he sat up and just shook his head and wobbled in the chair. Stacey pushed his head back down between his knees.

"Breathe. Slowly. In and out," Stacey ordered. Rand complied.

The dogs watched him without moving. Misty groaned and went back to watching Connie fix breakfast. Mandy continued to set the table.

When the lightheadedness passed, Rand sat up. Still pale, he stared at the dogs. They looked at him then back at Connie. After a few minutes, he asked, "I'm safe?"

"Yes. Absolutely yes, I wasn't expecting you for breakfast after the fire last night. If I had, I would have put the dogs in their room. You would never have known they were here. I'm surprised you're awake this early."

"It was the smell of the coffee," Rand confessed.

Connie put the bags of frozen vegetables in the microwave. "As long as you don't do anything to threaten me, you are completely safe," she said as she continued to make breakfast.

Connie started the microwave oven to thaw the diced zucchini and chopped spinach. With the vent fan over the stove turned on, she started bacon in a frying pan.

"Ace, go lie down," Connie ordered the German Shepherd. He complied and belly-crawled to lie next to Magic with his ears back against his head. He was not happy about leaving Connie's side.

With the bacon frying, Connie diced tomatoes to put in the eggs.

Stacey poured a cup of coffee and added three ice cubes from the fridge before gulping it down. She poured Rand a cup of coffee and set it on the table in front of him. She asked Connie, "What can I do to help?" as she poured a second cup and placed it on the counter to cool.

Connie's cell rang, and the ring tone told her the caller was Sharon. "Take over the bacon," Connie said. Stacey did. Connie answered her phone.

Sharon said, "I'm being called in to work an early shift in the E.R. Can I stop in for a minute? I got a phone message I forgot to give you yesterday."

"Sure, we're all awake. I just started breakfast, are you coming now?" Connie asked.

"Yup, Paul's driving me, he just got home from a house fire. Can he be fed too?" Sharon asked.

"Sure, why not?" Connie decided.

Sharon said, "We're on the way. We'll be there in a few minutes."

Connie got out more eggs and bacon so she would have enough to serve six for breakfast. "Mandy, we need to set place settings for six people now. Would you mind setting a couple more places at the table?" Connie asked.

Outside, Allen had worked for several hours. The propane tanks were spaced along the walls of the B&B. Each propane tank was surrounded with bags of fertilizer with road flares uncapped and inserted halfway, ready to light. Then he had added handfuls of nuts and bolts for shrapnel. He had splashed diesel on the sides of the building and made sure to pour fuel into the bags of fertilizer. He threw plastic pop bottles he had filled with gas onto the roof in several places. He had finally finished his masterpiece that would be a huge surprise for the inhabitants of the B&B this morning.

Since he had still had some boxes of ammunition of various calibers, he dropped a handful of ammo into each fertilizer bag next to the road flares. Allen ran diesel-soaked cotton clothesline coated with petroleum jelly to each road flare, circled the fertilizer bags then ran it on to the next flare with its bags of fertilizer until the B&B was completely encircled. He laid more fuel-soaked, petroleum jelly coated clothesline out away from the building to give him a fuse.

With everything ready, Allen opened the valves on each of the propane tanks to trickle out the propane gas. One hundred feet from the B&B, at the end of the clothesline fuse, he lit it. Allen stayed and watched for a few minutes, as the fire raced down the clothesline to the B&B.

He ran through the desert and across the road. As he crossed the pavement, headlights swept across him and illuminated the reflective tabs on his sneakers. "Shit!" Allen yelled. He hoped the driver mistook him for a nighttime animal fleeing traffic. He scampered up the hill to the mine to watch the fireworks.

Paul saw moving flashes in his headlights as he approached the B&B driveway. "Did you see that?" he asked Sharon.

"See what?" Sharon asked.

"I thought it was reflective tabs on the heels of sneakers. Like a jogger or something?" Paul replied. "But someone running away from the B&B and heading up the hill." Paul glanced at the clock on the dash; it showed 4:17 a.m.

Paul turned into the driveway of the B&B, and he saw flames running up the walls.

Stacey finished the bacon. It was crisp, dark brown, but not black and smelled delicious. She placed it to drain on some paper towels on a rack Connie had set out. Stacey refilled the coffee carafe with water and started a new pot.

Connie put the final touches on the veggies for scrambled eggs. Finished with putting place settings on the table, Mandy sat and nursed a cup of half milk and half coffee. Rand hadn't moved from his chair at the table. He couldn't take his eyes off the dogs.

Connie finished sautéing the zucchini in bacon grease and was about to pour the fork whipped eggs with the chopped tomatoes and spinach into the skillet when KA-BOOM! The building shook. Mandy screamed.

Allen rejoiced. He jumped up and down after the first propane tank had detonated. He was still only partway up the hill to the mine entrance. It was much more difficult to get up the hill in the dark without any light to illuminate the way.

For the occupants of the B&B, the exploding propane tank was deafening. The lights went out. Connie snapped off the stove. She activated the flashlight feature on her smartphone. The explosion drove Ace and Magic to Connie. Ace for shelter and reassurance and Magic to provide protection. Misty flattened out on the floor and peed in fright. Out of the kitchen window, that looked onto the enclosed porch, all that was visible were flames.

The explosion flipped a mental switch in Rand. The blast kicked his FBI training in, and he stopped letting the fear of dogs control him. He went into dispassionate trained FBI agent mode. "Get down! Everyone down!" he shouted.

Stacey ordered, "Everyone into the middle of the room. Stay on the floor. Get away from the walls and windows." She crouched below the level of the counters.

Rand started to crawl to the hallway, out of the kitchen towards his room. Connie stopped him, "I know it doesn't look it, but this is the safest place in the house. Tom told me this part of the house is the original adobe. The walls are two feet thick." Connie pleaded, "Stay here. I can't have anyone else die."

Rand turned, he saw Connie looked stunned and lost. Tears ran down her face.

Rand ruthlessly explained, "If I can get out, I can catch this guy!" Another propane tank detonated, closer than the last. Shrapnel broke through the window hit Stacey in the shoulder and upper back. The impact spun Stacey and flung her to the floor.

Mandy screamed, "Oh, no, Allen found me. He's going to kill me."

Rand snatched a dishtowel from the counter and pressed it onto Stacey's wound to staunch the bleeding.

Magic stood between Connie and the last explosion all her fur on end, growling menacingly. Her growl terrified Rand, but he ignored the dog to care for Stacey. He reminded himself that Connie said he was safe. Right now, he had to believe her. He had to care for Stacey.

The explosion scared the puppies who had been asleep in their crate. They whined, barked, yipped, and shook. The smoke alarms shrieked to add to the cacophony.

Mandy screamed, "Oh, my God! Oh, my God!" over and over.

Misty quaked in fear at the loud noises. Abruptly, she ran to the nearest corner and began to try to crawl up the walls to get away from the noise.

On the B&B driveway, debris from the second explosion rained down on Paul's truck as he drove up. He heard Sharon call 9-1-1 and talk to the dispatcher. Paul left Sharon in the pickup parked at the yard gate. He entered the yard and went to the metal shed that housed the tractor.

At the tractor, he hooked the battery up, flipped the seat down, and quickly got it started. As he drove out of the shed, he saw fire surrounded the whole B&B.

Mandy continued to scream, "Oh, my God!" over and over as she crouched under the kitchen table.

Connie pulled the puppy crate into the middle of the room, away from where it had been against the wall. She went back and dragged Misty by the collar to get her away from the wall. She pulled her belt from her pants to leash Misty.

"What else can I do?" Rand asked as he still applied pressure to Stacey's wound.

"Help Mandy. Get her to be quiet! It's not helping, her screaming like that," Connie snapped.

Rand pulled Mandy over to Stacey. To distract her, he showed her how to maintain pressure on the makeshift bandage he had made for Stacey's shoulder.

The smoke alarms continued their piercing wail from all the newer rooms that surrounded the old adobe center of the structure. Connie directed Rand, "Please disable that smoke alarm." She pointed to the device on the wall nearby. The noise was ear-splitting, and enough was going on without that racket added to the mix. Rand took a kitchen chair with him to stand on so he could disable the alarm.

Four more spaced explosions sounded over the next few minutes, interspersed with random gunfire.

Sharon told the 9-1-1 dispatcher, "I'm at the Mesquite B&B on Tingle Creek Road. I have heard several explosions and gunfire. My husband is firefighter Paul Grant. He's trying to fight the fire with a farm tractor. I know there are people in the B&B." Sharon heard more ammunition discharge. She continued, "Someone is shooting at us! We need help! Now!"

The sound of gunfire concerned Paul as he drove the tractor towards the burning building. He knocked down the privacy fence that surrounded the dog yard and went around the B&B until he felt he was closest to the room next to the kitchen.

Since Connie had been making breakfast, that was where Connie was most likely to be. In the kitchen. He could find the rest of them after he saved Connie. She was his only connection to his best friend.

The heat from the fire was staggering without the protection of his gear, but he kept working the controls of the tractor. He dropped dirt on the fire at the base of the building. Then he lifted the bucket and used it to break a portion of the burning roof away from the rest of the structure. He shoved it aside with the bucket and went back to scrape burning, shattered walls into a heap.

With the bucket of the tractor, he scraped fire, and bits of the porch roof, and the porch wall remains away from the B&B as he tried to make a path from the burning building. It had to be wide enough to get the occupants out. He hoped Connie had all her dogs with her in the kitchen. The roof over the dog room was already in flames.

Sharon watched her husband fight the fire with the old tractor. She wanted to leave the protection of the truck to help somehow, but that would only distract him. She had to stay in the truck.

Aloud, she began to pray, "God, Saint Florian, Archangel Michael, please protect my husband and friends. Keep them safe until the fire is out. Please keep my husband safe! I know Paul is a trained firefighter, but seeing him work is so different from hearing him talk about it after the fact. Help me do the right thing. Thank you, Amen."

To occupy herself, Sharon did a quick inventory of her medical pack that she carried everywhere. She heard sirens approaching. "Thank you, God!" Sharon whispered.

Rand called 9-1-1 on his cell phone. He identified himself to the dispatcher and said, "The suspect in the kidnapping of Amanda Bradley, Benedict Allen Stout, is possibly the arsonist who torched the B&B. Please rebroadcast the ATL for him. Include that he is armed and dangerous. Also, we need a paramedic. Shrapnel or some other projectile that came through the window and hit FBI agent Stacey Baune."

"They're already on scene, just waiting to enter the building," the dispatcher told him.

"I haven't heard any sirens," Rand said.

ABANDONED MINE

Most days Allen enjoyed the sound of approaching sirens, today it incensed him. "They shouldn't be here yet. It's too soon. How were they already here?" he fumed. He ran to his rifle in the mine and prepared for a firefighter turkey shoot. "No one gets to put out that fire until Mandy dies!" he shouted at them.

MESQUITE B and B
TINGLE CREEK, ARIZONA

CONNIE WAS FURIOUS. SHE DECIDED THAT WHOEVER THE SON OF A BITCH was who did this, as soon as she found him, she was going to kill him. The B&B was all she had left of Tom and his family. All her good memories were here, in this building. Connie began to tear up, then reminded herself, "Hold it together now, fall apart later, just like in dispatch." She had to protect and take care of her dogs.

Stranded by fire all around them, they huddled in the center of the kitchen, behind the kitchen island that normally sat three. As they waited for rescue, they heard more gunfire. Different sounding shots from the initial shots they had heard. As if the shooting was from farther away.

Mandy whimpered as she held her hands over her head, then moaned, "This is all my fault. I should never have agreed to come here."

"Why would you think this is your fault?" Rand asked as he maintained the pressure on Stacey's wound.

"It's Allen!" Mandy cried. "It has to be! Didn't you say he shot my dad?"

Rand muttered profanities under his breath. He checked Stacey's temporary bandage as Stacey tried to console Mandy from where she was on the floor.

Paul frantically worked the controls of the tractor. He poured dirt on the fire and scraped burning debris away from the dwelling. He knew the history of the building since he was a kid.

Tom had been his best friend since kindergarten. He hoped to find everyone in the adobe walled kitchen and get them out before the fire got into the roof.

The heat was nasty. Paul wished he had his turnouts and shielded helmet, cold water would be sweet, but you work with what you have. The wind blew the fire into an inferno. Embers relit some of the wreckage he had pushed aside. He scraped up dirt to pile on the flaming debris then added more soil against the building in the area he was trying to clear. After what seemed to Paul like hours, fire trucks arrived. When the fire chief arrived, Sharon filled him in on the sequence of events as she knew them.

Shortly after the fire department arrived, Deputy Sandoval showed up, and Sharon told him about the person Paul had seen fleeing across the road. The person had headed up the hill to the east before the first explosion.

The town ambulance arrived. Sharon went to talk with the paramedics and directed them to set up a triage area in the metal building. She told the paramedics that there was a minimum of four people and five dogs that would need care, not including first responders.

A pressure gradient caused the intensifying wind that blew embers from the flaming B&B across the road. The fire chief directed his people and equipment as they arrived. First to arrive on the scene was the brush truck. It was to provide a cooling spray over Paul as he worked to get into the B&B. The first engine on the scene began to put water on the roof near where Paul worked as that was where the people were sheltering in place. The firefighters had to prevent the fire from spreading to that part of the building until everyone was out.

The chief hoped to get the occupants out before the fire got that far. The water tender arrived, and resupplied both trucks, then left for more water. A second engine arrived. The firefighters from that truck added their water to the blaze. Steam billowed where the water hit the flames. Visibility diminished as smoke and steam blended in the air.

Strong wind gusts sent sparks floating across the road like a manic swarm of fireflies. The hill across the street was all dried weeds, grasses and scrub-brush waiting for an ember to ignite. And it did.

The hillside ignited. Small fires began in the scattered clumps of dry buffle grass.

The fire chief needed more trucks and men to combat the fire at the B&B. Even now, he could tell the structure was going to be a loss. "Dispatch, tell state land that they have fires starting on the hill to the east of my location," the fire chief said into his radio. "Advise them embers are catching across the road. If this fire gets away, the whole town could go. Page all off duty firefighters to respond."

"10-4," the dispatcher said.

Paul frantically tried to find the doorway into the kitchen. He knew he was close. It had to be here somewhere. A spray of water splashed against the side of the house where he worked, it was a cooling relief.

Help had arrived. Paul knew it was up to him. He had to save Connie. For Tom. She had survived too much to die now. He had scraped away the burning wall and knocked down the burning remains of the porch and shoved it away from the house. Paul finally reached the adobe part of the building. He scraped everything away until he could see only the adobe wall along that side. Now he just had to find the doorway into the kitchen.

Water showered Paul. More water went onto the house where he continued to work. Steam billowed. The wind blew the smoke and steam away from him.

Rand needed to do more. He had heard the shots. He knew it had to be the guy he was looking for. The one who had taken Mandy from her father. Rand wanted a piece of this guy. But, Stacey needed him. He sheltered Mandy and Stacey with his body.

Connie held on to Misty by her scruff and her other hand wrapped around her body. Misty fought Connie. She wanted to get away from the noise; her fear of loud noises made her deaf, dumb, and blind to help and safety.

"Magic," Connie called. When the dog turned to her, she ordered her to lie down next to Misty. At least in the kitchen, they had the appliances, and all the cabinets to protect them from the flying projectiles that peppered the structure.

B&B FIRE

ALLEN SAW THE TANKER TRUCK LUMBER UP THE DRIVEWAY. "DAMN IT! No!" Allen yelled. He looked through the rifle scope. He figured the tanker needed to be his first target, even before a firefighter. Allen missed his first shot. He was frustrated and aimed for the tank on the water tender and fired again. He hit the wheel of the large truck. "Fricking wind, it's messing up my shots!"

Deputy Tjosvold had just arrived and parked next to the tanker, away from the hoses that fed the fire engines. When he got out of his department SUV, he heard Allen's shot as it pinged off the wheel of the tanker. On his radio, Deputy Tjosvold said, "Shots fired at personnel at the B&B fire." The deputy dropped and scurried around his vehicle for cover. Then he ran to the metal shed for shelter.

Deputy Sandoval got on his radio. He asked dispatch, "Mike-59, is DPS Air flying right now? If so, the suspect is on the hill to the east, shooting at us. We're pinned down here."

In moments dispatch advised, "Mike-59, Ranger-98 is close and on the way to assist. Also, two road officers are on the way from DPS, responding from Sierra Vista."

Deputy Sandoval replied, "See if Cochise County or Pima County have anyone closer who can assist."

Inside the B&B, they were aware the fire department had arrived, and rescue was imminent. They heard the sounds of the tractor as it scraped against the burning dwelling. The billowing clouds of smoke generated by the fire reflected the blue and red flashing lights of the emergency vehicles outside. The water from the fire hose was loud as it splashed on the roof. Rand still held on to Mandy even as she struggled to get free. "If I go out there, he'll leave everyone else alone," Mandy explained.

"Too late, not gonna happen, kid," Rand said.

Mandy cringed as they heard another volley of shots hit the side of the B&B.

Allen managed to flatten a tire on the tanker. He reloaded the rifle.

"Mike-44, we're still being shot at, any assistance en route?" asked Deputy Tjosvold.

"Pima County is sending a deputy, and so is Cochise County," replied the dispatcher.

Angry he wasn't hitting what he wanted, Allen shot at the metal shed where he had seen people take shelter.

Deputy Tjosvold said, "Radio, Mike-44, Be advised, we're taking fire. Shots fired at the metal shed from the east."

Before dispatch could respond, Deputy Tjosvold heard over his radio, "Ranger-98 copies, ETA less than two. We'll be using infra-red to find your shooter."

That was followed by:

"Sam-683 from Pima County copies and en route. Be advised I'm a canine unit and five out."

"Cochise-27 copies, be advised, I'm cross-trained as a SWAT officer. Seven minutes out."

"Radio copies," the dispatcher acknowledged as the requested assistance from other police agencies announced their arrival on the radio.

Sheriff Martin Barrett of Maley County came on the radio. "Radio, Mike-1 copies, have Cochise-27 bring some flash/bangs if he has any with him and Radio, call out day shift early please, get them out there. Also, show me en route."

The dispatcher responded, "10-4."

Allen was furious. He didn't know how he had missed the damn tanker truck. His hands shook as he peered through the rifle scope again. The smoke and steam from the fire and water had reduced the visibility of his targets. The wind gusts were perfect for growing the fire, except it was blowing the embers in his direction. The fire was supposed to burn where he told it to, not freelance anywhere it wanted.

His next shot hit the tanker truck but nowhere vital. Allen wondered why he couldn't hit the water tanker near the bottom. It was where he was aiming. He needed to make the cursed thing useless. Make it leak or undrivable. He shot at the tires.

That went for all the emergency vehicles at the fire. Allen shot out the tanker tires on the left rear axle and one of the Maley County Sheriff Department vehicle's rear tires. He then tried to get a bead on the actual fire truck putting water on the fire, but the tanker shielded it. If he got higher, he could put some rounds through the engine. He heard the approaching helicopter and disregarded that idea — he saw no need to get out in the open and be seen.

DPS helicopter Ranger-98 was on the scene and began the search to the east of the fire using infrared scanning to find the suspect. The hunt was on for the shooter.

Deputy Tjosvold relayed the approximate location to the helicopter. When Ranger 98 thought they had something, they advised the deputies on the ground. "Ranger-98 to Mike-44, we saw what appeared to be shots coming from a little more than halfway up the hill to the east of the fire. The suspect has some cover that he ducked into."

"Sam-683 and K-9 Thor less than two minutes out" was followed by "Cochise-27 still about four away."

Deputy Tjosvold said, "Mike-44 copies."

Deputy Lopez came on the radio, "Mike-29, in service. Where do you need me?"

"Mike-29, Mike-1, I need you to stop all traffic coming from town before they get to the B&B. You need to block the road until we get the sniper. We don't need any unsuspecting citizen getting caught in the crossfire," Sheriff Barrett directed.

"Mike-29 copies," replied Deputy Lopez. "En route."

Not able to do anything more useful, Rand peppered Mandy with questions. Rand asked, "Where would Allen park your dad's truck? How many weapons does he have? What kind? Did he ever mention why he was doing this?" He paused for breath. Mandy didn't say anything. "Come on, kid, this isn't about just you," Rand added, "Get it together, you're the only one who knows."

Mandy described her dad's pickup and the rifle she had seen Allen use to shoot the snake in New Mexico. "I don't know any of the other stuff!" Mandy cried.

When the flames were visible from the road south of the B&B, Sam-683 stopped and parked his patrol SUV sideways across the roadway, with all blue and red lights flashing. He didn't wait for back-up from the Cochise 27.

In the dog area of the Pima County Sheriff's Department patrol Tahoe, canine Thor was excited, yipping and bouncing on his front feet. He knew he was about to go to work.

Sam-683 had Thor stand in the open back door of the Tahoe while he put on the bulletproof K-9 tactical vest with a twenty-foot leash attached to the built-in harness. Thor was then allowed to exit the vehicle. Thor went to work, nose in the air as he inhaled deeply.

The Cochise County Sheriff's Department Tahoe slid to a stop nearby. Cochise-27 grabbed a couple of stun grenades out of his supply in the rear storage area of his vehicle. Then he met up with the K-9 handler and his dog.

As Sam-683 and Cochise-27 conferred, Mike-1 arrived. "Radio, Mike-1 is with the out of county deputies."

"Radio copies."

Mike-1 joined Sam-683 and Cochise-27 so the dog could smell him. The sheriff informed the deputies there was an abandoned mine up there, about halfway up and a small, shallow cave about three-quarters of the way up on the west side.

"From what my deputies at the fire are telling me, I think our shooter is at the mine," said Sheriff Barrett. They set off up the hill, the K-9 and his handler led the way.

The DPS helicopter circled high overhead and stayed out of the line-of-sight of the shooter. The spotter on the DPS chopper watched for movement by the suspect on the hillside through the infrared camera as he also monitored the progress of the deputies as they made their way up the hill.

Cochise-27 and Mike-1 were behind and a little off to either side of the dog and his handler, weapons drawn, and ready as they made their way up the hill. They had to avoid cactus, brush and small trees with sharp thorns on them as they worked their way up the steep hillside. On the way up, Mike-1 heard additional units come up on the radio.

"Mike-46 in service." followed by "Mike-38 on shift. What have we got?"

Mike-1 answered, "Mike-46 and Mike-38, work up towards the abandoned mine from the north side, and be aware there is a K-9 unit working the hill on the south side. We have a sniper up there shooting at personnel at the B&B, which is on fire."

Allen was blind mad. He couldn't understand why those fucking firefighters wouldn't quit and save themselves. Gunfire had always worked in the past; why not now? He reloaded his rifle again. He shot at anything he saw moving. He was beyond caring if he killed firefighters or cops. Mandy had to die in a fire. She had to, for betraying him, and more importantly, she had betrayed fire.

Ranger-98 saw the increased amount of shooting that came from the mine entrance. "Ground units, Ranger-98, be advised, the shooter has reloaded and is targeting the fire scene again. Seems less controlled than the last time," the spotter said.

"Mike-1 copies, thanks."

Then the pilot said, "Ground units, Ranger 98, also be advised there are embers that have caught fire above the shooter's location, in several areas."

"Radio copies and will update State Land."

Mike-1 inserted the earpiece for his radio so he could monitor the situation at the fire without giving away the position of himself and the two deputies with him. The deputies continued their way up the steep hill. Occasionally one of them slid on the loose gravel or dirt that let go under their feet as they climbed towards the mine opening.

Thor was at the end of his twenty-foot lead, nose in the air as he worked back and forth, searching for the scent cone that would lead him to the suspect. Thor's handler watched him as they worked their way up the slope. As they got further up the hill Thor's side to side sweeps narrowed. Sam-683 said quietly, "We're getting close."

Mike-1 let everyone know that they were near the abandoned mine entrance, that was where the dog had focused.

"Mike-46, and Mike-38, we're almost to the mine entrance on the north side."

Allen was unaware of the deputies as they closed in on the mine entrance. The racket from the fire, the fire suppression equipment, and the nearby but unseen helicopter had disguised the sounds they had made on their way up.

From high above, Ranger 98 lit their spotlight and focused it into the mine entrance. The deputies saw the suspect raise his gun in preparation for another round of shots. The bright light blinded Allen. The rifle barrel began to track the helicopter.

Allen tried to shoot out the spotlight on the helicopter. When he had used all his rounds, he had to reload.

Finally, Paul found the door into the kitchen. The heavy spray on him and the side of the building where he worked, and a steady stream of water on the roof over the same area, had kept the fire from getting into the kitchen. He stopped the tractor with the bucket raised over the doorway. Two firefighters rushed in to assist him in getting everyone out.

Magic barked sharply at the firemen when they entered.

Connie grabbed Magic's collar to keep her from attacking the firefighters and also held tight to Misty so that she couldn't bolt out the door.

Ace leaned against Connie as she ordered firefighter Troy to pick up the crate that contained the two puppies and take it to the metal shed.

Paul helped Stacey stagger out as he held the makeshift bandage to her shoulder. They left the burning building and walked into the mud, created by the water that stopped the fire from reaching the kitchen.

Rand guided Mandy out of the burning building.

Connie felt Ace's panic rise as he leaned against her legs, harder and harder. In her sheer terror of loud noises, Misty pulled and lunged first one way then another against the belt Connie had fashioned into a leash.

Magic stood protectively in front of Connie, between her and the firefighters who entered the structure. Paul and Rand evacuated with their charges. Protectively geared firefighters pulled hoses to fight the fire from the inside.

Ace leaned against her legs so hard, Connie fell to her knees.

Firefighter Corey saw Connie's predicament, and he hurried to her. He scooped up Misty, and he easily carried the struggling dog to the metal shed.

Connie heard the fire as it fed on the B&B. She knew they were out of time. They had to evacuate. The fire had consumed most of the B&B except for the kitchen.

Hands free of Misty, Connie pulled Magic's collar with one hand and grabbed Ace's collar with the other and led them from the burning building to the shelter of the metal shed, following Corey with Misty.

Firefighter Troy returned from the shed and moved the tractor away from the building. The fight against the fire changed to saving what they could of the building to preventing the spread of the fire to surrounding brush.

At the metal shed, Corey bent to put down Misty so he can head back to the battle against the blaze.

"Corey, wait!" said Connie. "Put Misty in that crate, don't put her down or let her go. She'll run until she's exhausted," Connie explained as she pointed at a large, sturdy kennel against the wall of the shed.

Rand felt bad for Misty being so scared; he could relate, being around all these gigantic dogs. He held Mandy as she shook and wept despondently on his shirt.

Once Misty was safely secured in the crate, Corey drug it over to where Connie sat on the floor of the shed with Ace in her lap and Magic on guard at her side. As Misty began to feel more secure from being in a crate and further away from the noise, she settled down. Connie sat right next to Misty with Ace and Magic.

Paul and Stacey finally arrived in the shelter of the metal shed. As soon as Paul got Stacey into the safety of the shed, Dr. Sharon Grant and the paramedics descended on her. Stacey gratefully stretched out on the ambulance gurney for evaluation and pain management as she was patched and prepared for transport to the hospital by the ambulance.

Allen fired again at the helicopter spotlight and missed. He refocused on the B&B.

Mike-1 decided there was no other choice, "Mike-1 to all units, suspect is tracking his next target. Fire if you have a clean shot." The deputies carefully converged on the mine entrance simultaneously while they stayed out of the sniper's kill zone.

Through the scope on his rifle, Allen had watched a man lead Mandy to the big metal shed. Other people and the dogs also went into the shed. It would be a difficult shot, with most of the building blocked from view by fire trucks, and all the people milling around, but he had to kill her. She knew way too much about him where he had been, and what he had done.

He briefly saw Mandy as the medics swarmed someone else in the shed. They worked on that person as a group. He kept watching. He knew if he waited, he would get his kill shot on Mandy. He saw her again. Allen tracked Mandy with his rifle.

Multiple bullets ripped into Allen as the deputies from the north side, and the south side all shot into the mine entrance. He fell and dropped his rifle.

"Don't move!" ordered Sam-683. "Roll on your belly and put your hands behind your head!"

"I'm hurt," Allen whined, he continued to flop around in the dark of the mine as he felt around for the rifle.

"Freeze, or I release the dog!"

Allen stopped his search for the rifle but continued to squirm around, as he moaned, "I'm hurt. I need help. Help me."

"Freeze means do not move!" Sam-683 bellowed.

Allen continued to wriggle.

Sam-683 released Thor to subdue the suspect. The dog raced into the mine, his handler, ready for anything, waited at the side of the mine entrance. Peering in, weapon drawn and flashlight trained on the suspect, Sam-683 watched as Thor approached the bad guy.

Allen persisted in flopping around. Thor charged in and grabbed him by the ankle. He began dragging Allen to Sam-683.

"He's biting me! Make him stop!" Allen screamed, then rolled on to his back. He pulled a handgun from his belt as Thor drug him toward the mine opening by his booted foot. Allen sat up as Thor dragged him by the foot and lined up on the deputies at the mine entrance. He was fatally shot in the head by Thor's handler, Sam-683.

The distant sound of multiple gunshots reached the metal shed. Dr. Grant and the paramedics worked on their patients. When Dr. Grant came to check Connie over, Connie was having none of it until she made sure all her dogs were okay and healthy. "Where are my puppies?" Connie bellowed, worried about her Schipperke puppies.

Rand pointed to the far corner of the shed, where Deputy Sandoval sat next to the Schipperke puppies in their crate. Connie stood to get them, but Dr. Grant pushed her back down. "I need to check you over, now," Sharon said.

"Can someone please bring the puppies to me?" Connie begged as she ignored her doctor. Deputy Sandoval carried the small occupied crate to Connie. He held it as she looked in at them. The puppies huddled together in the very back of the kennel. "Thank you," she said to Deputy Sandoval when he placed the kennel in front of Magic. Connie pulled the enclosure closer.

Rand heard a single gunshot.

Dr. Grant approached Connie again. "I need to check you for smoke inhalation," Dr. Grant told Connie. "I also need to see if you have any other injuries."

Dr. Grant stood in front of Connie as her dogs surrounded her. Ace leaned against Connie as he shook and panted. Magic was in full-on protection mode, as she stood in front of Connie, fur standing along her spine, ears full forward and nose occasionally in the air, scenting.

"Not right now," Connie said. She stared at the ruins of her home.

"Can I get in here guys?" Dr. Grant asked the dogs, as she held her hand out, palm down for Magic to sniff. Magic sniffed at her hand but still wasn't letting anyone close to Connie.

"I guess that's a no, huh, Magic," Dr. Grant said to the protective dog.

Dr. Grant turned her attention to the hysterically crying Mandy. She still hadn't settled down any since Rand had brought her out of the B&B and into the shed.

"Mandy, you have to calm down. Being this upset isn't good for you," Dr. Grant said.

Mandy continued to cry into Rand's shoulder.

He shrugged when Dr. Grant gave him an enquiring look.

"Mandy, I'm going to sedate you if you don't settle down," Dr. Grant threatened.

Still bawling, Mandy held out her arm. "Shot. Help me," Mandy cried.

The deputies converged on Thor, who still had a grip on Allen's foot. Allen wasn't moving. Cochise-27 approached with Sam-683 and kicked the pistol far away from the suspect's hand.

Thor wagged his tail enthusiastically with Allen's booted foot gripped in his mouth, as he continued to drag Allen's corpse to the opening of the mine.

Sam-683 told Thor, "Leave it, then come." Thor dropped the foot of the suspect and went to his handler.

Sam-683 praised Thor lavishly and gave him his reward, a Kong squeaky ball he pulled from his pocket. Thor happily panted around the toy in his mouth when he was ordered to stand. Sam-683 removed Thor's tactical vest. Thor shook vigorously before he sat at heel again, toy in his mouth. Thor made the ball squeak as he held it in his mouth, tail still wagging happily.

Mike-1 announced on his radio, "Suspect DOA, code 4. Radio, we'll need forensics and Pima County OME (Office of the Medical Examiner) notified please."

The dispatcher replied, "10-4, the time is zero five zero eight."

Mike-1 then said, "Ranger 98, thanks for the assist. I appreciate it."

The helicopter pilot responded, "Any time," then banked his aircraft and flew off to the southwest with just his craft lights flashing in the predawn sky, blinking red on the left, blinking green on the right and a solid red light on the belly of the helicopter.

The news that the shooter was dead spread through the fire scene. Everyone was relieved. Fire fighting began on the east side of the building. No one had been able to go over there due to the sniper, and the fire had burned unimpeded.

Strapped on the gurney, Stacey rode in the ambulance to the hospital. "They can turn off the stupid lights and sirens," Stacey told the paramedic working on her. "I'm not that hurt."

The overall stress level in the metal shed dropped with the news the sniper was dead. Magic finally relaxed and let Dr. Grant approach Connie. Connie still wasn't ready to be assessed. She cried as she clung to Ace.

A second ambulance arrived to take Mandy to the hospital for observation, evaluation, and treatment. When Mandy left, Rand moved closer to Connie. He went very slowly as he still was uncertain of Connie's humongous dogs.

Still a few feet from Connie, Rand asked Dr. Grant, "Other than Stacey, we were all okay?"

"Everyone seemed okay. No one has any apparent injuries or much smoke inhalation," Dr. Grant replied. She motioned towards Connie, "I still need to check that one out. I'm afraid this may be the straw that broke the camel's back."

"It's just a house, and she can rebuild it. Memories are in the heart," Rand said. Connie heard him, shook her head, and cried harder.

Dr. Grant said, "It's that her whole life with Tom is gone, physically. And rebuilding wouldn't be the same. Now all she has are her memories. Nothing else."

Paul came over to Dr. Grant, and she checked out her husband. Fighting fire without protective gear hadn't been ideal.

"So, how's my favorite firefighter?" Dr. Grant asked Paul.

"Hot, thirsty, and fine, wife," Paul said, as he smiled at her. "I need to get back and help with mop-up."

Rand ached for Connie's loss. He'd hug her if it weren't for those dogs of hers. He could provide her with a shoulder to lean on. He decided he needed to stop being so scared of her dogs. She had said he was safe and they hadn't hurt him, or even threatened to hurt him. Not today, though. He also decided he could stay afraid of all other dogs.

Rand used his smartphone and called Dan Bradley. The message he left let Dan know Mandy was safe, but she had missed her flight. He finished the voicemail with, "… so no need to worry. I'll make sure she gets home to you safely."

Connie still sobbed into Ace's fur when Rand had finished his call to Dan Bradley. "Sharon, shouldn't we do something for Connie?" he asked.

"She needs this. To cry and grieve. She had less than a day to miss Tommy before his mom died, and then she had to be a rock for Jack. Then Belle her medical crisis, and Connie has been a rock for Art. She hasn't let herself grieve because she hasn't felt she had time to grieve. At least, that's what she told me. If she doesn't let it out now, I worry about how it will eat at her," Dr. Grant replied.

"Is there anything I can do to help?" Rand asked.

"Be a shoulder to lean on and cry on, someone to hold her while she falls apart. So eventually she can find herself again. She needs someone to help her put herself back together," Dr. Sharon Grant said.

The puppies demanded food. Their yaps and howls had reached deafening levels. The small critters made sure everyone knew they were hungry.

Sharon led Rand to the Yukon XL parked in the metal shed, opened the door and flipped down the visor. Keys dropped onto the driver's seat. She scooped them up and held them out to Rand.

"The first thing you can do is run into town as soon as the driveway is clear. Go to the feed store for puppy and dog supplies, food, bowls, toys, whatever. I'll call Todd to open the store early to get you what you need."

Rand nodded. He took the keys and got in the SUV. He wasn't in the mood to wait for the driveway to clear and maneuvered around all the emergency response vehicles and went to the feed store. By doing this, he was helping Connie. Sitting around made him feel useless.

At the mine, Sheriff Martin Barrett had to sort out who did what, when they did it, and what still needed doing. The Sheriff walked up to the 40-ish dark-haired K-9 handler and shook the hand of Sam-683, and asked, "What's your name deputy?"

"Ron Steffens, Sir."

"I wanted to thank you and your partner for the assist." He paused and looked at Thor, then back at Ron. "I'm sure you hear this all the time, but can I pet him?"

Ron looked at the black German Shepherd sitting at his side. "Standard answer is no, but today, if Thor decides to let you, yes."

"You leave that decision up to the dog?" asked Sheriff Barrett.

"Yup. It's safer for everyone that way, no unexpected bites," Sam-683 said.

"Makes sense," Sheriff Barrett said.

"Now, get down on one knee and hold out your right hand in a loose fist, palm down," Sam-683 instructed.

Sheriff Barrett followed the instructions Deputy Steffens gave him and was delighted when Thor reached out his nose to sniff his hand. "I always wanted a K-9 unit, but we don't have the funds in this county. Dogs are so darn expensive and then there's the training, also expensive," Sheriff Barrett said.

"Doesn't have to be. Thor was in a shelter when I found him, and he didn't know anything. He'd been on a chain in someone's backyard until the owners dumped him at animal control. Rescue groups also have great dogs that need a home and a purpose. I trained Thor first with a basic training group and then through Utility and then Search and Rescue for tracking and working along with other people and dogs before I started the specialized attack training I did myself. But then I've been training dogs since my teens. It's doable cost-effectively. It just takes time and effort and most of all, commitment, to the dog and the training." Steffens paused, then said, "Sorry for the speech, Sir."

"Not a problem. Great information in that speech," the Sheriff smiled at Deputy Steffens as he continued to hold his hand out to the big black German Shepherd Dog.

Steffens told Thor, "Okay. Go visit," once he was sure that Thor liked the Sheriff and wouldn't bite him.

Thor got up and moved closer to Sheriff Barrett, and the sheriff gave him a good rub on his chest. When Thor had enough, he went and sat at his handler's side.

The sheriff grinned like a kid at Christmas, then stood, and brushed the dirt off his knees before he turned to the Cochise County deputy. Cochise-27 was a tall and slender blond-headed kid. He can't be more than twelve years old, Martin Barrett thought, he resisted the urge to ask who bought his bullets for him. The kid had the bearing and confidence of someone who had served in the military.

"What's your name, son?" asked Sheriff Barrett.

Cochise-27 responded, "Bill Connor, sir," as they shook hands.

"Thank you for your assistance," the Sheriff said. "I greatly appreciate it."

He turned to include both out of county deputies, "Thanks to both of you for your help." He handed them each a business card with his contact information on the front and the Maley County case number was handwritten on the back. "If you could, please send me your report case numbers for your agency so I can get copies to attach to our reports. I'd appreciate it."

Both deputies nodded and pocketed the cards.

"I'm releasing you both to go back to your respective counties, again, thanks," said the sheriff.

Sheriff Barrett huddled with his deputies to figure out scene preservation, paperwork, diagrams, photos, etc. and the order in which they would occur.

In the shed, Deputy Tjosvold looked at Connie and knew it would be a while before Connie talked to anyone. He asked Deputy Sandoval, "Can you go to the hospital and interview, the injured FBI agent, Stacey Baune, and Amanda Bradley if she's settled down? I'll take the other FBI agent, Dr. Grant, Paul and Connie when she's ready."

Deputy Sandoval agreed and followed the route Rand had taken around the still present emergency response vehicles and left for town.

The firefighters struggled to squash every wind-driven spark around and in the smoking remains of the building.

Paul used the tractor again to push everything he could away from the adobe part of the building. A few of the town firefighters were putting out spot fires on the hillside across the road alongside the state land firefighters who swarmed the hillside fires after the sniper was dead and the scene declared secure.

Daybreak and sunshine finally out-shown the blue and red strobe lights on the emergency vehicles that had lit up the night along with the now subsiding fire. The wind picked up with daylight.

Connie was finally cried out. Magic lay at her feet, and Dr. Grant was finally able to check her over. The puppies continued to wail that they were still hungry.

The fire was finally out. Most of the formerly sprawling B&B was ash or smoking rubble. Firefighters saved the adobe walls of the structure. But there was significant roof damage, along with the smoke and water damage inside.

The walls and floor would be salvageable. The rest of the B&B, all the additions had burned to the foundations.

Everything Rand, Stacey, and Mandy owned and had left in the B&B burned. Everything Connie owned other than her dogs and what she was wearing, burned up in the fire. Including her photo albums of her parents and her husband.

As mop-up continued, a thirty ton, four-axle tow truck and a tire supply truck arrived. The shot-out tires on the fire trucks and sheriff's department vehicles were replaced. Trucks and firefighters began to leave as they were no longer needed, and their vehicles repaired and made driveable. The water tanker was towed due to engine damage from rifle-fire.

Rand returned from the feed store with the dog supplies he had retrieved. The pups were still squalling when Rand exited the SUV he had driven into town. Rand asked Sharon, "Is there anyone we can call for Connie? Family or someone?" as he handed her the puppy feeding supplies.

Dr. Grant replied, "No, her mom is in the hospital in Tucson after a stroke, and her dad is in Wyoming, getting the ranch ready to sell so they can move down here." Sharon opened the bag of puppy kibble and spilled it into the pups' kennel, through the wire door.

"No siblings?" Rand asked. The puppies quieted as they began to crunch on the kibble.

"No, she was adopted after a drunk driver killed her parents when she was young," Sharon said. "As far as I know, she still has three funerals to plan."

"And now insurance folks to deal with for the fire," Rand said. "I plan to stay and help her. I was supposed to be the best man at their wedding.

I never made it. My flight from Denver got canceled by tornados. I never intended to meet Tom's wife as his widow. I'll do what I can to help until she sends me home."

"I'm glad. I don't want Connie to be left alone for a few days. I don't know how much she can take," Sharon worried.

As he scanned the remains of the B&B, Rand knew he was fortunate to have all his reports on the kidnapping and the firefighter and arson case on the FBI office cloud server.

EPILOGUE

CONNIE

After the fire, Connie and her dogs moved into Jack and Kate's RV. She and Rand put up a new, temporary fence for the dogs that enclosed the metal shed and half an acre outside it. The last month and a half had emotionally battered and exhausted Connie. She taught Rand how to care for the puppies and the dogs, then allowed herself to sleep for a few days. She only got up for water occasionally, and that was with Rand's prodding.

With Rand's help, Connie arranged the memorial service to celebrate Tom, Kate and Jack Sullivan, all three of them together. After the memorial service, she felt so empty.

She had the Sullivans cremated, and she buried their ashes together on the B&B property. She and Rand planted some trees around their resting place to grow over time into a place of refuge.

Connie felt Tom's absence strongly; as if she was missing a part of herself.

Rand's company and assistance had been priceless to her. Before he went home, Connie had let him know his presence was the only reason she had been able to do all that had needed to be done.

RAND

Rand had stayed for a couple of weeks in a camper he borrowed from Paul and Sharon. He had it brought to the Mesquite B&B property for him to stay in. He helped Connie with the funeral arrangements for her husband and her in-laws. He also helped her set up new fences for her dogs. He enjoyed the physicality of using the fence post hammer to pound in the fence posts.

Rand dealt with the insurance adjuster when he showed up to survey the damage from the fire set by Allen. The adjuster assured Rand there would be no problems with the fire damage claim.

He forced himself to get comfortable with Connie's big dogs. When Connie needed a few days to sleep, he took on the care of the puppies and enjoyed it immensely. They were always getting into something or learning something new.

Finally, Rand had no more reason to stay and was almost out of vacation time, so he went home.

Back home in Dallas, Rand realized he missed Connie. He missed her a lot. Even though they had terrified him at first, he missed her dogs. They were very friendly once he got comfortable with them.

Rand gave thoughtful consideration to a job offer Sheriff Martin Barrett had made him before he left. Martin had asked him to join the department as a detective with the Maley County Sheriff's Department.

STACEY

STACEY WAS RELEASED FROM THE HOSPITAL TO RETURN TO DALLAS FOR follow-up care after her shoulder was cleaned of shrapnel, stitched and bandaged. She was lucky and had no significant damage to her shoulder. The doctors had told her she should be able to go back to work after some time off to heal and a little physical therapy.

Stacey called Connie to check up on her after Rand came home. Stacey made it a point to let Connie know she wanted to return for the mesquite bean picking season. She wanted to learn how to make jam.

She loved visiting Tingle Creek and enjoyed the dogs immensely.

MANDY

MANDY IDENTIFIED ALLEN FROM A MORGUE PICTURE AS THE PERSON who had taken her from Dallas to the Pima County Fair. Mandy flew home to Dallas with Stacey the day after the fire.

She was overjoyed when she reunited with her father in his hospital room.

She told him she was never going on a date again unless she had her own transportation. She wasn't ever going to rely on anyone else again.

ART

Art returned to Tingle Creek after selling the ranch in Wyoming, to help plan the rebuilding of the B&B. He also needed to find a place for him and Belle to live either in Tucson or preferably, in Tingle Creek.

For now, he stayed with Connie in a rented RV. Connie and her dogs took up all the room in Jack and Kate's RV.

BELLE

After showing some signs of improvement, Belle was due to be moved out of the hospital and into a long-term stroke rehabilitation facility in the next month. Eventually, she would be released and needed a home adapted to her needs.

Glossary of English and German commands for the dogs:

ENGLISH	GERMAN
Sit	Sitz
Down	Platz
Stand	Steh
Stay	Bleib
Heel	Fuss
Come	Hier
Jump	Hopp
No	Nein
Safe	Sicher
Easy	Einfach
Good dog	Guter hund
Make friends	Freunde finded
Eat	Essen
Back	Zurück

Follow the author and keep up with new books or book readings:

www.sguetter.author.com

email: sguetter.author@gmail.com

Facebook: www.facebook.com/AuthorGuetter

Instagram: sguetterauthor

Printed in the United States
By Bookmasters